LATENCY
PARA
DOX
OF
BARRET
TRUFFLE
HARD

Author of

Precognitive Ultimatum of Minokori Scuttlesworth

ULTRA KWON

LATENCY PARADOX
OF
BARRET TRUFFLEHARD

Latency Paradox of Barret Trufflehard

ultrakwon.com
@ultrakwon

Cover art by Domenico Di Francia K
Copyright © 2015 by Ultra Kwon
All rights reserved.
Edition 0.1
ISBN-10: 1515029409
ISBN-13: 978-1515029403

To be determined....

LATENCY PARADOX
OF
BARRET TRUFFLEHARD

chapter 1

For the past twelve hours, Milton Grainjar had been making the rounds, investigating private dwellings to track down illegal conspirators of the Jade Association.

This involved rapping on the doors of suspected jadeites and enumerating them. His part seemed simple in theory, but it was a gritty function, made worse by bureaucratic regulations and tedious data collection procedures, not to mention the drudgery of trudging through the obstacles posed by social ignorance. If only the denizens understood the critical role somebody like him played in these ambiguous times.

Milton Grainjar was almost certain he was done for the day. Almost, because in his line of work, you were never really done. Yet despite assuming this provision, he was mildly disappointed, when a personal message from his superior had directed him to one more unit.

It was right around the corner, according to the GPS, when the Bureaux message utility took precedent. The three-dimensional, holographic map on the dashboard was superimposed by a loading disclaimer. The progress cell filled to deliver another personal message from his superior. It was a follow-up: Kyra McVeronica informing him he had failed his most recent physical evaluations, part of the Bureaux's annual emergency testing protocol.

This did not mean desk duty for Milton. There was no such reprieve in his work place. It meant he would have to take the evaluations again, at his own time and expense, just like he had before, with the purpose of achieving a passing score. Until then, his failure would be reflected in his pay.

Still none of that bothered him as much as the mandatory pep talk that would result from it. Somehow, he knew there would be a confrontation. Kyra never let anything slide. As if she thrived off the tension, he thought. Everything is a test with her.

He had had enough. The hell with what they called those emergency tests, he said to himself. It wasn't what I signed up for. Or was it? I'm fried, he realized. I'll put in my notice first thing tomorrow. I can't keep on going like this. It's detrimental to my health. And then, he thought about Kyra and how she'd react to the news of his departure. He did not want to dwell on it. Good riddance, he thought.

When the topographic hologram reemerged, he discovered he had missed a turn. He shook his head in lethargy. Such notifications always seemed to distract him at the timeliest moments. Now he was being rerouted. He shifted the purple beetle from the lodgment of traffic, relinquishing its position from the unending line, performing an Immelmann turn by accelerating up into a half-loop and rolling the car laterally until it leveled out. He adjusted his flight path, decreasing altitude until the clogged tiers of the holoway cast over him. Blocky buildings shuffled past his periphery. Among the uniformity, the GPS pinpointed the unit, highlighting a structure that was coming up ahead. Milton started searching for parking.

The valet utility informed him the rooftops were all car-capped and full. It offered him the nearest vacant slot. He circled around and pulled into it, lowering his purple beetle to the ground level parkway. An unnerving torsion shrilled against the base of his car, and his seat made a violent jerk, shuddering to a halt. All signs indicated a successful landing. He relaxed his hold on the dual steering sticks and eagerly searched his pockets for some change. Something grasped.

He pulled out coins, smooth and polished, reflective without any sharp corners. He checked the date of the pixels. It was this year's. Above the vehicle's console box was a glass panel featuring a lit display of advertised sustenance. He dropped the coins into the corresponding vertical slot and selected the original flavored Health Bar.

Nothing happened.

He searched the receptacle chamber to make sure. He slammed the glass panel and shook the dashboard. Still nothing printed. It always happened. Yet he was mildly disappointed. Now it was even harder to look forward to his last assignment.

He switched off the engine with defeat. The mobile clock grimly displayed 8:26 p.m. It was for him, the thirteenth hour. One last address, he assured himself. After this, you're home safe. He sidled out with two large briefcases, basking in the glow of the hovering street lamps. He reached up for the door, pulled it shut, and stumbled forward with his briefcases.

Milton had parked three miles away. The distance complied with the instructions to park his vehicle far off to avoid making any kind of noise or scene that would foreshadow his arrival. Visitations were encouraged to entail soundless operations. Consequently, Milton was off to a proper start, and he would have been right to hold his chin high, with the air of pride alluded to obtaining results without producing a racket. If only such professional sentiment was more than mere pretense he would have abruptly set aside, had a spot on the roof been available. After all, Milton thought, my legs hurt. And besides quietude and stealth, numbers are the bottom line of an enumerator.

Since joining the bureaucratic agency, Milton Grainjar had compiled the highest record of enumerations. Technically he was still a trainee in title. He preferred to think of it as a statutory glitch in the system. His tally at the moment was 33,285 and counting; he was averaging 6.6636 enumerations per day. More than any of his fully certified peers. Nobody else had ever posted quintuple digits, as far as his awareness. The exception was Barret Trufflehard, who was before his time. And in some ways, Milton thought, always will be.

Barret Trufflehard was the man, the myth, the legendary icon of the world: a herculean, patriotic protagonist, declared the Pride of the Ekonomy and Champion of Humanity.

As difficult as it was to believe for Milton Grainjar, who had, since watching the first Trufflehard blockbuster, aspired to be like his hero, the numbers did not lie.

Milton was the penultimate. The next best thing. Deserving of department royalty, by virtue of his credentials. And yet, he was mildly disappointed.

Where was the special treatment? he asked himself, staring ahead, strolling through the dimly lit streets. It was a thankless job with a staggeringly high turnover rate, and he had known this prior to willingly accepting it. But God, he thought, I didn't know it was this thankless.

By the by, Milton was feeling the onset of second thoughts, affliction, a breakdown in his constitution. This business of tracking down illegal members of the Jade Association, had once been his life purpose. Barret Trufflehard had a lot to do with it. He was a big influence for him, as it was for everyone else, growing up at the zenith of the Green Scare.

Watching recruitment campaigns and the cinematic adaptation about Trufflehard's symbolic heroism of greatness in the social service, was what attracted him to the job in the first place.

Suffice to say, Milton Grainjar wanted to be just like Barret Trufflehard. He regarded the man with esteem and deference like the paternal figure his absent father never fulfilled for him. And without even ever having met the old guy. He adored the children of Trufflehard, yearning to live vicariously through those who lived vicariously through their father's live-action triumphs. Imagine having the coolest dad in the world, he thought, as he advanced through the sidewalk bridge.

From his periphery, he picked up the 3D contours popping out of the holographic banners on the adjacent wall. He approached the redundant headshots of Barret Trufflehard and lowered one of his briefcases to trace one side of the protruding, fine jawline. What an implacable mug, he said to himself. Underneath it ran the slogan for Indoctrin-Aid fruit juice - *"Get with the program!"*

He retrieved the briefcase and came upon rows of complimentary banners, magnetically displaying Trufflehard's refined wrist fashioned with an Atomix watch. The next set of images focused on an angle of Trufflehard's tapered back, while he glanced over his squared shoulder with OmniIwarE sunglasses. Then there was Trufflehard in full body armor, flexing his shredded biceps and striking a kosher grin for vitamin gummies molded in his image. Similar projections of the remodeled personality proceeded ahead, having in common Skyler Skyler, the newest actor cast to play the legendary role. So the rumblings were true, Milton thought. The new Trufflehard would be dimpled and epicene, atypical of the grizzled and hulking prototype I grew up watching. The market power of the patriotic hero howbeit, spanned a gamut of goods, including ice cream, cereal, toothpaste, tableware, sneakers, phones, briefcases, and more, ensuring consumers they were premium goods that were certified Anti-Jade Agenda.

Exiting the shed, Milton stole one last look at the bushy brows and steely blue voodoo eyes of Trufflehard in a fragrance ad, to pump himself up with the spirit of patriotism and self-confidence.

That man is my role model, Milton said to himself, pausing to take a breather. He lowered a briefcase to the floor again and reached inside his jacket pocket. Drawing out a lime flavored taffy with a strawberry flavored wrapper, he popped it into his mouth and let it stew. Ponderously, he picked up the briefcase with his free hand and forged ahead.

Deviating from the parallel hodgepodge of broad and tall buildings that expanded across his field of vision, he recalled fondly of yonder years watching the muscle-bound Humberto Shortsnaker - the original actor who played Trufflehard - mowing down dozens of jadeites under one roof. It seemed so romantic when he was little, the concept of being outfitted in homeostatic full-body armor that was an impermeable, protective shield against laser beams, wielding a giant gun, saving damsels in distress, all of it. A man in uniform was what he strived to be. He never thought he would be dressed in civvies – his own apparel, some of which dated back to the year his growth stunted. That was a while ago, he thought. When it came to the giant gun however, he got that, divided and concealed in two heavy duty briefcases. His shoulders were throbbing already, as he lugged them across the front steps that wound up to the portico. Critical of the glowing glass walls sectioning the boxed residential complex, he resorted once again for the eighth time that day, wondering what Trufflehard would do.

This is my world, he told himself, something he imagined Trufflehard would say. *I am in control here.* The transformative exercise should have begun taking place, making him feel reinforced about himself already.

He exhaled and imagined freezing his target. *I decide the outcome*, he said to himself. *I own this residential complex.*

He took a deep gulp of air like he was vacuuming his enemy's attributes. Just like what he was instructed to visualize by his Friend, who he could no longer afford. He sighed at the fruitless labor of it all. The routine was getting vain.

But at least it made him think of Amber Blacklight. Just the thought of her revitalized him with prospect and fortitude. How she would come visit him whenever he would schedule an appointment, whenever he had the money. Those days were hard to come by. Alternatively, he had tried others - Bosom Buddies they were called - but there was an inherent cheapness to them that left him mildly disappointed.

Amber was always there for him, as long as she was not booked for the day. She was the one person who sincerely cared about him. The only thing that helped him alleviate the buildup of excess. Maybe that's what I should visualize, he said to himself. Just her and me, like always in the backseat of my car. The company car. "That's what Friends are for," she would say, the tagline of the Friendship®.

I really need to save up, he thought. She's the only Friend I have. And I need her now more than ever.

The motion sensor at the foot of the portico entrance detected his presence, and a silhouetted operator appeared before the holocube intercom monitor. He took it the residents here respected their privacy.

"Pine Cone Lodging," blared a heavily distorted voice. "How may I assist you?"

Milton shifted forward, putting the briefcases down and stepping into view. His voice boomed with confidence and authority. "I'm Enumerator Milton Grainjar. I'm here to speak to one of the residents in your building."

"I didn't get any of that sir," the silhouette said. "Could you please step in closer to the mic and repeat what you just said?"

Milton pulled up the digital bureaucratic insignia on his phone and flashed it toward the camera above the holocube.

"Well I should be ashamed. I don't recognize your enterprise."

The bureaucratic agency which employed Milton's services was truly secretive, such that it was unheard of in the public sector. The Domestic Defense Division was an independent entity that took on many forms in its history. A history that existed longer than anybody probably was aware.

For these reasons, Milton had offered an ersatz ID that presented him as an enumerator from an innocuous civil agency called the Census Bureaux. It was, in his opinion, a poorly conceived cover that still failed to register with the residential masses, and in the rare occasions that it did, garnered no cooperation whatsoever.

"You can call my bureaucratic agency and cross-check my badge number," Milton said.

The fuzzy head on the holocube fidgeted. "I'm sorry sir, this is a private property. We have a zero tolerance policy for unauthorized loitering on these premises."

Milton stated, "While I understand your concern, a professional disclaimer should better warn your actions as interfering with patriotic affairs."

"It's not mandatory, though," the silhouette said.

Milton recited the pretentious line fed to him by his superior. "Any denizen who refuses or willfully neglects to comply with the requests of an enumerator shall be fined not more than fifteen pixels."

"Please vacate the premises before I alert the authorities."

To his left, the cleft of the sliding glass doors gaped open. From the entry way, came out a self-absorbed tenant in a brown jacket, heedless of the enumerator on standby and bobbing toward the streets.

Seizing the opportunity to avert further hassle with the noncompliant operator, Milton entered the building. Off to the far right, he made out the sharp features of an automaton encased in a clear hull, occupying the front desk, yammering instructions in a timid, singsong voice through a filter. Milton passed by unnoticed, across the lobby. He considered initiating the misinformed automaton, but the impending visitation with a suspected jadeite was paramount. Matching the name of the tenant to the unit code, he accessed the conveyer chute that corresponded with his destination.

"I'm not opening the door," the tenant said. "This is your last warning. If you don't leave this instant, I'm calling security."

As per usual, convincing the suspect to grant him voluntary access, entailed some process, but it was required for obscure bureaucratic purposes. Enumerators were not authorized to infiltrate private property by strongarm methods.

Milton was holding onto a thin, transparent, pliable, phonographic rod - lasikally grafted with the patented Sara Bell technology by the Instant Instinct Institute. It read his mind, opening up with a menu that greeted him with an assortment of options.

A holocube popped up, swiftly processing the next action to take through his chain of thoughts, isolating only the executive function of his cognitive processes, generating the suspect's file. He took the unproductive interlude to review the dossier again. It listed everything he had to know. The accompanying profile projected a gray haired male in his mid-30s, average height and weight. It referenced at the very top that the suspect's name was Arthur Melanogastor. Job Title: Artist. He was suspected of attending Jade Association functions, party fundraising, and promoting the Jade Agenda through musical performances. Curiously, he glossed over some of the songs and lyrics.

Eventually, he gave up. Extracting political meaning buried beneath sexual innuendos was never his forte. Why do I even go there? he said resignedly to himself, feeling out of it.

He transmitted another conscious wisp to switch modes. The bolt on the door became neutralized, and it yielded to the polished glass floor, encompassing pipework and circuitry beside. The living room was plastered with floral wall paper. A glass wall overlooked the streets. Amid an entertainment setup, a trio of couches surrounded a coffee table. He also made out several shelves furnished along with a desk to the far right. Nothing out of the ordinary.

In front of him was a male with a shiny black wave on his head. His wide-eyed demeanor could have expressed any multitude of feelings. Save for the dye job, his face for the most part, matched the animated profile in his dossier. He had on an orange coat and yellow bow, with slippers and no pants. Presumably in the middle of changing.

"But how?" he asked, nonplussed. "I locked the door."

The thin, clear phone in Milton's hand reflected the ubiquitous passcode utility; the application was not provided to him by his agency. The Bureaux derided such applications, even classifying it as one of the foremost contraband utilities under one's possession.

Enumerators were held to the highest regulatory standards. Special agents were after all, servants of the public. Thereby they were not only expected to act and behave with accordance, but do so under the guise of anonymity. As much as the Bureaux mandated a steady series of physical and psychological evaluations, they did not enforce random searches of caches. Otherwise, they would have excavated among other hacking utilities, the ubiquitous pass he had failed to report from a prior raid.

Any denizen caught with a ubiquitous pass would be charged of a first class felony. Milton imagined he was not exempt. He had formerly glimpsed the disrepute.

On one particular occasion, he had made the rookie mistake of disclosing to a co-worker his tools of the trade. At the mere mention of one item in his personal repertory, the amplifier lens, he was shunned. And it was yet to be banned at the time.

What was most depressing was, he thought they had a connection. Goowi Dara was her name.

He fancied her, but she never saw him the same way again. In fact, she never saw him, period. Maybe she would've changed her mind, he said to himself, had she not retired from the job the day after. And Milton to this day wondered, What if?

Now every time he used the amplifier lens, or any other banned items and utilities in his possession, it reminded him of Goowi Dara. One day, he thought, I'll find her and ask her to marry me. His goal-oriented mind was interrupted.

"What do you want?" the suspect asked from a distance. Behind him were stacks of large boxes and shelves with multi-jointed figurines and miscellaneous household products.

Milton slipped the phone into his pocket, picked up both briefcases and entered. "I don't mean to trouble you," he said. "I'm only here to conduct a survey. Strictly routine."

The suspect backed away with caution. "Routine for you, maybe. I've never had anybody break into my home before."

"Nothing was broken," Milton said with assurance, surveying the dwelling. Kneeling down, he unclasped his briefcase and removed a transparent sheet. Beneath it, snuggled between glowing cylindrical parts, was the electronic face of a golden gadget with a handle: the genomic polygraph.

Milton felt the restless glare of the suspect, as he configured the device.

The man slicked a hand through his black hair with unease. "That doesn't make me feel any better." He paused. "I can't do this right now. I can't…"

"I'll make it quick," Milton said, heaving himself up.

"Yeah, you do that," the tenant said, "and you'll be sorry you did that." His voice lacked hospitality.

"I express my apologies in advance."

The suspect blinked slowly to convey his exasperation. "I'm not interested in an apology, and I'm not interested in your stupid little survey. I told you I'd rather pay the fine."

Milton stated neutrally, "I'm not in the business of billing you for not complying."

The man gestured toward the door. "You couldn't do the survey from outside?"

"I need to have a look around," Milton said.

The man's face twisted. "I thought this was just a questionnaire."

"Don't be alarmed," Milton said, putting his hand out, trying to put a name on the suspect. Arthur Mega-something. He took his phone out and raised the dossier again. A holocube emanated from the rod. He enlarged it and accessed the details, reading the suspect's name out loud. "Mr. Arthur Melanogastor, do you mind if I call you Arthur?"

"But we're not on a first name basis," Arthur Melanogastor said.

"We can change that," Milton said. "You have that power."

"Absolutely not."

"Mr. Melanogastor, this is just a routine background check."

"There's nothing routine about this," Melanogastor protested.

"Mr. Melanogastor, the sooner you cooperate, the sooner this'll all be over."

"And once it is," Melanogastor said in a sardonic tone, "I will do everything in my power to ruin you."

Milton warned him, "I advise you to stop looking ahead of your current setting. There may be no further proceedings for you, if my findings don't check out."

The man's expression ruffled with disbelief. "I'm calling the authorities."

"I work for the authorities," Milton said.

"I'm pretty sure you don't," the man contended. "I'm buzzing building security. We'll see if they know who you are."

Milton looked up from his setup. "I can't let you do that."

Melanogastor's eyes flared with astonishment. "You're gonna come into my house and tell me what I can and can't do?"

"Of course not," Milton said. "I'm asking you nicely."

Melanogastor was headed toward the overview of the neighborhood, with a transparent rod pulled out. Before he had time to react, Milton pinned him against the glass wall. Melanogastor tried to free himself. "Hey why is your-" Milton thrust his forearm against the suspect's neck. With the suspect's mouth and pampered jowls squished up against the glass, Milton flashed his digital bureaucratic insignia. This was the initiation.

Milton leaned in and stated, "My handle is Milton Grainjar." The suspect tried to speak, but Milton forced him to look at his own reflection, frosting it over. "And I come all the way from XYZ."

The man cringingly offered up his phone. Milton released him and tossed the rod to the wayside. Melanogastor crumbled to the floor, letting out a sickly moan.

Circulation returned to Melanogastor's stamped cheek, turning flush. He shuffled himself to face Milton. "Was that really necessary?" he protested, lurched forward, running his hand over the side of his jaw.

"Formalities. I didn't mean to shock you."

The suspect tried to orient himself, affected by the acute ache of having his head jammed. "You don't mean a lot of things, apparently. Let's skip the shenanigans and address why you're really here. What is it you want from me? Do you want pixels?"

Milton stated, "It's against the law to accept bribery."

"You know what else is against the law?" Melanogastor asked. "Breaking and entering and physically harassing."

"It was a last resort. I have vested in me the authority."

The suspect shot him a look of utter denial. "Authority from who? I don't see a warrant."

"From the Bureaux which employs me."

"The Census Bureaux? I've never heard of the Census wielding such authority."

"XYZ."

"What the hell is that?"

"The cipher for my agency."

"What kind of agency?"

"Special."

"You didn't tell me you were from a special agency."

"I just told you right now, and I was about to get more into-"

"When?" Melanogastor asked. "Did you say something during the physical you administered? I didn't hear anything but the sound of my body slamming against the wall. And if you said something afterward, my ears must've been ringing."

"My deepest condolences."

The suspect's eyes expanded with befuddlement. "Do you even mean any of what you say? You also said you were from the Census."

"Briefly," Milton said. "For undercover reasons. Would you have opened the door if I told you I'm from a special agency?"

"Why not?" Melanogastor said.

"Then allow me to proceed."

"If you can prove it," Melanogastor stipulated.

"I can," Milton said readily. "I have my badge." He took out his phone and flashed his digital insignia.

"It could be counterfeit."

"You can call the number to the office and crosscheck my ID."

"Let me look it up. Can I find your agency on the list of public directories?"

Milton replied, "No."

"Then how do I know it's a real office?" he asked.

"You can see for yourself," Milton said, offering an invitation.

"Give me a rain check," Melanogastor answered. "I've had a long day."

We all have, Milton thought. "Let me pull up your folder," he said, projecting a holocube from his phone. "Is your name Arthur Melanogastor?" When he looked up, he saw the suspect dash for the bedroom.

Milton, realizing what was transpiring, was slow to the draw. His reactionary time was compromised, by desensitization of mental acuity, not just from general fatigue and hunger, but the formulaic monotony, compounded by the mild disappointment, stemming from his failure to secure the suspect. I should've known, he thought. It's not like my first enumeration.

"Melanogastor!" he shouted, dropping everything and chasing after Melanogastor into the dark room. The motion sensor activated, and the lights switched on. There was a bed and a small white stand beside it, with windows hanging from the walls. To his left, was another doorway. He went inside and found himself in the powder room. Rushing past the glass sink and toilet, he poked inside the opaque, holographic shower curtain. There was nobody there. He looked up. Back where he had entered, adjacent to the doorway, Melanogastor's lower half was slithering into the opening of a silver air vent that lined the ceiling. Milton went after him, leaping into the air and grasping the fading foot. He took hold, and for a moment, he dangled in the air. The slipper slid off, taking Milton with it to the floor. The foot above him disappeared, and there was clamoring across the duct.

Milton sprang up and returned to the living room, where the two briefcases stood side by side. He crouched down, popped them open, and drew out all the pieces of the plutonizer from their respective compartments. In all, there were eighteen pressurized cylinders. Each cylinder housed key components - molten rock, volatiles (e.g. hydrogen sulfide, uranium dioxide, zirconium alloy), high-energy neutrinos, radioactive isotopes, unstable atoms, dissolved gas, gas bubbles, suspended crystals - to create a complex high-temperature fluid substance. The tubes were inserted into the reactor ratchet. The magma chambers flubbed with waxy, red and pink and orange globules, as he finished drilling the thermal and blast-proof muzzle extension into the barrel of the main frame.

The assembled result was cradled back to the powder room. Estimating the speed and direction of the assailant, he pointed the plutonizer and blasted ahead where the duct merged into the top corner that connected with the outer air shaft. The affected area of the duct melted on command, ejecting its contents to the floor.

A disheveled Melanogastor scrambled to his feet and bolted past Milton and through the doorway. He swung around the bedroom and raced for the opening that led back to the living room. Milton trailed closely and bound his arms around the suspect to drag him headlong to the floor.

"Yes." He wheezed. "My name-" He panted. "-is Arthur... Melanogastor."

Arthur Melanogastor sat defeated, behind a desk. His shoulders were slouched and his bow was misshapen. His hair was sloppy; strands of it had turned gray.

Milton Grainjar sat across from him in his pale green jacket. He referred to a document on the phone. "Mr. Melanogastor, what is it that you do?"

"What kind of question is that?"

Milton clarified, "How do you get by?"

"I don't know," Melanogastor said. "I never stopped to think how I get by or what is it that I do."

"It's not a difficult question," Milton said, lifting his glance from the holocube resonating from the phone.

"I'm unemployed."

"My files indicate otherwise," Milton said. "I have here a digest that advertises your performance at the Boilermakers Arena."

"I kind of have my own thing going on, playing wherever I'm paid to play." He paused, with aversion slowly creeping across his face. "Why am I telling you what I do? You tell me what you do."

"I'm an enumerator," Milton told him.

"Enumerate my busted back!"

"I guess you can call me somewhat of a specialist."

Melanogastor grunted, "Specialist for breaking into the homes of denizens, or their backs?"

Milton looked away from the documents and fixed his stare on the suspect. "I thought I went over that. You keep bringing up the past."

"Why are you doing this to me?" Melanogastor asked resentfully. "I've never done anything to you."

"I haven't even told you what I'll do," Milton said.

"You did. You told me you were about subject me to some survey." He threw up his hands. "Until that turned out to be bogus."

"No, the survey will still be conducted," Milton said, "because you see Mr. Melanogastor, I've been mandated to clear a report that suspects you of illegal activities."

Melanogastor bent closer to the desk, craning his head sideways. "Meaning what?"

"It pertains to the conspiracy theory," Milton said.

Melanogaster leaned back. "The hell are you talking about?"

Milton rose to his feet. "According to my papers," he said, circling behind the suspect, "you've come under scrutiny for leading a false lifestyle that contradicts your true form, or true agenda."

Disdain shriveled the suspect's countenance. Milton pulled up around the desk, beneath which the suspect fidgeted defiantly with his fingers. Milton went around, inspecting the drawers.

"Keyword," Milton said. "Agenda."

Melanogastor shifted in his seat. "You're not suspecting me of what I think you are. There must've been a misunderstanding somewhere down the pipeline." Watching Milton pick up a golden gadget, he asked, "What are you doing?"

Milton ventured around the residence, scanning the atmosphere with the genograph. "Looking around the sugar bowl."

"On what basis?" Melanogastor asked, fidgeting in his seat. "I never volunteered consent."

"Matters of security breach fall under exigent circumstances." Milton proceeded to the shelves, and tossed various items over his shoulder. He swept the shelves. Packages, jars, and frills tumbled to the floor. He paused momentarily, to shake a snow globe and listen to a sea shell. More scouring followed.

Melanogastor glowered with indignation. "Can you stop rearranging my furniture? I have my interior designer for that."

Milton worked quickly, orchestrating the genograph to and fro. "Mr.

Melanogastor, does your interior designer know that he or she's working for an enemy of the Ekonomy?"

"I know what you're trying to do. 'Know' is a factive," Melanogastor said. "It presupposes your statement as truth. Ergo, there isn't a right answer to that. You're setting me up."

Milton was hunched over, punching open boxes upon boxes of generic goods. "It's a yes-or-no question."

"I'm not a member of the Jade Association if that's what you're inferring. I believe that's what this is about. Isn't it?"

Milton moved through the kitchen. "My bureaucratic agency instructed me to your residency to rectify the records."

"What are you gonna do?" Melanogastor asked.

"With your legal status in doubt," Milton said from behind the counter, "standard protocol mandates your willful participation in a quick survey to help discern your allegiance."

"You keep saying survey," Melanogastor said. "Survey of what?"

"It's a survey for data collection purposes," Milton said, keenly analyzing the ripples on the variegated holocubes of emissions readouts. Years of experience helped him interpret the graphs, the spikes confirming single-nucleotide polymorphism analysis matching the genomic sequence of a jadeite. Also charted were electromagnetic sine waves conducive of anti-Ekonomic presence within closed quarters.

"What kind of data?" Melanogastor asked.

Milton came out of the kitchen with the genograph lowered and approached the seated suspect. "Have you ever held anti-Ekonomic views?"

"You said survey, not an interrogation."

"The survey will have to wait. But first," Milton said, motioning for the suspect to stand up, "have you ever been accused by anybody you work with, for holding anti-Ekonomic views?"

Melanogastor, getting up, balked at the suggestion. "I've been sooner called a luddite than the J word."

"Hands on top of your head," Milton instructed, as he grazed the genomic polygraph about the suspect's outline. "These are yes-no questions, Mr. Melanogastor. I advise you to keep opinions to yourself and answer as clearly as possible to avoid complications. You could sit back down."

Milton entered his final entry into the utility and took a seat. The genograph had reached its conclusion with a 98.7% rate of accuracy: Arthur Melanogastor was a jadeite. But it was not enough. Ninety-eight-point-seven percent was not the be all end all, when it came to Bureaux standards. It was merely referential, secondary to the survey.

He restored the genomic polygraph and closed the corresponding utility on the phone. Then he opened the dossier > past history > activities. A multitude of holocubes and sub-holocubes splayed from the light source of his phone. "The Bureaux has information obtained through unconfirmed reports that you've taken part in numerous entertainment functions. I have listed here dates and locations, where you have performed. One of them was at the True Nation Memorial. May I ask you whether or not the True Nation Memorial was under the auspices of the Jade Association?"

"I refuse to answer questions derived out of unconfirmed reports," Melanogastor said.

"I don't believe there is any more authoritative source on hand," Milton said.

"Then I don't believe you've done your due diligence." Melanogastor shrugged. "You have nothing on me."

"Let's try not to reach conclusions," Milton said calmly. "I'm not the one who compiled this list." He scrolled down the digital document further, and cleared his throat. "I'm looking at a newsletter which carries the title Revolution Marathon. The advertisement states, 'This is your chance to fight back and show them who you are and what you stand for,' exclamation point. Slated for the program are marching troops and cheerleading squads, along a multitude of check points to celebrate the 'spirit of revolution.' One of the checkpoints lists entertainment by Arthur Melanogastor. At the bottom appears, 'Helpers of the Ekonomy,' and at the top, 'Tonight,' with the date." He whipped the holocubes aside and astutely settled his eyes on the suspect. "Did you lend your talents to the Helpers of the Ekonomy under the auspices of the Jade Association on the occasion indicated by this pamphlet?"

"No, I don't remember ever taking part in anything like that," Melanogastor said.

"Then why does the pamphlet advertise your performance?"

"Any number of reasons," Melanogastor said indifferently. "Somebody got it wrong, or there's someone of the same name. I was never there."

"Are you positive you weren't there?" Milton asked.

The suspect raised his right hand. "I swear on my mother's epitaph."

"I have here a video of your performance." Milton showed him the accompanying clip displayed from a separate holocube, confirming the suspect on stage, helming an organ, mic burrowing his aching face.

"That's not me," Melanogastor stated flatly. "There's a difference in the chin. They'll be hearing from my lawyer soon."

Milton compared the chin of the performer in the 3D clip, to the suspect's, but he was no expert at facial recognition. "Do you have evidence of being elsewhere on that date? Possibly an alibi?"

"I can probably call around or dig something up, but why should I be the one saddled with the burden of proof?"

Milton returned his attention to the phone. "I'm looking at a copy of the black market organ Ivory Exchange in a column entitled *Highlights*, where it mentions a fundraiser concert called *If I Had a Zap Gun*, which featured songs playing on the themes of the Jade Agenda. And then follows a statement: 'Among those singing was Arthur Melanogastor.'"

"Well, I never," the suspect said with vehement rejection. "I never performed for those ends."

Milton presented him the accompanying clip, once more showing personage resembling Arthur Melanogastor, crooning in front of a large audience. Milton had the suspect officially cornered. This was not nothing. "What were the circumstances under which you were requested to take part in that performance?"

"It's an impostor," Melanogastor said, paying no regard to the recorded footage. "Somebody who looks like me is out there accepting public engagements, defaming my name."

"As the Bureaux suspected," Milton said. "Hence why I've been alerted to your residence."

"I'm being framed, can't you see? Here you are accusing me of something I didn't do, while someone out there is spreading lies, disinformation."

Milton reverted his gaze to the holocube and broached the next item. "I have before me another issue of the black market organ Ivory Exchange, which has an article entitled 'Shades of Jade Festival Put on by the Musical and Cultural Education, SE Division.' This article emphasizes a production called *We Come with a Peace*, describing it as the following: '*We Come with a Peace* was a smashing show of live entertainment and razor sharp squib. New songs and film strips walloped the Ekonomy and its consumers in what the singers called hyperbolic language.' Denizens among the credits, include one Arthur Melanogastor, who was recited to be headlining singer and the master of ceremonies." Milton lowered the phone and viewed the suspect. "Mr.

Melanogastor, were you involved in the aforementioned capacity of the Shades of Jade program by the Musical and Cultural Education Division under the auspices of the Social Engineering Division of the Jade Association?"

Melanogastor was unmoved. "You could read me as many of these allegations as you want. All it proves is that somebody is out there using my name and my songs without my permission.

Milton adjusted his phone and scrolled further on down the holocube. "Did you also perform and entertain at certain functions held by front organizations, such as the Feminists for Eugenics? I have here a copy of the Ivory Exchange indicating such programs were conducted in dozens of states. Did you entertain this function under the auspices of the Jade Association?"

"No."

"Were you a Jade Association member at any time during the various entertainment features in which you were reported to have engaged?"

"No."

"Are you a member of the Jade Association now?"

"No."

Milton lowered the holocubes spanning his perspective and examined the man leaning across from him. "Have you ever been commissioned for your talents to raise money for the Jade Association?"

"Absolutely and positively not," Melanogastor said, unblinking.

"Have you ever performed in order to raise money for Jade Association causes?"

"No."

"Very well," Milton said, reverting back to the phone. He opened another holocube, which documented erroneous fiscal activities of the suspect's personal bank account. "Last year, you made forty million pixels. But according to your account records, you spent none of it digitally. You withdrew the entire sum, absorbing the 50% transaction fee, which amounts to twenty million pixels. That's twenty megapixels, half of what you made."

"I prefer money I can feel," Melanogastor said, "even at the incursion of a charge."

Milton glanced up from the holocube. "That's a lot of untraceable pixels to be carrying around."

"I don't carry it around."

"Do you stash it?"

"I earned the money," Melanogastor said. "It is my Ekonomic right to spend it or keep it."

"An expired pixel holds no value in the Ekonomy," Milton said.

"I spent it all."

"Can I ask you where you spent it?"

"Food, clothing, general living expenses," Melanogastor said. "My man, is it hard to conceive it all tallying up?"

Milton informed him, "The transaction of pixels is forbidden at black market vendors with no business permit."

Melanogastor nodded. "I know that. I did not barter with black market vendors."

"It is illegal to pass off expired pixels as legal tender."

"I'm also aware of that."

"Mr. Melanogastor, do you still harbor any of the expired pixels in your residence?"

"No, I did not save it."

Milton ordered the suspect, "You will need to provide me in full detail, to the best of your memory, where you allocated twenty megapixels without a single pixel to go unaccounted. I have the form with me." He raised a holocube with the form and slid his phone to the suspect.

"Great, I'll make sure somebody gets it back to you. Is there a specific timeline?"

"Right now," Milton instructed.

Melanogastor crumpled within his seat, intoned forcibly, "Then I lost it."

It was evident to Milton the suspect was not contributing to his aims. "How much of the pixels did you lose?"

"All of it," Melanogastor said.

"All twenty megapixels?" Milton asked, focusing on the suspect.

"Forty megas," he answered monotonously, "as you said, when you account for the tax. Is that a problem?"

"It's your money to lose," Milton said, consulting the holocube. "But," he started, "I don't see a record of it. Is there a reason why you never got around to reporting it?"

"Is it against the law to lose my own money?"

"No, but it's the obligation of a denizen who cares about the Ekonomy. It seems trivial, but there are positive ramifications from notifying your local bookkeeper. It's about helping Execs make informed decisions with timely and accurate data. Any patriotic denizen understands this responsibility and what's at stake for its community. Ekonomic decision makers count on quality, current statistics to plan services and policies."

"I earned that money," Melanogastor quipped. "It is my Ekonomic liberty to do with it whatever I please."

"Even if you aren't moving untraceable pixels to privately support the Jade Agenda, you're still conspiring with anti-patriotic forces that stagnate optimal fluctuations of economics," Milton said. "It is a crime to partake or advocate any activity promoting the overthrow of the preexisting governing bodies of the Ekonomy by force or violence, or for anyone to become a member of or to affiliate with any such agenda." Milton rose from his seat. "Now before we could begin the survey, you must direct me to the money."

"Was that not the survey? And what money?"

"Twenty megapixels of it," Milton demanded.

"That's preposterous," Melanogastor said, his face vexed with baffled disdain. "I told you, I don't have it. What do you think I subsist on? You're reading far too deeply into my financial prerogative and making up irrelevant associations. I have no hidden agenda." He paused and shook his head.

"I can't leave without it." Or else, Milton thought, it's coming out of my pocket. "I'm under order to confiscate it, regardless of your involvement with the Jade Association."

"All of my money is stored in the safe. You can check, but you won't find any spoiled pixels. You won't find anything."

Milton stood up. "Take me to the safe."

As Melanogastor got up to his feet, Milton armed himself with the plutonizer. He waved the muzzle at the suspect to lead the way.

"I'm trying," Melanogastor said, against a wall in the bedroom. There, concealed behind an ersatz window, lied an inset safe. The biometric authentication software measured brainwaves of the owner to identify the right passthought. Behind Melanogastor, was Milton Grainjar, waiting for the lock to spring open.

It had been nine minutes of lollygagging. Milton asked, "Why aren't you opening it?"

"It's hard to concentrate with your gun pointed to the back of my head," Melanogastor said.

"It'll get even harder if you can't get it to open."

"I don't know why it's not working," Melanogastor said tentatively, looking over his shoulder.

"I'll have to start counting down, if you don't open it this instant."

"I promise it's not opening," Melanogastor said, shaking his head.

"Promises are made to be broken." Milton preferred to circumvent the bureaucratic hoops and cut to the end game. "Step away." He pointed the plutonizer toward the corner diagonal from the door and away from the powder room. "Right over there. And try not to do anything ill-advised. Another stunt, and I will not hesitate to call it a night for you."

He hoped that would get the message across and lowered the plutonizer to his side. With his free hand, he fished the phone out of his pocket. Without delay, the ubiquitous passcode utility emitted from the rod. A clack resounded before him, and the safe shuttered open, revealing rolls of pixels. As Milton had suspected, the pixels were dated.

"See," Melanogastor insisted from the corner. "I told you, you won't find anything."

Milton weighed the money in his hand. "I discovered three rolls of expired pixels."

"That's only tantamount to thirty thousand pixels."

Milton looked over to Melanogastor. "Where's the rest?"

"That's all there is."

"Do you have another safe?" he inquired.

"No."

Milton fired his plutonizer at an adjacent window. It fragmented into shards of glass. What remained was the wind in the twilight sky. Melanogastor hugged himself.

"Show me," Milton said, "before I'm forced to tear the whole place down."

Melanogastor, with concerned lines etching his face, furiously shook his head.

Milton marched over to the night stand in a tantrum and yanked out all the drawers. The lamp was flung across the room. He wrangled the mattress and pillows. The bed frame was inverted. He turned toward the corner to find Melanogastor where he last left him. A horrified man cowered from flying objects amid the snow of feathers. Milton stormed out to the living room and approached the desk. He swiped the surface with his plutonizer, clearing everything, and overturning it. He squealed open the filing cabinets, before tilting them to the wayside.

Melanogastor manifested from the bedroom, overwhelmed by the wreckage. Milton halted to regard the pantless man. Melanogastor's mouth remained half-open, portending to say something, but he remained silent and stationary, seemingly stuck in time. The atmosphere coagulated with dead air. He blinked every once in a while.

Cabinet covers swung open. Pots and pans drummed. Drawers pulled out to the clatter of utensils. Wares serenaded the kitchen floor. The dining room table toppled over. Chairs were kicked down.

Milton ripped open the couch cushions and fired a beam from his plutonizer at the entertainment setup. A resultant spark landed on the nearby wallpaper, which started to smolder and scroll up, unraveling behind it a wall of stale pixels.

A bone-chilling screech spun him around. Milton confronted kitty-cornered pupils, underscored by a gaping, lipless orifice, on a bright green face craning over him. It was an eight-foot tall jadeite standing in lieu of Melanogastor, sporting a frayed coat and a distorted bow. An arm protruded from its body, with wispy green fingers elongated around the grip of a zap gun.

Milton's plutonizer was pointing at his feet. His hands were down, as though it was his first day on the job. Now it'll most likely be my last, he thought with mild disappointment. All because of a minute lapse of judgment. Minute, but fatal. He wished he could say he had a good life.

But he could only say, "Well played, Mr. Melanogastor."

Milton jumped. Laser beams hotly pursued him over the countertop. He distributed the blow of the fall evenly across his body by bouncing off the landing and rolling over in one motion. The plutonizer crashed beside him. He went to retrieve it. Pantries exploded, pelting him with plastic shrapnel from the composite material. Shaking away the chipped and clotted particles, a goblet dinged him on the head. Before his vision perforce dimmed, he clung to the plutonizer and reared up behind the counter, gritting his teeth. He could feel his back reverberate from the impact of the jadeite's laser beams. The sink above him tore off. He was inundated by a massive downpour of water. Hate when that happens, he thought. Drenched, he slumped beneath the fountain of water and touched his back for holes. He struggled out of his soggy jacket. It was not tattered, as he had expected. Just encumbered from the saturation.

He squirmed back into the jacket and with nowhere left to turn, crouched beside the ruptured pipe that lambasted him in the face. Blindly extending the plutonizer over his head, he fired. A projectile stream radiated across the room, wiping out everything in range. Milton fumbled for the water valve and shut off the leakage. The geyser waned to a dribble and ceased. He listened for the jadeite, over the rhythm of his arterial palpation.

He mustered himself against the demolished corner of the counter. He brought forth the periscope utility from his phone and took a gander. It jerked out of his hands, and he immediately turtled in response to the disintegrating cupboards. Amid the cascade of splinters, Milton heard the faint click of an empty tube. He sprung out of his defensive shell and ventured around the counter. He took aim at anything that was large enough to conceal a jadeite. All of the furniture was reduced to a shamble of igneous rock, exposing a supine figure.

Wet and mushy from head to toe, Milton squished over to the

mangled body, a canyon formed within the torso, the eyes omitted of life on its contorted green face.

Meanwhile, his back was flaring from the altercation. He stripped off his jacket and cautiously inspected every inch of himself, making sure he was still okay. As always, he thought, a miracle. No direct contact with a laser beam was evident, although it did not denote he was physically untouched. He reached behind with limited flexibility and tried to knead the flesh between his scapulae. Hives and welts from the radioactive aura, high-energy light waves indirectly permeated by the zap gun. Over time, Milton had developed an allergic reaction to the atmospheric exposure to the clothes-penetrating, gamma radiation. The symptoms were commonly referred to as phantom bullets in his field.

Wringing out his jacket, clumps of heavy water sloshed the floor. He sheathed himself gingerly. Times like these he regretted the neglect of adhering to the recommended water-repellent, biohazard armor that was rented out by the Bureaux. He had decided they were bulky and unwieldy for dodging oncoming beams of laser. Not that he could afford it anyway, at his current rate.

Kyra used to tell him he would be required to suit up, once he was fully certified, but it never did pan out. Too late anyway, he thought. Damage had accumulated. He chalked it up to one of the occupational hazards that came with the job. Something he had to live with. For now. Perhaps even forever.

He recovered his phone and saw projected, seven missed calls. He concentrated his cognitive efforts on the menu of the holocube, thoughtfully summoning his superior's contact and executing the call. He curved the rod and clipped it over his right ear. A ringback tone emitted.

"Grainjar, what took you?" Kyra answered, filled with intolerance. "We've been trying to reach you all night."

"I'm here at Melanogastor's. He- It's been enumerated."

"You did it?" she asked. "You got it?"

"Yeah," he said.

"Are you sure?"

Below him, he glanced at the plural pieces of the jadeite and the innards on display. "Might as well be," Milton said. "It's blown in half."

"You don't sound too sure."

No, he thought of saying, the legs might still be kicking. But he managed to compose himself, wiping the bead of water trickling into his left eye. "Yes, I'm…" He strained tortuously and contracted his back.

"If you're not sure-"

"I'm sure," he said.

"We can't afford to botch it like before."

He had botched it once. His first assignment. She never let it go. "I know, Kyra."

"I'm glad you didn't wet the bed this time."

"About that, I'm completely covered in water from a pipe burst."

"How refreshing," she said. "Meet me at headquarters. We have to discuss something with you." There was an ominous break. "You know what I'm talking about."

It donned on him then, the failed test. The fatigue came rushing back. The adrenaline was wearing off. He stood there, feeling clammy and cold, dripping and drooping with resignation. "Yes," he said after a moment.

"How long will you be?" she asked.

"I've found an entire section of outdated pixels," he said, scratching at the embedment of phantom bullets that tingled his back. "It should take me a while to haul it all-"

"Could you get here in fifteen minutes?" she pressed.

"I'll finish the write-up and dry my clo-"

She cut him off. "Okay, hurry up." The line went dead.

For a while, Milton just stood there, indecisive, with his shoulders depressed, legs bowed, weighed down by the sodden baggage that leeched his heat and zest for life. Like I'm wearing the frigid, gelatinous skin of a carcass, he thought. The carcass of whatever died trying to consume me.

Beside the well of water accumulating under his feet, the deceased remnants of the jadeite were flickering wildly, until at last, there was nothing there. The last image screened into his memories was its yawning mouth, conveying a frozen scream that was inaudible to human ears, shrilling through the hollows of his mind.

Everything in the room had turned inert. The debris crackled beneath his pulpous velcro shoes; it felt like his insoles were swapped for cold, wet sponges. He stopped before the wall of money, grabbing handfuls and armfuls of rolls at a time to unload them into multiple duffel bags he kept folded up for these occasions in the bottom compartment of his briefcases. When the duffel bags were filled to capacity, he zipped them up and proceeded to dismantle his plutonizer. Each component was carefully stored into its respective compartment and insulated with more rolls of pixels. Milton squandered zero space, tightly packing as much money as he could into both briefcases. Sitting on the covers in an effort to get the clasps around the nooks, something caught his eye. In the corner of the exposed wall, was a deluxe canvas bag. Indigested calcium, he supposed. They were helpful in identifying future suspects.

He stood up to sounds whining from the opposite side overlooking the city. The blast radius of the recent crossfire had caused a breach in the soundproof glass wall. He could hear murmurs coming through, the neighborhood abuzz. Alternating lights crept along the dark horizon.

Draping both duffel bags on each side of him, he lifted the briefcases, turned to leave, scrubbing the floor. He halted, and thought, I almost forgot. He put one briefcase down, and went back for the deluxe canvas bag. Hoisting it across his shoulder truncated his posture. As he had supposed, it was heavier than both duffel bags combined. Balancing all the cargo, he dragged his feet to the lone briefcase, secured it, and endeavored toward the doorway, leaving behind a fluid streak exuded by the damp strain of his structure.

chapter 2

The manatee gently poked his nose in the air and reeled it back into the collapsing warmth of the ocean. His body remained still, drifting like a log, half-dunked, exposed to the surface, bathing in the sun. He was perched between two worlds. A common puffin surfed on the floating island of wrinkled flesh scaled in algae and barnacles. It took flight, as the manatee submerged himself into the blue space. Vaguely, he lumbered around, paddling his flat tail through the pink shades of coral reef, washed over by the migrating sockeye salmons. Underneath the psychedelic wallpaper of jellyfish he walked, flossing his whiskery mouth on an anchor rope and rolling on his back among the frolics of starfish.

The warm beams from the noon sun inundated the ground level, residential extension of the Kokiri House. Sea breeze ruffled the translucent fibers implanted on Eldridge Kane's head. Instinctively, he turned toward the calling, the open wall, where the waves greeted him from the coastline. The creamy rumbles of the tides lulled him deeper into his sleepy opulence, tugging at him. He stretched prosperously on his silky bed sheets, his body moaning in the aquatic ubiquity, and mindlessly sensing as he always did on the precipice of his waking dawn, somewhere in the root of his acidic design, a flash of concord, a vestigial yearning for an ancestral past.

He turned his head slightly in bed and neurally activated the phone inset on the wall. Below it bulged a refrigerator that doubled as a nightstand. "Ahem," he uttered slumberously.

"Good morning to you too, Lord Kane," said his secretary Dolores Gilmoro. "I'll have Mr. Lazaro come serve you right away."

It was too early for him to form words. He babbled something in agreement. His staff interpreted it as a hypnopompic thank-you, but it was more of a modulated bedlam to intone acknowledgment.

"Don't mention it," Dolores Gilmoro said, ringing off. She was trained along with the rest of Eldridge's personal staff, to cater to his idiosyncratic genius.

The refrigerator, monitoring for a specific encephalographic signature, immaterialized its door. Eldridge shifted creakily and looked inside. Freshly-chopped bamboo stalks were arranged in a neat stack, side by side, one on top of the other. He pulled one out, spun off the top and refreshed himself.

He appreciated the seaside of his vast bedroom, unobstructed by the wall programmed to open moments before he shifted out of dormancy. The guards stood out behind the corners, ordered to stay invisible to preserve the pristine nature of the majestic vista. Eldridge sat up and stared sightlessly, anticipating his vision to coalesce. The scentful ocean gradually calibrated into focus.

The briny scenery was often imitated by the popular ersatz windows and vistas that provided live video feed from cameras planted in all the beautiful places in the world: mountain ranges, under the sea, deep space, etc.

Even though it was the penthouse view from the 515th level of the Kokiri House that was advertised as the LCEO's point of view, this too, was not that shabby, his first level, domestic vantage point in the restricted expanse of Malibay. He imagined there were consumers out there somewhere, enjoying the same ocean view as he did this moment.

With modern technology, the ersatz windows were frighteningly realistic. The effervescent fizzle of the foaming waters, radiating across the sands. Seagulls screeching against the endless percolation of waves reconstituting in the background. Cheap chemical packs replicating the essence of sulfur and seaweed in the olfactory centers. But no amount of realism could duplicate the tactile location itself. Eldridge took great satisfaction in that. Knowing he can step out onto the connecting porch, down the steps, and marvel at the waterfall of sand cascading betwixt his fingers, inhale the breath of the sea, and wriggle his toes in the oceanic swirl engulfing his feet. A luxury he made exclusive to himself between the twenty-seven miles of the sandy coastline stretching in both directions. The privatized beach was sealed from the public, since its acquisition.

Out of the conveyer chute, the Executive Chef Rocky Lazaro smiled, leading a party of handsome women, bikini-clad, draped with their respective provincial sashes and crowning tiaras. They carried golden platters and lids. Eldridge neglected to notice the sous chef trailing behind.

"Good morning, Lord," Lazaro said.

"Good morning, Lord," the sous chef said.

The beauty queens, beaming cheerfully, greeted in chorus, "Good morning, Lord!"

Pleased, Eldridge nodded at them.

Miss Frankingmuth leaned over to tie a napkin for Eldridge. A table was set over the bed, and breakfast was presented one at a time by each of the ladies.

Miss Jaxonville presented the first platter, uncovering it, and smiling. Chef Lazaro described the dish. "We have here, dry-aged filet mignon, fresh from this morning's slaughter, served raw, marinated in soy, garlic, sesame oil, and topped with a raw quail egg and matchsticks of crisp nashi pear."

As Miss Brekkenridge came forward, Chef Lazaro announced, "Then we have king crab steamed with lemon and butter. On the side, we have black king kong shrimp, dipped in microbrewed beer batter, rolled in coconut, fried golden, paired with a creole marmalade made from seventeen different citruses."

Miss Lynchburg stepped up after her, followed by Miss Edgartown and Miss Gangnam.

"Carved into immaculate pinions from only the core of noirmoutier potatos, fries encrusted with seven of the most expensive nuts," Lazaro said, "and fried in duck fat and seasoned with minced garlic clove, sage, rosemary, salt, pepper, and thousand island made with the latest award-winning white wine. A pitcher of tropical juice, flash-squeezed and cold-pressed from sumo oranges and rareberries, and a pitcher of opal apple juice."

Eldridge was not listening. He was reflecting on all the beauties he had encountered from around the world. A new set of Misses were routinely flown in to cater to him every morning. His personal favorite had been the preceding year's Miss Chincoteague, not that this year's winner was wretched by any means. There was just something about the cheery-eyed former queen that had imparted an enduring impression on him, perhaps an immaculate oblivion in her utterance. Ear candy, he mused sagaciously. And she wasn't sugar-free on the eyes either.

Then there were the ones that stood out for alternate reasons.

Reasons that did not garner adoration and his bright side. Miss Snowhomidge came to mind. The only special talent she had was scaring off crows, he said to himself repugnantly. Even then, she couldn't win a pageant against a straw hat on a clothes hanger.

Hits and misses, he thought, that's how these went. But today, they were all crème de la crème. Noble specimens, no doubt.

Aside from their provincial sashes, he could not tell them apart. They could have swapped geographies for all Eldridge cared. They were all assorted hybrids of races, what with generations of multi-cultural intermingling. Stragglers of so-called purebreeds were still around. There was still an ever-dwindling market for them, but they were often plain and unattractive. But not here, he thought. They were by comparison, inferior to the genetic combinations showcased in front of him.

The voice of the sous chef broke his thoughts. "For dessert, we have a warm toffee cake served with tempura fried banana ice cream, glazed macadamia, and butterscotch whiskey sauce."

The next platter was being uncovered. Eldridge raised a hand somnolently. The sous chef halted, his jaw frozen slack on the brink of prattling off more descriptions. He knew what the gesture meant. Eldridge was not interested.

Chef Lazaro spoke up. "Lord, if you have any questions-"

Eldridge flitted his hand, his answer being No. Everything was prepared per his instructions; their livelihoods depended on it. It also meant to move out of the way. They were blocking his view.

Chef Lazaro turned to notice the gathering of varsity cheerleaders flown in from Little Kyoto. Squads were present, stretching and warming up to perform an early screening of their district championship. The wall facing Eldridge parted to reveal a gyrating stage powered by blinding white lights. The first group was stepping on stage in their sleek and spiffy uniforms.

"Enjoy, Lord," the Executive Chef said, chagrined, ducking away to the side.

The sous chef mimicked the meek exit, bidding, "Enjoy, Lord."

"Enjoy, Lord," the beauty queens announced altogether, dazzling with their smiles.

Before they all left, Eldridge pointed out Miss Frankingmuth and Miss Lynchburg, the private selections to dine beside him during the program. But wait. He was not finished. They were all invited, sans the creatures from the kitchen. Back to work for them.

Energetic music vibrated from the walls, startling the reigning queens of the world, as they pranced on the bed, giggling uncontrollably. The lovelies tumbled over each other, resulting in a spill. Then they girdled the LCEO for warmth and took turns sliding victuals into his cavernous mouth. Across from them on stage, the coordination of athletic chants, incessant flipping, and pyramid formations were underway.

chapter 3

In the seven years of employment under Friend, Amber Blacklight had established a rolodex of clients that ranged from all walks of life. The relationships formed within the protective sanctum of client confidentiality, exposed her to the innermost thoughts and daily dilemmas of those who sought her counsel. These denizens included men and women who held various professions, from syndics and school teachers to missionaries and hotshot Execs. Regardless of the individual's background, everybody needed some company for whatever, whenever, and that's where she came in.

Amber Blacklight was the all-purpose Friend, and an accomplished one at that.

She sat on one end of a three-seater, tending to an emergency appointment that bled beyond her normal hours of operation. She had been offered a unique financial incentive by a customer she rarely saw: Milton Grainjar. Of all the customers that Amber had encountered,

Milton was the poorest. Hence, the reason she barely and more rarely saw him, and furthermore the ironic surprise, when he offered triple her usual rate if she could come down as soon as possible. She practically beamed herself there.

Milton was slumped in a furry bubblegum-colored bathrobe, with patches of yellow that made him look like a pink prominent moth, and ersatz spider-skin slippers he probably picked out from the bargain bin thinking who-knows-what. He had on a white tank top and bumble bee striped briefs underneath. On the whole, his attire could not have made him look more insectoid. Shameless, when she paused to consider the fact that they were all no-name brands.

"So I said," Milton said impassively, "'No matter what you say, just don't say you don't wanna die, because it's out of our control.'"

"What'd she say?" Amber asked.

"I don't wanna die."

He was in the middle of telling one of his amazing stories. That was the other thing about Milton Grainjar. He wore the famous gimmick that he hunted down jadeites for a profession. She would play along, anticipating him to eventually ditch the fanciful paranoia thematic of a Trufflehard narrative, and as a consequence wavered for his exhaustive efforts to continue the charade. But upon several more sessions with him, she realized the act was not going anywhere. For years now, she had continued making sporadic visitations. The more she got to know him, the more she realized, this was how he just was. A sad man, she thought.

But one whose antics were harmless. In a way, she thought, the rest of my clientele's not much different. They're also wannabes on the basis of how they perceive themselves. Larger than the existence they inhabit. Only Milton Grainjar wasn't just embellishing the truth, she thought. He was making it up as he went.

Lying across from him, she asked, "God, do denizens really say that?"

The table was set with his late supper of assorted snacks. Milton leaned out of his arm chair and filled another bowlful of chips and sour apple ranch dip. "I was trying to be reassuring to her."

"Grim words of comfort," she said.

"Kyra says denizens will say anything when they're staring down the barrel of a zap gun. Even what you just told them not to say. Apparently I was supposed to have some kind of statement memorized to defuse such instances. But it's too long."

"VIPs are such a hassle," she said. "Just do what I tell you, Milton, and you'll go far." Well, further, she thought.

"Shut up and kiss her," he said, regurgitating what he had been told by her from a prior session.

"Worst case scenario," she said, "you get backhanded, and she forgets how overwrought she is with consternation."

"I learned the hard way."

"So what happened?" she said.

"Fortune had it, I was able to escort her away from danger and enumerate the jadeite."

"What'd you do to celebrate?" she asked him.

"Celebrate?" he said, as if she had posited a foreign concept. He paused what he was doing and glanced up. On the table, were neon-colored candy separated into distinct piles. It was slowly coming back to her, his perverse ritual for gummy larvae. He would freeze it, and then sort out the red and green and clear gummies from the unwanted oranges and yellows.

Amber, inflecting in a neutral voice lacking regional dialect, said, "Now that you've restored balance and prosperity to the world, what are you gonna do next, Mr. Enumerator?"

"I was contented to squeeze in a nap in my car before the next assignment," he said dimly. "Just filing the proper forms for it took hours."

"I would've thought a breakthrough, ultra-specialized agency designated to fight the war on jadeites had denizens for that."

"That would be me," he said, munching on chips.

"Trufflehard never had to file any reports or conduct all these endless documentations and adhere to bureaucratic standards and protocols and-"

"But I'm not Trufflehard," he said.

"Then what are you?" she asked.

"Not him."

"Talk about a hero's welcome."

Mindlessly, he started chucking the gummies into his mouth, red first, then green and clear. "That's not true. I came out with a 200-pixels-off coupon for an 86-pack of muffins when I purchase a 12-pack of disposable welcome mats at Ekonomy Mart. Which I don't know what I'm supposed to do with."

She grinned, showing off her perfect teeth. "You can apply it at checkout for 200 pixels off."

"I don't mean the coupon itself," he said.

"What do you have against muffins?" she chided.

"Muffins are fine. It's the welcome mats I have no use for, twelve of them no less. I only have one entrance."

"A twelve-pack of disposables will only last you six days, if that, before their greetings turn to sour frowns and ridicules and you have to renew them. But then, there are some consumers who rather like that."

"I don't have an account at Ekonomy Mart," he said dully.

"Then you need to get one." As a practicing Executivist born to countless generations of proud and devout Executivists, this was a point of contention that proved of significant interest to Amber. In her previous interactions with Milton, it was disclosed that he had never been to Ekonomy Mart, an avoidance she found utterly reclusive for his plump age. This was often the case with most of her clients. They were in essence, fanatics of an extraneous plane of existence. And much like them, she thought, he's stuck in a loop that occludes self-improvement and subconscious development. She had, to her credit, done her best to tip him in the right direction. For now, he was considered a work in stagnancy.

"I've determined I don't need one," he said.

"Sure you do," she said, "Everybody does. And if you enroll today, it only costs 30,000 pixels for an annual Executive membership."

"I live in a single-consumer household. I don't need the Ekonomy size for anything."

Amber was tired of explaining the importance of Eko Mart to him. Milton was stubborn to a fault. It's his bane, she assessed regretfully, as though he was predestined to be baseborn and godless. It seemed almost unfair. "You're depriving yourself of more than just paltry savings. It's also about the personal connection you feel to the experience itself."

"What personal connection?" he asked.

"Before you go in, there's an automat adjacent to the entrance, where you'll see families properly seated under jolly canopies, gorging on pizza and cinnamon pizzles and Trufflehard ice cream bars, with cartloads next to them."

"I've driven over it several times," he said. "It's not the most breathtaking aerial view."

"My parents and I used to brunch there," she said wistfully. "I always got the same thing - a cinnamon pizzle and a Truff bar. Twenty years later, I still have to swing by for a pizzle and a Truff bar when I'm done with my shopping. See Milton, it's not all about giant-sized, discounted goods."

"Those Truff bars do seem palatable," he remarked. "You don't need an Executive account to get a Truff bar, do you? The automats are right outside?"

No, she thought, you don't need an Executive membership to tend to the outdoor cafeteria. "But you need to go inside," she said, exasperated by his philistine outlook. "You'll see stacks on stacks of products so high, you could crane your neck and squint up to see virtually no end."

He said casually, "I've seen the commercials with the golden statue of Eldridge Kane and the automatons with permanent smiles and beard nets, handing out samples."

He's totally missing the point, she thought dejectedly. "It's one thing to see the commercials. Being present in body and mind is what makes it such a life-changing, religious experience."

"Well," he said, taking a swig of his banana-melon wine cooler and making a pass toward her, "I'm present here, so why don't we start our own religion?" He sat beside her and proceeded to nosedive into her face.

She was fazed by his emotional unavailability of appreciating her conviction. His advancement was repelled tartly. She was put off by him. Not to mention that face. She was not attracted to it. Nor did it ever grow on her. It was the hardest face to remember. Even after she had gotten to know Milton Grainjar relatively well and seen him on numerous occasions over the years, she had a hard time picturing what he looked like in her mind when she was away. Not that she exerted much effort in that activity. More of a fleeting thought, spontaneous in its origin. His face was in every sense of the word, forgettable.

"My blunder," he said, backing off. "Payment upfront."

It was, as he rectified, Amber's policy to receive payment before services were rendered. "Let's be professionals about this," she said, rising up to seat herself, while straightening her fur coat.

"Let me go and get it," he said, getting to his feet.

"No," she said. "Sit."

"I'm sorry. I keep forgetting."

"No, it's not that," she told him quietly. Something else bothered her. He was impossible to convert to Executivism. Not only because he's stubborn, she said to herself. But above all, he's just a piteous boy. A piteous boy who has no other option than to be what he is, was, ever will be. A simple organism of simple mind, lacking the farsighted perspicacity to understand something greater than him. He lacked faith in the LCEO. She wondered, How could I be in the mood to make this eternal pact with this poor little thing?" He was impoverished and ungodly. Damned, in her eyes. Goddamned.

"What a rush," he said in a vague stupor.

"Milton, I just spilled my heart out to you, and you completely changed the subject."

"I have a short attention span," he said.

That's just a glorified way of calling yourself an idiot, she thought. "I came up with the best most rebuttal, but I won't say it lest I hurt you."

"I'm not perfect," he said.

"You could've fooled me."

Milton stood up. "You don't have to suffer me gladly."

Amber said nothing. After a while, Milton sauntered over to a duffel bag to grab the pixels, and Amber turned on the projector.

Before her, a holocube warped into view. It was the official female automated spokesperson of Ekonomy Mart, amid issuing a statement.

"-philosophy and world conquest, we must assume the worst and strive for spiritual growth through Executivism. Consider the hardships and sacrifices of those who've made it possible for our independence. Of utmost priority is fulfilling our patriotic obligations, continuing our lives without interruption, in spite of the alien agenda that encroaches upon our economic principles. As usual, we will remain operational, open for all affairs and business, in efforts to take precautions protecting-"

Amber changed the channel. The sprites reconfigured to a six-armed automaton, handling a dozen plates, wheeling past bright red vinyl booths seated with model parents and model children.

"-we have the best of everything. Burgers, pasta, fish tacos, mozzarella-and-twelve-other-cheeses sticks. And don't forget to reserve space for our ambrosia salad, ranked number one for the past 28 years at the National Ambrosia Cookoff. You haven't had ambrosia salad until you've had the best ambrosia sal-"

She flipped the channel.

"At Ekonomy Café, we are committed to carbon neutrality. Our sustainably sourced, organic gurgle blend - dark roasted for a rich, robust, cocoa profile with notes of hibiscus, cedar, and whole white peppercorn, with a velvety mouthfeel-"

She went up another channel.

"-Armageddon nacho dressing! Get it at Ekonomy Mart before the jadeite invasion! Don't get stuck with bland tasting meat and veggies in your cellar, when the world ends! Spice up your death! Portion of the proceeds will go toward fighting the Jade Agenda! Anti-jadeite cellar sold separately."

She went up another channel. *Trufflehard Saves the World* was being televised. A classic scene was unfolding, as the camera panned around Barret Trufflehard to feature the flanking jadeites. The strapping hunk of carven brawn, a comically proportionate physiology that was reinforced with an attractive, protective body of gleaming, pearlescent armor, found himself at a dead end. "I came here to dish out lollipops and laser beams," he said, inadvertently flexing his jaw muscle, "and I'm all out of laser beams." He produced a large box of lollipops and commenced doling them out. The candies detonated. The holocube went white.

"*We interrupt this program with a message from the LCEO of the Ekonomy,*" the audio blared.

Milton returned, and Amber motioned to turn it off.

"Please, not on my account." Milton sat down on the couch beside her and transferred a hefty sack.

Amber did not see the need to count the money. It felt like 300,000 pixels in tangible tender. The sack was already tearing from its abrasive contents, jagged edges of expiration shining through.

"Your eyes are sensitive to light," she said.

"I'll just turn away and watch you," he said.

The remark prompted bashful laughter from her, but she repressed it for his welfare. While it was the opinion of her colleagues to mistake Friendship® for agreeing and laughing at everything their clients said, Amber disagreed. She believed different clients demanded different needs. Case in point, Milton Grainjar did not appreciate laughter. In fact, he felt every time you laughed at something he said, you were laughing at him. Ironically enough, this just made everything he said all the more funnier. He did not know that sometimes, his candor could be unintentionally amusing. "You're not taking this seriously," she said.

"I'm trying to make it up to you," he said.

The Ekonomy Ink's LCEO Eldridge Kane was delivering a live speech.

> "There are no glass ceilings in the Ekonomy. How high do you wanna go? How high do you wanna fly? The only limitations are your wingspan. Reach as far and wide as you want. I'm not telling you to have faith. I'm asking you to open your eyes and see for yourself. Look around to the material facts, because we have a system in place. A system that works. Everything you want is tangible. You just have to walk outside and go get it."

Milton flipped the channel.

The holographic figure of Eldridge Kane blinked and refocused.

> "-inequality gap is a lie, a fallacy perpetuated by those who don't want to work for what they want. By those who want to stick their grubby hands in your pocket of hard-earned pix and-"

Milton flipped the channel again, but it was the same stream of the same face.

> "Nothing is free in a free world, and there is no such thing as luck in this Ekonomy. No inheritances. What you have, is what you earned. There are no poor consumers in the Ekonomy. We are all rich shareholders of the Ekonomy.

Everybody shares a piece of the pie in the Ekonomy. We all own a piece of our success. The question is, how much of the pie do you want? Just a little nibble? Not unless you're on a-"

Milton surfed the channels, the holocube adjusting with the adamant image.

"Maybe you want it all to yourself, and there's nothing wrong with that. That's not greed. Not in our Ekonomy-"

Milton manually inputted a channel. Another angle of Eldridge Kane materialized. Milton kept trying more channels to no avail. With each remote command of his conscious whim, the stream remained unchanged. Eldridge Kane commanded every station. Every living room. The head at the table of every dining room. Served on a platter as the main course.

"-the Ekonomic dream. Ladies and gentlemen and children of all ages, welcome to the land of butter and riches. Right this way to the Ekonomic buffet. Load up your plates, but make sure you eat it all before it spoils. That's what we're about. That's what the Ekonomy is about. Everybody gets their turn. How much of it do you crave? How large is your appetite? What will it take to satisfy-"

The holocube broke in with a loading disclaimer.

"And now, we interrupt this interruption with an important message from our sponsors."

Individual ingredients orbited around the company's logo, as a cheerful, electronic spokesperson exclaimed:

"Hurry on down to the Burger Galactic for our signature classic! Double beef patties, a slab of onion dredged in our award-winning garlic and butter batter, and deep-fried to golden perfection, on our patented donut pizza bun!"

The frying process captured the floating donuts from the viewpoint of the submerged side reacting with the lard. Afterward, it was thoroughly spray-painted with a glossy pink finish and strawberry flavoring, whereby it was spangled with freeze-dried fruits and specks of confection. A blade of laser sliced it crosswise, revealing what smoldered inside the donut halves - spicy tomato sauce and melted cheese. Chopped tomatoes tumbled onto the open-faced halves, followed by a bed of spinach, banana pepper, pineapple, mushrooms, bacon, and anchovies. The buns enclosed two beef patties divided by breaded onions. The electronic spokesperson added:

"You could also upgrade to free range cricket patties by ordering protein style. Or if you're feeling adventurous, try our special, mouthwatering-"

"I would literally die for a Galactic burger right now," Amber said.

"Are they open, finally, for business?" Milton asked.

Amber left his side and walked through the projected holocube. "No, they just have commercials."

"I saw one recently and tried entering the drive-thru, but there was no response."

"They're everywhere nowadays," she said, absentmindedly padding over to the bookshelf against the far wall. "They look open from the outside. The lights are on 24 hours. You could even park and walk up to the glass and see the menu and the uniformed automatons. But the doors are locked. At first, I thought they were training, so I tried banging on the door, but I couldn't seem to draw their attention."

"Maybe it's a new promotional tactic," Milton said.

"It's been years that way now."

Amber moved along the shelf of random belongings: plush dolls of a praying mantis here, a frog and a lady bug there, a cheap collection of cereal prizes and trivialities. Geometric puzzles with mismatching colors, and a rock beside, red and rectangular with eight round pegs.

"I know a place that has the crunchiest waffles," he said. "Their banana-rum sundaes aren't bad, either. But their waffles-"

"What's the story of the red space rock?" Amber asked, as she headed toward the powder room.

"Remember when I asked you whether or not to confide in Kyra about my burnout?"

"Yeah," she said.

"Well I did what you told me," he said, "and I was issued a pep talk."

Inside the powder room, Amber unslung the turquoise fur coat and leaned over the sink, examining the mirror. Snow white eyelids blinked back at her. She tossed back her rhapsody white hair which frilled down to the white garter belt around her waist.

"It was her belief I wasn't overworked," Milton said from the living room. "I just had inherent motivational issues. So she told me to plant holonotes all around the house to remind myself that I can do it."

Amber puckered her white lips and watched her bust spring to life, hopping up and down. Such vigor. Such buoyancy. She twirled her slender body and caught sight of something on the small of her back. She ran the tips of her fingers across the bumps on her skin. It read,

"Benedict Calhoun Quon" in Morse code. It was the client she had raced back from. In her haste, she had neglected to erase it. She glanced up at her ruefully white cheeks. I doubt Milton would mind, she thought to herself. "What happened after you told her that the notes didn't do anything for you?"

"She asked if I'd ever tried throwing a stone over a bridge."

Amber popped her head out from the doorway. "Oh no she didn't."

Milton continued. "'Do that Grainjar,' she said. 'It's your homework.' I protested the logistics of it, because as you know, I really don't need to be weighed down in my profession. But that was exactly what it represented, according to her. She said it was a symbol of my inner burden. I tried my damdest to get out of it. I told her I had a bad back. She blamed it on my posture. Well, when you've been carrying two briefcases for over ten years, it really does one in. I already have the weight of the world for that. You want I shrug that off? I forgot we ever had the conversation until one day, I walk into HQ, and there on the surface of her desk, awaits a giant piece of rock. She says, 'Try this.' I told her it's too heavy and she goes on to explain how its shape and size proportionally reflected the extra weight I'm lugging around. Only when I'm ready to let go and shrug the mental burden I'm carrying on the inside, am I allowed to throw it over a bridge."

Amber asked, "Was it more helpful than the email she sent advising you to find a relaxed environment that's conducive to thinking more positively and strategically?"

"I called her the next afternoon and said, 'It worked. Holy shit it worked.' And I never brought it up again."

Amber giggled to herself, threw the coat back on, only to walk back out the doorway, and then, let it melt off her shoulders. The coat slid down the length of her figure and truncated around her pumps. She strutted in his direction and came to a stop. "Did it really work?"

Milton looked up haggardly from where he sat. "Do I look like it worked?"

Being the anonymous face of planetary defense had its pitfalls and added pressure. Good Kane, she said to herself, look at him with his head drooping. And that constant crestfallen expression, she thought. At times, it was easy to forget he suffered delusions of grandeur to cope with the monotonous pressures of bureaucracy. What a dreadful reality to occupy for him.

She gave him a spiritual lift, breaking into poses and modeling an assortment of full body articulations. Spinning on her heels, she drifted in the opposite direction and came across a mass of cables and wires. Next to it were a row of holobooks on a shelf, vertically displayed. They were the disposable variety that was sold at newsstands - thin and lightweight stems, with a customizable ergonomic grip. A holocube saver of the book cover emitted from the tip, as the neural scanner detected her scrutiny. She tacitly riffled through a couple titles. She grasped a pink-colored reed and conformed it to her hands. "What's this one about?" she asked Milton.

"I don't read," he said haltingly.

"Then why did you buy it?"

"It had a pretty cover."

"Can I borrow this?" she asked.

"Keep it. It's just charging space on the bookshelf."

Dexterously whirling the book between her fingers, she returned to the couch and carefully inserted it into her gargantuan purse. She cozied up to Milton and turned her attention to the holocube, blustering with the executive voice of Eldridge Kane. The words of God, transmitted from the Malibay Dome to the darkest corners of the universe. And look how sharp he looks under the solar rays, she said to herself, spellbound and utterly captivated by the crystal clear projection of the charismatic leader. She was awestruck by the sight. My Kane, look at all those pores, she thought. He owns a fortune. At an estimated net worth that was exponentially growing each year, was it any wonder why they called him the High Resolution Man?

His speeches evoked praises and shouts from the crowd of awe-inspired followers. The scene panned across the empty seats of the soldout appearance. Not a single audience member was sitting. It was still bright and sunny there. When wasn't it at Malibay? she thought. The city where the sun never sets. A part of her longed to be there and bear witness, shoulder to shoulder with other Executivists. Even if she could fortuitously get hold of a golden ticket for admittance, the drive was practically halfway across the world. It would take days, accounting traffic.

Middle-aged women were respectfully aiming their panties at the face of God. Young girls about twelve, no more than sixteen, were either balling histrionically or falling unconscious. Front rows of women were depicted with the whites of their eyes, chanting in glossolalia. Medics rushed through the aisles, tending to collapsed members of the audience, as Kane proclaimed his divine harangue on stage.

Milton shut off the set. It bounced back on. He shut it off again, but the program recovered once more with the inexorable presence of Eldridge Kane. Milton ceased his efforts and enveloped Amber's hand in his. "Had I known Executivism meant so much to you," he said, mumbling over the turbulent vociferations of the holographic construct, "I would've given it a lengthier consideration. Maybe I can take you out on a picnic sometime. It'll give us a chance to… acquaint each other even better."

A picnic? she wondered, turned off by the ear-shredding, catchpenny suggestion. "Milton, when's the last time you actually wined and dined a girl? Not counting of course, the time you took that girl out to Grassfed Kitchen of Organic Fine Dining and Gluten-Free Drive Thru."

"I'd have to check my calendar utility."

She sidled over to her reserved seat on his lap. "Hopefully somewhere fancy, like Atom or Sucrose, followed by a trip to Eko Mall to get her a new bottomless bag and mittens and muffs, not to mention a personalized necklace, along with a nice pair of shoes, at least?" she asked, pitter-pattering her lashes at him.

"Not in this world," he said.

"Falling in love should be an excursion from your cut-rate reality," she said, her intonation elevating fervently, "comprising of shopping sprees and traveling. Unlimited expenditures."

"But how could they ask me to relinquish my responsibilities, my moral obligation to protect humanity, just to let myself go fudging around with my darling dearest?"

"Not to mention, you're broke," she said. "You're so broke, it's cute."

He tenderly graced the side of her cheek with his knuckles. Blocky knuckles from hands that always seemed inclined toward a closed fist, since her first encounter with him. She imagined his grip strength was tantamount to holding something and never letting go. Something of great weight. His briefcases, perhaps. He had always mentioned how heavy they were.

Milton asked her, "What do you expect when my job is to save the world?"

"Expense accounts and vacations," she said, simulating a smile.

"I say this over and over," he said. "I have a duty to uphold, to serve and protect humanity. You might not think it's the most important job in this material world, but what part of planetary security do you not understand?"

"The 'security' part."

"Aren't you afraid of the Jade Agenda?" he asked her.

"And the repercussions it could pose to our institutions?" Sullenly, she got up from his lap and fumbled through her purse. Unable to find what she was looking for, she knelt down and spilled the contents of her purse, producing a mound of belongings. She sought something to enhance the experience. Or take her out of it.

Scavenging a vaporizer, she asked, "Is the preservation of said institutions worth risking your life over?" She took a deep puff and suppressed a cough. Languidly, she crept toward his boot and groped her way back to his lap. "What do you fight for, Milton Grainjar?" She peered wanly into his godforsaken gaze. "You have no family, and you're beyond redemption. Nor are you marriage material." She hesitated, consciously reconsidering her frigid critique. "Not that anybody is. But it doesn't stop us from getting married and divorced." She proffered him the vaporizer.

"Every love story draws to an end at some point," Milton said.

"So why worry about it? It's inevitable. Focus on the climax."

She moved the vaporizer toward his mouth.

He declined. "It makes me sleepy."

"You're always sleepy," she said. "It'll take the edge off."

He reclined and lolled his chin to the ceiling. "I can't just kick back and relax until kingdom come."

Amber swiveled on top of his lap and mounted herself, saddling over his pelvis and thighs. She stripped away the layers of his clothes, the robe first, followed by his top, and wrapped her arms around his nude shoulders. "You've been through a lot," she said. "More than enough. You have to know when to hang it up and give it a rest."

His eyes were distant and far away. "What about the Jade Agenda?"

"The Jade Agenda," she said, "is not all that bad."

"Without a doubt," he said wearily, "the cannibalization of babies and virgin sacrifices should be fun for the whole family."

"And worse comes to worst," she said, popping off a brassier strap, "being a sex slave might be freeing in some ways."

Amber thrust off and scrambled for the exit. The domestic security system recognized the neural response of the principal lodger and slammed the door shut in front of her. The physical revival he exhibited was rapid, and even after all these years, it surprised her. She had generated in him, a spark, a latent energy, a trigger-happy response. She folded in feverish anticipation, as he moved up and covered her.

"Oh Mister Enumerator," Amber said, bursting into despair. At the same time, her trim panties slipped to her knees. "I swear I don't know anything. Please, I'll do whatever you want. "

"Here's what I want." Milton jacked her right leg off the ground, and worked to free her, uprooting the strand of undergarment from the corresponding heel. With both arms wrapped around her stockings, he boosted her above him in embrace. Such garish demonstration of primal clout never ceased to sweep her with salient precipice. It was hard to conceive he harnessed such strength for embodying an average, if not flabby physique. The voltage flowed from his arms, his legs, his core. All the years of carrying dual briefcases had trained him for this exercise.

Finding her much faster than before, he said, "I want you, to transmit a message for me." She felt herself exalted fiercely against the door. The cold glass came as a shock to her flattened back, shooting an electric chill up her spine and neck that made her ears fizzle. Her arms and legs bubbled over with goosebumps. All at once, he was everywhere, her everything. He was her atmosphere, redolent of a lugubrious alleyway of empty bottles, burning barrels, and abortions.

"My God," she gasped, with neither heels touching the floor, "so powerful." She clobbered his chest with both her fists. Her head fell away in delirium. "No, I can't! You have no idea what they'll do to me if they found out."

"I'll protect you," he said in a conserved whisper.

"Just get on with it and enumerate me!" she said in anguish, viewing him from the corner of her shrinking eye. "I'll be your prettiest number."

"If I wanted to enumerate you, I would've done it long ago," he said, delaying the dynamics. "But how can something so darling be reduced to a statistical value?"

She took the respite to face him. "You don't know them! What they are." She looked away. "They're not humans."

He lingered over her exposed shoulder, with the brassier strap hanging off. "They are the ones who don't know me." He roused back to motion, her wet skin starting to break. "Because nobody does," he said, exhaling, propelling forward. "But they will."

She coddled his head and pecked him incessantly on his salted lips and eyes and nose, stalling him just a little while longer. This was not a show anymore. She could feel her legs going to sleep, the walloping mace of his chest versus her quivering breasts.

How incredible it was, playing along and deluding herself. It was moot, whether he was really saving the planet by neutralizing illegal aliens or not. She no longer posed the question. Not here, she thought. Floating in the air. Three feet off the ground. With my heels on. Panty clinging from my left ankle. In this moment of truth, everything goes. Anything is possible. She lathered his hair, rubbed his chest in a waxing motion, and finally braced him, fire-breathing into his ear. "Mister Enumerator, you're gonna let me go after all, so I can pass it along to the other party members. Through me, your legend will spread."

"Tell them my handle is Milton Grainjar," he said, impelling her to whimper sprightly. "That I come all the way from XYZ, for each and every one of them."

"Oh Kane," she said, sighing, trembling, sinking deeper into his clutches. This time, she did not resist, could not, capitulating under the force. She let in the warmth, the sun piercing through the midnight. She could see clearly now the composition of a passage, pebbled by green and violet and orange crystals of broken bottles. The vents burping pink pillows of smoke. The red spread of pantyhose beside the tie-dye puddle of frothy chemicals running off into the drain. Her eyes glistened and swelled with illumination.

chapter 4

Eldridge Kane arrived at his penthouse office in the Kokiri House. Between ice sculptures carved in the likeness of the Lord Chief Executive Officer, was the refreshment wall. Hundreds of the day's pastries were laid out, with holographic labels to discern the selection – coconut buttermilk biscuits, strawberry-plum fruit galettes, colossal cinnamon rolls, just to name a few of the everyday favorites, along what looked like edible little toys: a monkey juggling on the head of an elephant on a unicycle. A walrus lifting a barbell on its shoulders. A killer whale jumping through a ring of fire. All part of a diorama capturing the essence of a carnival show. Bite-size, he observed. Another one, mapping out the human genome. These were just a few of the many themes tastefully expressed in the cake section. Beside it were the state-of-the-art waffle and beignet terminals, and bars serving frozen yogurt and smoothies. Slender, lingerie-clad chefs stood at attention, accompanying their respective stations. A mere mortal would be overwhelmed by the number of offerings. Eldridge too, was indecisive, but only because he was sick of it all. He grabbed a stalk of bamboo water and headed to his command post.

On his desk, was his computer by default, a stack of colorful illustrations, and a crate, heaping with beach towels, backpacks, key chains, plush dolls, action figures with 200-plus points of articulation, lunch boxes, and chewing gum, all of which were themed after Trufflehard. More urgently, he eyed a basket beside the crate. It brimmed with confectionary: matcha-dusted honeydew cronuts and watermelon-glazed banana bread slices. Weaved into the basket was a customary holonote; he did not bother.

He seated himself on his executive chair. The holocubic menu of the computer activated upon his psychic advancement. Scanning Eldridge's thoughts, it deferred to his direction. A second holocube opened up with the news.

Eldridge thumbed a cronut and munched, returning his fixation to the main page. The text went dim. Another holocube generated. A gruff voice blared, "FRIDAY! SATURDAY! SUNDAY!" An enormous shutter factory was depicted with doll-faced babes performing quality control checks in white lab coats and construction hats, each of them respectively equipped with a mallet, a saw, and a drill. The frantic and boisterous tone continued, "For three days only! Ekonomy Shutter's annual going-out-of-business sale is finally here! And this year, all shutters have to go! Buy the highest quality shutters for prices so low, you'll shudder!" The lab coats were stripped away, and a sequence of wreckage flashed in tandem with the preceding claims. "Locks can be picked! Windows can be broken! Shutters can be penetrated! But not Eko Shutters' shutters!" A green head, who had a bikini body from the neck down, was shown beaming the shutter with laser. "Only Shutter Corp's shutters are plasma proof!" The shutter was still standing. "Don't put a price on safety! Protect your wife and daughters from the jadeite invasion!" A thousand images flickered in rapid succession - an exploding watermelon, superpowered heroes in color-coordinated spandex and visored helmets, a pro-wrestler getting flung from the top of a 20-foot cage, an elephant attack on a zookeeper, a man on a crucifix, etc. "SHUTTERS! SHUTTERS! SHUTTERS!" A mushroom cloud. "This message, brought to you by Ekonomy Shutters. Shuttering the world for fourteen generations." The ten-second commercial came to an end.

A doughy lump caught in Eldridge's throat. Frantically, he fumbled open the rain water and choked it down, slamming the empty bamboo stalk on the desk. Rosy complexion returned to his face. His ears were still ringing with the residues of a recurring resonance, and he was seeing squiggly lines drifting across his vision, when female attendants at the counter rushed over with kerchiefs and napkins. They dabbed concernedly at his face and his shimmering golden tank top and the spill on the desk.

By the time he gestured that he was fine, a full minute had passed and the commercials were still streaming. The holocube featured a buxom figure transposed against a prismatic, psychedelic backdrop. An ad for a water recycling system. Having exceeded the prerequisite worth of ads, he optioned out and read the featured news title.

CHEAP THRILLS LEAD TO SHRILLS

He expanded the story, enlarging the holocube.

Eleven consumers are dead as a result of bargain hunting gone wrong at the 812th Ekonomy Mart in Times Square. Shots fired by security officials to enact crowd control, fatally wounded four shoppers.

The security officials who fired the laser guns have been identified as Alvin Mitrione and Skeeter Brafflowski. However, both officials maintain they fired above the shoppers without malice. Further investigation identified pink laser beams in the surveillance recordings, along with the blue plasma signature matching the regulation arms belonging to the security officials. The pink laser beams were traced to a display gun.

The shots fired were the result of the security officials' ill-fated attempt to salvage injured shoppers of a preceding disaster - seven individuals were killed and eighteen more were injured when they were struck down by a tower of Lucky Rice Cake breakfast cereals. One of the fatal victims, 84, who did not find out it was Bargain Hunting Day until well after entering the store, was decidedly on her way out.

Blah blah, he thought. He skipped a couple paragraphs and left a bite mark on the banana bread.

The Ekonomy Mart staff was overwhelmed by the massive turnout of customers who grabbed the boxes easiest to reach in front of them. Employees simply were unable to fill in the voids in time, causing a structural discrepancy in the five-story tower of cereals being offered on the national holiday for 5% off. This was not the first time one of the product towers collapsed on unsuspecting shoppers. Last year, the 1,731st Ekonomy-

Crabbily, he glossed through the rest of the article until he read the following passage:

> *The manager of the store confirmed a box of Lucky Rice Cakes*
> *would be reserved at the discount price for the families of the*
> *victims.*

That's one consolation, he thought, smacking his lips and returning to the main page. He munched vigorously, ripping the bakery to shreds, the spongey texture soaking up his drenched tongue. Tart watermelon notes reacted pleasantly with the dominating flavor - banana, amplified, sweeter, and yet somewhat monotonous and less complex. Lacking in the ripeness and age. What lingered was the perfumey, volatile compounds encased in a matrix of vegetable fat to mimic fruit.

He opened a line to his personal secretary on his flat office phone. "Explain what's on my desk," he demanded in a muffled voice.

"The holoprints for the upcoming issue of banners," Dolores Gilmoro said. "Creative stopped by earlier to show you those for apprais-"

"Next to it."

"Trufflehard merchandise that made it to the final stages for the upcoming quarter. You sound just as surprised as I was to find the test demograph-"

"I'm talking about the basket," he said.

"Those are the new flavors that were added to the bakery section at Ekonomy Mart. It was sent in as a gift."

Eldridge's temporal artery surged. He picked up the basket and flung it in a fit of blind rage. After which he bolted upright and blazed a trail to his private powder room.

The double doors parted to offer a bunny-eared, bosomy shape garbed in a magenta leotard and heels. Operating a cart full of cleaning equipment and towels, she greeted him with a bright smile. "Good afternoon, Lord."

She was abruptly pushed out of the way. He stormed into a stall and keeled over the neon orange bowl, with a rotund finger jammed inside his throat, gargling.

The attendant could be heard inquiring from behind. "Lord, is everything okay? Should I call a doctor?"

Eldridge rose up from his knees, grunting and gasping. The double doors parted. He manifested with a red and sticky countenance, a batter of saliva and mucus. A sorrowful look of surprise spilled across the attendant. He was able to identify her by the sash demarcating the month of reign: July. She raised a cloth to his nose, and he blew it like a trumpet.

"You poor, poor thing," she said, wiping the beads of ooze that flowed from the orifices on his face and ran down the trunk of his neck.

He returned outside to find his personal secretary standing at his broad, stately desk, among the basket and the scattered bakery. Her hair, which used to be vibrantly blonde at one point, had faded of luster. She had lost weight. Too much. Her taut, angular face was tired and compressed, subjugated to the demands and pressures of harried transactions.

"Lord," she said tentatively, "you look ill."

His bulky body galumphed forward, pointing toward the bespeckled floor. "This is prepackaged. It's not fresh. I only eat food with enzymes. Remove it from my office. I don't even want to breathe that stuff. Dolores are you trying to kill me?"

She snapped, horrified by the implication. "Lord, I would never!" She drew back, opting for respite, polishing her mini skirt and pressing the knotted bun atop her head. "Brody Combs sent it to you."

Eldridge leaned on the desk for support and slid down on his chair. "Is that name supposed to mean something to me?"

"The CEO of the Ekonomy Bakery."

"CE-who?"

"He said he knew you."

Who doesn't? he wondered. "That really narrows it down for me," he said caustically.

"His company was ranked 14th last year by Elephantine, among the fastest growing companies," she said. "He just wanted to know what you thought of the newest additions to join the fine bakery items that went on sale this month."

He flashed her a portly sneer. "The next time you try to peddle ersatz food into my office and poison me, have my king's taster go first."

"Lord -" Her voice faltered. "I'm deeply sorry."

"Sorry for the attempted assassination, or sorry you were caught?"

The vascularity in her forehead amplified, as she cried out defensively, "I affixed a note on the basket!"

"The perfect alibi, confirming your premeditation," he said astutely. "You betrayed me, Dolores."

The secretary's nose blushed. "I've been loyal to you for twenty years," she said, sniffling.

"Indeed aged by the refining forces of governance your position charges inside the Kokiri House. Your experience in the mantle of the Ekonomy, has not hardened you into a precious stone. It has earned you eroded stripes to the visage, perhaps weathering you with confidence to work anywhere. But I would omit citing time served for the Lord CEO. Your record here will be thoroughly cleansed from the system. You'll be discharged in t-minus one minute. Unless you need more time to clean up this mess that you caused. And go retrieve the Executive Graper before my tongue breaks out in hives.

"Of course, Lord," she said in a deadened voice, tears streaking her imploding cheeks. Her head hung low between her pointed shoulders, as she turned to kneel down and gather the debris. Silently she sobbed to herself. The attendants behind the refreshments looked on passively and beautifully; they understood personnel matters were beyond their purview.

Milton Grainjar stayed in bed, listening to the distant rumble of a car, crackling with thrust, gaining momentum, until the bass of the rocket exhaust was completely drowned out by the sky. It all happened so quickly. One minute, he was eating it up with his best Friend. And then, he was sober and alone with nothing but the consequences of ducking Kyra and depleting expired money confiscated from the latest rounds of enumerations. He stared at a phone with eighteen consecutive missed calls and anonymous alerts inquiring if he knew such and such. Some things never changed.

You've reached a new low, he told himself, getting up from the bed and checking the time. Where did all the hours go? he asked himself. He bristled his hair with a hand, racking his mind for an explanation. He had to tell Kyra something. Perhaps the car broke down at the same time my solar-powered phone ran out of solar energy, he thought. It could happen. It happened once before. And she didn't believe it then, he thought dejectedly. Why would it all of a sudden work now? He knew he had gone too far this time. It was bound to happen sooner or later.

Eldridge ignored the distraction and flipped through the pile of 3D holoprints on his desk.

The first one rose to feature iron-clad babes hauled out in caged transport by a green and baldheaded oppressor who helmed the wheel. The depiction was titled, *"CONQUEST,"* with the message below warning, *"THEY'LL TAKE OUR LOVED ONES!"*

The next archetype was spangled with the block letters, "INFILTRATION." It depicted a boardroom full of green Execs in suits.

The message underneath it warned, *"ARE THESE THE CONSUMERS YOU WANT TO ENTRUST W/ YOUR DAUGHTERS?"*

Another featured a profile - greenskinned - that boldly protested - *"WE ARE NOT MASCOTS!"* A veiled pop-cultural reference, he suspected. But all of them, Anti-Jade Agenda posters. Part of the public relations campaign established to counter views and opinions that resisted the monopolization of economic policies.

Under Eldridge's direction, the Board of Execs had authorized the formation of a diametric political complex to discredit the opposition, an opposition that would eventually become clustered with the rest of an unnamed party that operated under the Jade Agenda.

He remembered the plot like it was yesterday.

Two-hundred-and-nineteen pages of the infamous manifesto were the only tangible evidence of the party's nature. Eldridge and Execs had never planned on producing any members of the derivative following, jadeites as they were aptly coined by the press. Much unknown was promulgated to shroud the Jade Association, by surrounding it with the ambient association of fear and anxiety extrapolated from the disseminated doctrines. Keeping the conspirators faceless would serve to dehumanize the true identities and project attributes appealing to public boredom. Indifference incited to intrigue, exploited by the malleability of who, or possibly what they were.

And that was when the headlines were made to declare war. Not a conspicuous war that grandma and grandpa fought in clear view. But a vague and shadowy struggle to uncover an anonymous spy network whose imminent threat loomed in the form of planetary annexation. Failing that, the sociopolitical fallout pending revolution, forebode a drastic shift among the fundamental institutions of religion, marriage, home, civility, and the progressive way of life.

A panel of Execs and paranoid experts were regularly featured on numerous programs to pontificate on the sinister implications of the invisible enemy, interpreting passages from the Jade Agenda. Cryptic verses of text ascribed to promoting crimes and offenses that would undermine the Ekonomy, diluting it for the penultimate phase. The Jade Agenda was, as one reliable source put it plainly, an instruction manual for the revolution.

The usurpation of Execs proposed within the manifesto, was not what was considered indefensible. Such sentiments had begun to pervade a desperate subpopulation of the cultural zeitgeist, and prevailing themes of anarchism circulated as possible solutions to the growing inequality. But the implications of such foreign revolt would inspire agoraphobia and xenophobia in the media, a stigma of implications that grew crisper with subsequent declassification: new editions of the manifesto, expanded and revised, adapting with the times. The most recent volume stood 6,723-pages long to accommodate in-depth speculation among other ideals, mass genocide as a viable means of population control, as well as virgin sacrifices and the cannibalization of babies.

Eldridge reached the illustration of a metropolitan island of cloud emerging with a flourishing, golden cityscape. The wonky text declared, *"BEWARE!"* and *"LOOM OF REVOLUTION!"* The utopia was thrived by a population of beautiful women sheathed in tattered bikinis. Ominously overlooking the praiseworthy paradise was the gigantic, hairless head of a tea-colored abstraction, eyes slanted and directionless, ever narrowing into a small, gaping mouthpiece, with its outstretched canopy of fingers. Symbolic attributes of a jadeite that borrowed heavily from the Barret Trufflehard legend - now a major motion picture and a couple remakes.

Originally illustrated as nebulous silhouettes lurking in dark alleys, the franchise had infused the unseen conspiracy with vivid dimensions.

Its constituents were eventually popularized into physically deformed anomalies, domineering and strange, otherworldly in appearance, abnormally large, smooth heads consumed by blacked-out eyes amid the emerald complexion. The uncanny semblance was maintained and canonized through various mediums. Before long, the so-called jadeites were synonymous with shapeshifting aliens under terrestrial subterfuge, on mission of genetically engineering the perfect sexual slave race.

The plan had worked out better than anyone had conceived. Quashing civil unrest and provoking patriotism were executed with sensational deliberation, through hyperbolic threats from an abstract entity and the persecution of the associated stigma.

Who but he could've known?

Eldridge Kane. Lord CEO of the Consumer's Ekonomy.

But even he, lauded for his commercial aptitude, underestimated the lucrative industry to emerge from the political contrivance. Crossing his hands behind his head with crooked arousal, he had to admire himself for the progeneration of commodities: lovechildren begot from his visionary endowment. His directorial delegations made the world. A world that he was breathing. A dream that he awakened to. There was nothing before me, he thought. Nothing but clay that I made from scratch.

chapter 5

Her short, auburn lump of thick, voluminous hair was handsomely swept to one side. The dim, blue ambient lighting of the Bureaux facility applied a sapphire pallor to Kyra McVeronica's face. Leather jacket with lapels flayed, collars flared, sleeves ribbed, zipper diagonal, no buttons. Her leather leggings caressed her long, slender legs, clinging to her skin, tapering to the ankle-high leather boots, with red heels and zippers slashing the length of her inner ankles.

Kyra wedged her knee into his thigh.

"Grainjar," she said, "you have no idea how long I've been waiting to do this."

She leaned closer, and drew a deep breath between her glossy lips and pronounced, "YERRRRRRRRRRRRRRR!!!!! FIEYUUUUERRD!!!!!"

Her delivery blew his hair like a sudden gust of wind.

"Do you have any idea what you've done today?" she probed.

Milton's chin was held frozen by her icy hands. Unable to look away from the darkly azure eyes, he muttered, "Yes, you've made it known for the past hour."

"According to our estimates, you still owe the agency 3,629,625 pixels for recovered funds. And that's not covering the preexisting balance you owe."

Where was she getting that math? Milton wondered. "Like I said, I only had enough space and time to bag 17,410,375 pixels, and I only spent about 40,000 of it."

"Your quota was twenty megapixels."

"My quota is to keep the world safe."

"Then you're falling short on all counts," she said.

Perhaps on that supposition, he said to himself, she has me there. There was nothing to gain by arguing otherwise. Granted, he found her delivery method less than amicable. But she was right, wasn't she? he thought. He saw no reason to argue the merits of his service. Certification was not within reaching distance for him. And by requesting his withdrawal from the Bureaux, he would be disqualifying future consideration for candidacy. "So that's it," he said.

"Not until you surrender your gear."

That was an understanding he thought he had conveyed by the briefcases containing the plutonizer and the genomic polygraph placed before her. He bent down and slid them closer to her feet.

"Your badge and key will be reset," she informed him. "Don't bother to pull it up. You've been revoked the permit to exercise the authority."

He did not mind the loss of the badge. It was useless. But relinquishing the key to the beetle meant he would have to rely on the public transportation system. He did not look forward to the dozens of transfers it would take to reach his studio in the town of Cherry Gushing Hilltop. Might as well get started, he thought. "Am I free to walk now? I have to get going if I want to reach home by the next morning."

Unadulterated reversion glinted from her eyes. "Yes."

Milton had a hard time believing it for the moment. It was over now. And he felt then, an urge to apologize for himself. Regardless of the poor working conditions and whatever tension existed between them, he believed he owed her that much. To close it out by accepting full responsibility. In parting, he said, "Kyra, I'm sorry I didn't live up to expectations. It's not your fault. It was all my mistake." He glanced back, swallowing piteously. "I hope you don't harbor resentment toward me." He turned and started toward the conveyer chute.

"Is that the best you can do?" she called out to him.

Now what? he wondered. I've taken the fall for all parties involved and accepted judgment. Termination, in this case. There was no longer cause to argue. No certification to vindicate my hours, my failures, my financial dependence and self-worth. He glanced back, swallowing deplorably at the crippling premonition of receiving a seven-digit bill on damages. "I hope you don't harbor resentment toward me." He continued on his way, picking up his pace now, impelled by an avid rush to face the reality of unemployment.

"Aren't you forgetting something?" she asked from behind.

No, he thought. Nothing came to mind. His genomic polygraph? His plutonizer? No, he had surrendered those items for a reason. He was not involved with the Bureaux anymore. Those were not his to own. They were not for keeps. Just the memories, he thought. In his muddled speculation, he was struck by a great epiphany. My severance check, he realized, captivated by the prospect.

He peeked over his shoulder to see Kyra trailing. Beside her was a gentleman he had never seen before, with gray hair and gray suit, carrying the briefcases Milton had just dropped off. *Where did he come from?* he asked himself.

He turned to receive them slowly and reluctantly. "I'm sorry," he said blankly. "Again."

Catching up to him, Kyra said, "Sorry's not enough." She folded her arms.

How much more blame could one individual shoulder? he wondered. Milton was unclear about the steps to take. "You just fired me a minute ago."

"Grainjar, you didn't think it would be that simple," Kyra said.

His processing capabilities were taxed. Her words lacked gestalt. He had to caption the statement in his head to read what he had just heard. "I don't understand," Milton said. "You just told me-" He broke off, noticing the man beside her, eyeing him sternly. Milton turned to Kyra. "Does he need something?"

There was silence. The man's expression persisted stoically. At last, he spoke. "I understand there's been a breakdown in communications."

Who the hell are you? Milton wondered. "I'm sorry, who are you again?"

"Nelson Wattlecup." Grave lines carved his chalky face like a powdery white tombstone. He extended his hand. "Senior Superior."

Milton shook it out of courtesy.

Wattlecup said, "I've been listening the whole time."

No kidding, Milton thought. But why?

"As you can see," Wattlecup explained, "we erect a high moral standard for all of our agents here at the Domestic Defense Division. Therefore we enforce a zero tolerance policy for the list of violations you've been citied for over the past week."

"Didn't we already go over this?" Milton asked, looking to Kyra.

"Grainjar, just hear him out," she said.

"I'll get to the point," Wattlecup said. "Your actions over the past week have been a disgrace to everything this bureaucratic agency stands for. Normally, you'd be terminated abruptly and sentenced to the Reform Division to be administered electroshock therapy and chemical castration for your crimes. But as it stands, you're the only agent we have."

"What about Vicky Gracie, Abigail Ketchum, George Brecknock?"

"Gone," Kyra said, with no annotation.

"Wallace Buckingham, Joey Morecott, Anney Fitzgeoffrey?"

Kyra pivoted her head in a negative manner.

"Anney Fitzgeoffrey?" Milton repeated, making sure she heard him the first time. She was, not too long ago, touted as the best and brightest. The youngest enumerator to receive full certification.

"It's been a while since they've seen action," Kyra said.

"Are we talking weeks here? Months?"

"It's not important."

Milton was wondering where they had gone. "What about the latest roundup?"

Kyra said, "You mean Mona Jabagchourian, Sigourney Grayson Bartholomew, and Juanita Diffendaffer?"

"Sure," Milton said, assuming they were the recruits in question.

"They're no longer with us."

Goddamn, he thought.

"We decided to withhold the information until the time was ripe, but the time never came," Wattlecup said, pursing his lips. "We didn't mean to break it to you this way." He sighed uneasily. "But it can't be unbroken. You must've been close with them."

"Not really," Milton said, to which Kyra and Wattlecup exchanged glances. It was the truth. He recalled vague instances of exchanging small talk here and there, mostly hellos and goodbyes, and something about how privileged they felt to be granted the job of saving the world. "But I understand," he appended. "They died for a worthy cause."

"The politically correct term is early retirement," Kyra corrected him.

"Yeah, that," Milton agreed.

Kyra perused him tartly. "Grainjar, just never mind."

"You'll have to excuse Kyra," Wattlecup said, head bowed. He was concentrating on the phone he was holding. "She was hit especially hard."

Milton sensed neurological pulses. It was his phone, alerting him of updated settings.

"Go ahead," Wattlecup said, nodding. "Take a look."

Milton rummaged his pocket and yanked out the translucent rod. On the holocube, his shield had resurfaced. To his surprise, the key to his beetle was intact as well. "So I'm not fired then?" he asked.

"That you are," Kyra said. "Oh believe me, you are."

Wattlecup's eyes remained steadfast on Milton, unblinking. "After all the conduct codes you've broken, we were left with no other choice but to let you go.

"You've been terminated," Kyra reiterated.

"I got that," Milton said.

"And now, I'm officially rehiring you." Wattlecup brought his hand out.

Milton shook involuntarily, nonplussed by the roundabout verdict.

"Welcome aboard," Wattlecup said, fashioning a sallow grin.

"I'll take it from here," Kyra said.

Milton went oblique through the conduit pipe, up the spiral escalator and the conveyer chute, and stumbled out of the shed with a headache. He had not expected his leave to go easy and without disaster, but he had expected a leave.

The air drifted heavily with the decaying scent of vegetation. Underneath the dark gray sky of the early morning, was the purple beetle, standing on its base of multi-jointed spokes amid the shrubbery.

The soft, damp soil yielded under the imprint of his weight. Clutching a briefcase in every hand, he hauled over to the vehicle.

Presently, he stood motionlessly in front of the car, organizing the dissident thoughts with one hand resting on the hood. The shed door grated from behind, disrupting his meditation. Out came Kyra McVeronica. She hurried excitedly toward him, fist-pumping down the side of her hip. "Who's your favorite daddy?" she demanded. "Do you know how close you were to being fired indefinitely, if it weren't for yours truly? The only reason why you still have your job is because I really stuck my neck out for you."

"You should've just kept me sacked, Kyra," Milton said mundanely, tossing his briefcases inside. "I'll only drag you down with me."

"Then drag me down," she dared him. "Show me how low you can go."

Milton chronicled a snail humping across the bed of brittle sticks and crunchy leaves. "Before I joined the Bureaux," he said, "I didn't know what I wanted to do. It was like I didn't exist."

"Check you out," Kyra said, hands on her hips, leaning back. "You're a real hero. A real life superhero."

"No, Kyra. That's fluff."

"Hold on a minute," she said, a disconcerting shift in her tone. "I don't know where this is coming from."

"I can't be the only one who feels this way," Milton said. "But I can't turn to my colleagues." He paused, hesitating. "They're all gone."

Kyra came near and cupped the sides of his face. "I'm still here. You know you can talk to me. We're going through this together."

It occurred to Milton he had never seen Kyra outside of HQ. Her eyes were wide and clear, fried green eggs under the break of dawn. "You ever just feel like all this planetary defense stuff gets kind of clichéd?"

"No," she said, removing her hands.

Milton considered the ersatz redwoods encircling the scenery and the ridge of the hills beyond. "I don't feel like the good guy, anymore."

"Why, aren't you a bad boy," she said, squeezing his triceps.

"That wasn't where I was headed." He pried her hand from his arm. "I just wish denizens would give me the respect and authority of an agency that requires me to enumerate jadeites."

"Denizens respect the shit out of you."

Milton subdued himself from the mordant incongruity extrapolated of his experiences. "Who, Kyra?"

Kyra turned on her heels and waved a hand, conducting to the forested park. "Everyone," she insisted. "Just open your eyes. Whether you know it or not, they look up to you and depend on you."

Somehow, he was not convinced. "How hard should I look for these supposed denizens?" he asked. "'Cause when I come knocking, nobody seems to know who the fuck I am, nor do they seem to give a lot of shit."

Kyra swiveled back around. "What do you expect from jadeites? They don't care about us. Our way of life."

"I'm talking about normal denizens. Consumers of the Ekonomy, Kyra. Automatons, even."

"We've gone over this before," she said, expounding with exasperation. "Because those powers could be abused in the wrong hands. Or else, what's the difference between that and forcing entry? There is none. That's why you've been obtaining permission and doing it the proper, legal way."

He shifted his gaze. "If I told you otherwise, will I be fired again?"

"You're all I've got right now, so you can breathe a sigh of relief," she said with a sense of consolation. "At least until the reorder with the training center gets processed and they replenish my reserve with some fresh trainees." She regarded him intently. "Don't think there won't be some repercussions for this. We'll go into it in greater detail later. Right now, I need you to focus on your next assignment. You're not quite flipping pancakes and blending milkshakes."

"Thanks for the headsup," he said, commencing to step on the nerf bar of the beetle.

"See Milton? You're making progress. And if for any reason, you have something else on your mind, don't be afraid to consult me again. I'm here to make your life easier."

You know what would really make my life easier? he wanted to say. If I didn't put it on the line everyday. "Of course."

"Good luck and have fun. You're gonna kill it."

Literally, he thought and got inside the car.

chapter 6

Eldridge was still reclining when an anthropomorphic mechanism was fast nearing with long strides. Robotic arms swayed side to side, clamping in one metallic hand a transparent, phonographic rod. Reggie Johnson, Eldridge's newly-acquired assistant, could be seen in an ekosuit with his puny hands wrapped around the dual joysticks, operating the seven-foot prosthetic machinery from the abdominal cockpit. The synthetic body curbed before the desk, across from the LCEO.

"Lord, good afternoon." Johnson handed the phone to Eldridge, by the controlled movement of a sterling appendage. "The upcoming issue of Elephantine, scheduled to retail next week."

The holocube was set to the three-dimensional cover. Eldridge angled the image up to his eyes and twirled it with scrutiny. "Johnson, do I look fat?"

"Why," Johnson answered, looking out from the torso of his augmented platform, "it's the flattering portrait of health."

Eldridge's hologram postured rigidly, dressed in a blue leather jacket, waist high, with deep creases. The shoulders and sleeves were decorated by golden spikes. His belt buckle was golden and sizeable. He was braced stiff by his black pants, which cut off lengthwise at his ankles, showing no socks underneath his heeled shoes. This was the money shot, after two hours in the makeup chair and all day of standing amid bright lights and blowing fans.

Eldridge had no denial. A large part of his success was due to objective reasoning and judgment. He knew he was not the prototypical structure. But there was a difference between being fat and looking fat. And this 3D cover, he determined, made him look fat.

Incorporated below the Elephantine masthead, was the hook, "Fat Profits," followed by, "Battle of the Bulge." The title of the cover story was superimposed above the rest – "Dinosaur in the Room." A spin on an old idiom, he obtained.

"They swapped 'elephant' out with 'dinosaur,'" he said. "I'm being mocked on grounds of being old and fat by my own subsidiary, no less."

Johnson offered, "A 'dinosaur' conjures up a powerful brand of a dominant species."

Eldridge contested, "An extinct species whose ancient fossils are up for display at Eko Banks worldwide."

"Unstoppable in its prime," Johnson said, "ruling the world with superior bite force."

"Bite force," Eldridge gleaned. "Not brain force."

"A man of action," Johnson clarified.

"Act first, think later," Eldridge said.

"You get things done, decisively and efficiently."

"That's a gainful interpretation. But it's certainly not the first impression. The title compels readers to ask, 'What's a dinosaur doing in a room?' It's strictly unwarranted, unless it's at a birthday party or educating children, but even then…" He paused, turning away with repugnance. "There are better ways to encapsulate my competence. I despise the derisive connotations that could be drawn from the title."

And that was that. He could not be talked out of it. But Johnson persisted, "The featured article between the flaps should pacify you of any qualms. It puts forth a glowing case that you're at the top of your game. Despite how fast times are changing, you managed to hold position. It ends on the promising note that you're not going anywhere."

It only gets better, Eldridge thought sardonically. "I'm going nowhere. In a hurry. Their jab that I'm stagnant. And I know what you're about to say before you can even think it. That not going anywhere, is not the same as going nowhere. A subtle difference, mayhaps, but minutiae that is thoroughly lost on the general public nonetheless. Not that it matters. Articles are marginal garnish, compared to the disco raid of animated ads and flashy graphics that can pack thousands of powerful messages without any effort expended by the browser." He returned the phone, unmitigated.

Johnson studied the miniaturized version of the man sitting before him. "You look avant-garde and ironically hip, donning your… studded dinosaur jacket."

Eldridge remained unconvinced. "I look emotionally unstable."

Johnson motioned his mechanical arms in earnest. "But you're gushing queenly with regal splendor."

Eldridge had never argued that. "I'm the LCEO. I can be unclothed and still be gushing queenly with regal splendor. More so, even. But the double entendre does not eradicate the mind of the travesty."

Johnson stopped trying, with good reason. Even a dullard would have seen the rationale by now. "Tell me what to do."

"Justifiably," Eldridge pointed out, "I should discharge all the editors. But the LCEO does not allow a mere vexation to meddle in the way of sound business." He spun toward the glass wall, overlooking the clouds, the holoway, the cityscape. "Let them have their moment of amusement and run the title. And let the consumers snicker. It'll be at their expense, should it lead to purchase."

"Your benevolence is sovereign," Johnson said.

"My benevolence is sovereign, but it is not absolute. If we don't see a significant boost in sales for this month's edition, then the editors will never write again for another publication."

chapter 7

Eleanor Flutterby adjusted her visor cap and paused to make sure she had the right suite number - 61398F3. It was the rendezvous site for the day. Ever since automated proxies took over the market, transportation and parking enforcement was not the booming business it used to be. The Department of Public Mobilization was down to six safeguards, from 600,000 at its height, and the latest budget cuts had led to the foreclosure of the official offices.

When Eleanor entered the room, visors swung around, coworkers expecting to see the director. Realizing otherwise, they made no effort to acknowledge her, and instead went back to echoing gossip off each other. Eleanor as the new blood, this being her third year on the job, was not welcome to join the fraternity of seasoned, grayheaded veterans who had experienced the polarization of epochs - from the best of times to the modern day.

"Top of the morning," she said. The veterans ignored her, but Eleanor noticed sitting beside them a couple of young girls, who did not look as though they wanted to be there. So it was that time of the year again, she thought. They were daughters, brought over to commemorate Bring Your Daughter To Work Day. They were dressed in double-breasted uniform shirts and shorts, just like their matriarchal forebears. She waved at them in exchange for empty stares. They've been trained well, she said to herself. Coworker Unity was situated adjacent to the disposable cups and bowls of the refreshment counter, changing the diaper of her infant.

Why do we have to meet every morning? Eleanor lamented. The news bulletin was two hours of the same twaddle everyday. Trends and patterns, a rundown of the day's prime locations, a progress report, self-congratulatory comments from Team Captain Eugenia Hayworth, after which veterans would take turns excitedly sharing stories of outstanding encounters on the job. And somewhere in between, news about more cutbacks, who would leave, who would stay, when the new lease would expire, etc.

Eleanor chose a rickety chair behind one of the dilapidated desks and sat herself. She noticed one side of the room was boarded up. Another section of the wall seemed a slightly different shade of beige; it did not look intentional.

One of the veterans was overheard mentioning a guest speaker. In addition to the day being Bring Your Daughter To Work Day, it donned on her that it was a Wednesday. Wednesdays were appointed guest speakers. Eleanor did not mind. It certainly beat the alternative. I wonder which former pro wrestler we're gonna get in this time, she thought.

Director Claudette Bauzer came into the room. She was a tall woman, broad-shouldered, with her head nestled between the collars of her pink trench coat. The brim of the visor cap was tucked low, keeping her face concealed. "Safeguards, we have a very special guest with us this morning. Everybody give a warm welcome for V.V.N. Wiggins." Director Bauzer briskly stepped aside.

Eleanor was the only one to clap, as a much smaller lady presented herself in a white suit. She did not look anything like an ex-pro wrestler, other than the fact that she was old. But she was also pale-skinned, frail, flat-chested, with platinum blonde hair, cropped short and styled to an anterior jut, curtailing subtly at the tips. The heels of her boots beat on the floor, as she paced back and forth, sternly gauging the audience of visor caps. "You probably have denizens in here all the time," V.V.N. Wiggins said, "cheering you up, telling you you're worth something you're clearly not. I refuse to mother you like that, because you are not my babies. You are safeguards. Can anybody tell me what that means?" She picked Henrietta, who was combing her daughter's hair. "You there."

"A safeguard is a traffic control agent who issues citations to maintain utmost vehicular safety," Henrietta said with rehearsed confidence and poise.

"Somebody else?" Wiggins said.

Eugenia's hand sprung up. "She forgot to mention graffiti, vandalism, and littering."

"Try again," Wiggins said. "Anybody?"

"We're guardians," Gladys started, "because we guard the safety-"

"Next," Wiggins said.

Unity glanced up from tending to her infant, "We enforce and regulate the laws-"

"Nigga please."

It was Eleanor's turn. "To serve and to pro-"

"That's all there is to it," Wiggins said. "You serve citations. That is what you are, so don't pretend to be doing something greater, because that's the bottom line. This is not a job for the faint of heart. This is a job for finishers. And right now, I don't see a single finisher in this fleabag. I see denizens who are fine, and I'm not talking about your attractiveness. You're all hideosities if you ask me. I'm talking about your complacency levels." She leaned over Beatrice's daughter, hands linked behind her back. "Pray you take after your father."

Beatrice promptly pulled her child away from Wiggins, as though to shield her. "I don't know who her father is," she protested.

"Boohoo," Wiggins said sternly.

"I have an older daughter," Beatrice said, "whose father ran away when she was just two."

"Good for him."

"And another daughter, whose father refuses to pay child sup-"

"Let's not get carried away," Wiggins said, gesturing with a hand.

Unity interjected indignantly. Her infant girl was sprawled out on the spread, freshly powdered and ready to be bundled. "Tell that to our bastardized daughters."

"Tell what to who?" Wiggins asked tonelessly.

"That they don't deserve love," Unity said plaintively.

"Whoa," Wiggins said, "I never said anything about-"

"Do you have any idea what it's like to be a single parent?" Henrietta demanded, levying in a manner barbed with accusation.

"Denizens," Wiggins said, avoiding eye contact, "there are resources that help you plan out your parenthood. Research it on your own, because I don't have time for that odyssey. I was invited here to address your performance levels, or lack thereof."

Wiggins paced the room, her countenance unyielding. She opened her mouth, prepared to verbalize, and then, was given pause, shifted orientation, and aimed her focus on Unity. Unity was preoccupied, with a scowl adorning her freckled face, in the task of wrapping up her little girl. Wiggins leered as though she had never seen anybody pampering their offspring before. She burst into a coarse cackle.

The veterans looked on impassively at the solitary amusement displayed by the guest speaker, sharing an atmosphere of skepticism. But whatever humor that compelled Wiggins was walked off. In the next moment, she had collected herself. "I see some of you have brought your daughters along in honor of Bring Your Daughter To Work Day. While I'm as patriotic as anybody else, I'll need to remind you this is a work day, not fap day or holiday or anybody's birthday." Her amusement ceased. "If you're looking at me and thinking, 'She has no right to speak to us that way, especially not before my precious daughter,' yes I do. You're the ones who brought them here. This is a war zone, not a daycare center." She glided past Gladys, who was occupied with a pomegranate. "Or Let's-Eat-A-Pomegranate Day, not for another week." Wiggins halted at Timothea's desk and gazed down at her. "It's your wake."

Timothea was flushed by the morbid suggestion, folding her arms and crossing her legs. Wiggins walked away. "If I'm coming off a little harsh, it's because I've read about your performance output. I've seen your numbers, and quite frankly, I wasn't impressed."

"Don't judge us on our field numbers," Eugenia quipped. "We're not about the stats."

Wiggins turned to the diversion with uninspired regard, settling her attention on an old woman whose light smoky hair spired to the top of her head in a blow-dried updo beneath a visor cap. "And who are you?"

"Team Captain Eugenia Hayworth," she rasped decisively.

Wiggins faced her fully. "So you're the captain that sunk this ship." She scanned the room. "From now on, there is no team. You are individuals. Start acting like it."

"With all due respect," Eugenia said, "our priority is to protect the denizens."

"Save the sanctimony for the press and the public."

"There could be a fire," Eugenia tried to reason, "and if there's a car parked-"

"Stick a hose in it," Wiggins said, "or park on top of it."

"But some denizens come up with excuses."

"You're coming up with excuses."

Henrietta chimed in. "What about when they make an honest mistake?"

"What an oxymoron," Wiggins said. "There's no such thing as an honest mistake. You are the mistake for thinking you can tell who's being honest. There's no such thing as honesty, when they talk their way out of a fine. Polish their strap-on while you're at it, why don't you, so they can plow you in the back?"

"We uphold laws that are in place to protect denizens from traffic hazards," Timothea said.

"And you're fine with that, because you keep telling yourself that." She ran her gaze across the back of the room. "It's what you denizens do to feel fine. You make excuses and take a cold shower when you get home. And you call yourself a safeguard."

"I've never taken a cold shower in my life," Timothea muttered with indifference.

"But you admit you're an underachiever."

"Whatever." Timothea turned a cheek.

"You don't have to recite me what it says on your forehead."

Timothea sprung back with a lopsided glower. "For your information. I've been a safeguard all my life, and I'm one of the best in the field."

"I've seen your numbers," Wiggins said monotonously, "and I maintain I'm not impressed by your performance."

"I'm not trying to impress you," Timothea said.

Wiggins stood back. "Well, whoever it is, it's not working."

Timothea vacillated with perverted wonderment. "I'm not trying to impress you, or anybody else."

Wiggins calmly offered up a smile. A smile that was blank and emotionless. "But you brought up that you're the best. The best of the best of the obsolete. The last human employees of a field that's outsourcing its labor with proxies. You're an anachronism of technology." She perceived the rest of the safeguards. "That goes for all of you. You think you're fine, but you're finished."

The veterans fidgeted uncomfortably, swapping baffled expressions with each other.

Beatrice asked, "What kind of motivational speech is this?"

V.V.N. Wiggins unbuttoned her double-breasted jacket and opened the upper flap to show that it was inlaid with giraffe skin. To convey it was a genuine Bruno Hugo article, there was a patch sewn indicating its certificate of authenticity. She rolled up her sleeve and flashed the colorful bands of watches swaddling the length of her skinny forearm. "This clock on my wrist is a real Atomix, encrusted with pink diamonds. 600,000 pixels. And it's the least expensive of them all." She straightened her sleeve. "You see this kerchief in my breast pocket? This silk is 100% pure, unadulterated epidermis molted from velvet worms. It costs more money than all of your uniforms combined. I blow my nose with this. You think I'm lying? I don't blame you. The quality of ersatz has risen considerably these days. Sometimes, it even confounds the experts. They even come up with tags and receipts that look just like it was purchased in-store."

She kicked her foot up and stomped the desk before Beatrice, an impact that reverberated a strident shutter. The children were especially startled. Beatrice's daughter whimpered. Unity's baby erupted into a wail. Henrietta's teenage daughter sucked on her inhaler. Their mothers wrangled them close, in a consoling effort.

"Look at my shoes," Wiggins resumed. "They're genuine Hullburry pumps, made to order. You can't knock this. Need I mention, I don't wear anything twice."

She brought her foot back down to the ground. "You're probably asking what this all has to do with you. Have you even heard of these designer brands? Let me tell you a little about myself, now." She pointed at Eleanor. "I used to be sitting right there in that seat, just like you. Not the selfsame seat. This was back when the Department of Public Mobilization still had an officially designated location. But that's beside the point. I wasn't born wearing a scarf made of 97% pure green milkweed locust resilin. I used to be a safeguard, like you denizens. In my first year, I cracked the top ten. For the subsequent five years, I became the top performing safeguard when it meant something, among over twenty million members of my peers. Now when somebody says they're a top performer, it only means they're the best of the worst underachievers." She scrutinized the veterans, most of whom were postured apathetically, except for Unity, who held in her face, visible contempt, as she rocked a bundle in her arms.

Wiggins continued. "Today, I have an office at Kokiri House. You wanna know why? Because they wanted someone who could get the job done. You wanna keep peddling a cart chasing treadmarks and contrails? You will be living in the dust of other denizens. And you will never catch up to me, because I'm exempt. I'm not just a card-carrying Executive member of Ekonomy Mart. I am an official Board Exec."

"You want this." She frantically caressed the side of her face and frisked her shivering body, rustling her hands down to her legs and gliding back up to grope her breasts. "You want this." She flashed her watches for good measure, and flung the kerchief into the air. Beatrice and Henrietta both shot up to catch it and thumped into each other. "You want my life. You don't deserve it. You haven't earned it."

"Money isn't everything," Eugenia said.

"Then why are you in this business?" Wiggins asked.

Eugenia wavered. "Because I wanted to make a difference."

"You can make a difference flipping flytraps at the Burger Virgin and not burning them," Wiggins shot back. "Instead the only difference you made was to last year's revenue - the lowest on record in DPM history. Go make a difference some place else. Like the kitchen, and make me a sammich while you're there."

"And let the proxies run me out of town?" Eugenia asked. "They aren't capable of making intellectual decisions."

"Too late for that. The Department of Public Mobilization doesn't have so much as a pobox anymore, let alone an address, in case you were too busy making intellectual decisions to notice. Enjoy these continental breakfasts while they last." She gestured toward the counter of raisin bran and pitcher of milk. "Because at this rate, you'll be meeting at Sushi Bob next week. And the week after that, the junkyard. Just be sure to bring your own bean bags to the powwow. The Department won't be supplying any collapsible chairs, since it liquidated all of its office furniture."

Eleanor thought, We don't have to meet. Or if it really is necessary, we could call each other on the phone and meet with our holographic constructs.

"Now that you're with me," Wiggins said, "let's go ahead and begin the sixty-second lesson I had prepared for today."

Wiggins opened a holocube on her phone and enlarged it. An acronym materialized before them.

FINISHR

"Consider the word of the day, and make it your favorite word."
Wiggins then went on to decipher each letter.

FIND THE QUARRY
INITIATE THE PROCESS
NEVER NEGOTIATE WITH ANYBODY. NOT EVEN
YOURSELF.
ISSUE THE FINE
SEAL THE DEAL AND SIGN OFF ON IT
HUSTLE
REPEAT

"The DPM needs you," Wiggins said. "But not as much as you need it. Be an individual. Be a finisher and finish. The only member of your team is you. Nobody will hold your hands. Finish it, and put it to bed. Everything stops and starts when you get in and out of bed."

She moved on to the next set of letters - BED

BREATHE - DON'T WASTE YOUR BREATH ON
ANYTHING THAT DOESN'T GET YOU CLOSER TO
MEETING YOUR QUOTA AND EXEEDING IT

EAT - BREAKFAST, LUNCH, DINNER. EAT AS MUCH AS
YOU WANT WITHOUT GETTING FAT IN YOUR...

DREAM - WHEN YOU'RE NOT FLYING IN THE SKY,
OVER THE LAND OF GOLDEN CARS, WAITING TO BE
MINED AND LIQUIDATED, DREAM AND DAYDREAM
HIGH ABOUT IT

"This all makes sense in theory," Eugenia said, "but have you seen what it's like out there? When you were a safeguard, they didn't have automated proxies flying in circles, designed to spot a car askew from a thousand and a half miles away."

"There are a thousand and a half excuses and a cold shower to make you feel better about yourself," Wiggins said. "But not a single denizen in this room clutch enough to handle the heat and rise to the occasion to make a real difference. When I was a safeguard, they didn't need to have automated proxies, because I was the one flying circles around them. You consumers are worse than ersatz. Ersatz than ersatz. The only thing real in this room is excuses." She walked over to the holographic letters and directed their attention once more. "Finishers don't take cold showers. They take ice baths. Finish on your own terms and conditions. Don't let the denizens make excuses or make you make excuses for them, and least of all, don't make excuses for yourselves, because you have nobody to blame and lie to but yourself. Don't say the proxies are unqualified. Show it. You're writing a ticket, not a treaty. You see an unparallel car? Finish the citation. You see a parallel car? Finish it."

"Even if it's a parallel car?" Henrietta asked feebly.

"Finish it."

Henrietta floundered her eyes. "What if they contest it?"

"Your word against theirs," Wiggins said.

"But what if they actually go through all the trouble of recording a footage and packaging it with a form of appeal so they can secure a court date to show up and overturn the citation?"

"Let them," Wiggins said, reviewing the room. "We're in a new world, ladies and gents. Times have changed. This is the turning point." She stepped up to Unity. "What do you do if you see someone loitering?"

Unity hesitated. "Finish it?"

"Don't answer my question with a stupid question."

Unity snapped her posture and looked straight ahead. "Finish it."

Wiggins picked the turns. "What do you do if you see someone driving too fast?"

"Finish it," Beatrice said.

Wiggins acutely set her eyes on the next candidate. "What do you do if you see someone driving too slow?"

"Finish it," Eugenia said.

She moved on. "What do you do if you see someone walking too slow?"

"Finish it," Gladys said with conviction.

"Pull over and finish it, or tractor-beam it," Wiggins ordered, "or hit the road, get lost, jack yourself off under some hard rain. My time is money. Is your time money? I just made more pixels trying to get you to do your job, than anybody in this room made in the last year. So the next time you find yourself moping around at a pit stop, daydreaming of flying over the land of jalopies begging to be towed and compacted into diamonds, remember the clock never sleeps."

V.V.N. Wiggins went on her way. The director followed her out on the pretense she would be returning shortly. The group of safeguards in the meantime, sat erect and still, expressions blank with their chins up, eyes fixed forward. The daughters patterned their mothers, undistracted, legs uncrossed, hands neatly assembled upon their desks, visor caps on their heads. Nobody had broken posture even after a full three seconds had passed. They seemed to exist in a muted state of fervor ravishing with urgency and obligation.

What are we waiting for? Eleanor asked herself, rustling in her seat. She thought of sliding to her feet and making the journey to the refreshment counter to pour the sweating pitcher of cold synthetic milk into a bowl of ersatz raisin and bran flakes and picking up a polka-dotted mug to fill it with gurgle from the decanter, diffusing the air with a hot aroma of fruit tang, all while humming birds floated in the background. It was so quiet, she was unsure whether or not she was allowed to make munching or sipping noises. Any such compulsion was equally matched with preventative unease, a lackluster thought intruding her mind. She imagined V.V.N. Wiggins would barge in, drumming her fingers together, shivering hysterically, and instantly center her attention on Eleanor's dissidence.

After putting some thought into it, Eleanor decided it best to vacate the urge and blend in with the rest of the daydreaming safeguards. I'll close my eyes, she thought. Close my eyes and count to ten.

But each passing second made it ever evident, the guest speaker's impactful outlook and prudential methodology had resonated with contrast. Where is my enterprising outlook? she asked herself. My positive enlightenment? My upright composure?

Conversely, she never felt more noxiously afflicted and beset by woe, hearing her motivations outlined with implicit, barren economy. Everything V.V.N. Wiggins had said, merely licensed what Eleanor knew was asked of her by the DPM. She of all safeguards did not have to be enthralled by what she was doing. Not in this Ekonomy, she said to herself. There were no fanciful conciliations, nor idyllic justifications. Her modus operandi was common sense and adequate: she needed a means of supporting herself. And if it wasn't me to fine the driver, she thought, it would've been somebody else, or something else. A proxy.

Eleanor looked around at her coworkers and their daughters. They had not budged. Their eyes remained intent and wide, as if the guest speaker had opened up a whole new realm of possibilities that was previously unaware to them. Observing the moment of perpendicular silence, Eleanor thought, They all look empowered to go out there and prove something. But what that was, she could not be sure.

chapter 8

After an hour of rummaging through the six-room residence, Milton Grainjar located the stash of pixels in the last room. It often seemed to work out that way.

The room was beginning to look identical to the others he had scanned before it – a whirlwind of toppled furniture and damaged electronics, among foam balls and art supplies and inverted cushions. The entertainment setup was rendered nonfunctional, after Milton had fired at it in hopes something would turn up. He was surrounded by walls framed with ersatz windows, streaming a radiant oceanside view, accompanied by the seductive call of waves and occasional seagulls. He was getting ready to shoot them as well, provided the row of shelves and storage cabinets divulged nothing useful. But behind one of the capsized cabinets, he distinguished a safe installed within the wall's recess.

The peaceful waves of the framed ersatz window adjacent to him were broken up by the swishing doors across the hall. Here he comes, Milton thought. He finished emptying the safe and zipped up the duffel bags. Then, with the genograph in hand, he set off toward the hall and halted.

A balled-up, compact figure wheeled on by, past the doorway. Milton made him out to be the suspect. According to the background detail on his phone, the suspect's name was Thomas Grodzak, 87, artist. He was being charged with the general dissemination of Jade Agenda and fundraising for the Jade Association.

The compact, hunched figure appeared again, backing up in a hover chair and veering to a stop across from him. His shins were bare and exposed, jutting out from underneath the robe. He sloped forward, showing the nest of white hair. Thin skin clung from a narrow, gaunt face, gawking dolefully out of ridged, deep-sunk eyes.

His body language was flax, non-threatening. But his voice was direct when he spoke, "I suppose this is the part I ask, 'Who the fuck are you?'"

All day, as with any other day, Milton had seen the worst of folks, with their disgruntled attitudes and uncooperative, hostile temperaments. Could he blame them? He was in their homes uninvited, conducting protocol that suspected them of being jadeites. Nobody - jadeite or not - would be offering him cookies and milk for that. And I'm not asking for that, he said to himself. I'm not asking for anything. Maybe a little respect wouldn't hurt.

He stored away the thought to explain his presence. "I don't mean to trouble you. I'm only here to conduct a survey. Strictly routine."

"What kind of survey?" he asked.

"Mr. Grodzak, there's been a breach of security," Milton tried to explain.

"By you or someone else?"

"Someone else," Milton said.

"Who?"

"You."

"Me?" Grodzak asked with a dark, beady glare. "Last time I checked, I own this house."

Milton treaded closer. "I regret to inform you the scope of my affairs deals beyond the parameters of your address."

"You mind waiting here for a moment while I get security?" Grodzak swiveled in the other direction.

Milton gained on him and reached for the back rest. The hover chair swung in the air and bucked the suspect off his seat. He flopped to the cluttered floor.

Milton lunged forward, commencing the skirmish. The phone slipped out of Grodzak's control and clattered away. He tried to reach for it, but Milton clamped down on him, suppressing further movement. "Resistance is impractical," Milton said.

"Who the hell do you think you are?" Grodzak cried, wiggling in a vain effort to free himself.

Milton flashed the digital bureaucratic insignia from his phone. "My handle is Milton Grainjar." The suspect's pupils dilated. "And I come all the way from XYZ."

"And I came all the way from across the street," Grodzak managed to yell, squirming from the bottom. "Now get off my patch!"

Milton released the hold and detached himself from the suspect. The old man floundered to return to his hover chair.

"Standard protocol," Milton said, calmly rising to his feet and adjusting the lapels and cuffs of his jacket. "I didn't mean to shock you, believe me."

"Believe or unbelieve, you shocked the living shit out of me," Grodzak said, panting with irregular breaths, struggling to heave himself back onto the hover chair.

"My condolences. It was not my intention," Milton said, helping the man back up. The suspect was heavier than his scrawny frame suggested.

Exasperation furrowed Grodzak's forehead. "Please, I don't want any trouble. Take all of my pixels."

"I already have," Milton said.

"Well, what else do you want?" Grodzak stammered. "I'm just an old man who wants to die with dignity. Take whatever you need. Just don't shoot me."

"There's been a misunderstanding, Mr. Grodzak," Milton said. "I'm a specialist."

"Specializing in what?"

"Agency," Milton said, "of the bureaucratic type."

Bafflement plastered Grodzak's face. "If you're a special agent, then why didn't you let me call security?"

"Building security? They'll only get in the way."

"What about the JERQS?" he asked, gauging Milton with scrutiny. "I can call the JERQS."

"The Judicial Enforcement and Regulations Quadrant of Syndics? They'd only complicate procedures. This should be in and out."

Grodzak puckered his brows. "Where did you say you came from again?"

"XYZ."

"Never heard."

Milton expounded, "It's the same agency represented by Barret Trufflehard."

"Trufflehard," the senior suspect said, stopping to consider. "Why does that sound familiar?"

"The patriotic war hero."

"The belligerent from the political fable?" Grodzak asked.

"So you say."

"But I was told by my grandchildren it was just a movie."

"They told you that," Milton said, "to make you feel better. To shelter you. But you were misinformed."

Grodzak's posture tightened, and his eyes narrowed a slight degree. "You mean to tell me jadeites are real?"

"It's all over the news."

Grodzak was dismissive with a snort. "Since when has the news been credible? They're controlled by corporate subsidiaries-" He coughed.

"Now that we know your stance," Milton said, "I'm conducting a routine sweep, with permission."

Grodzak creased his countenance, frozen with incredulity. "You keep saying this is routine, as if subliminally suggesting the notion that this is all fine and dandy, will get me to grant you permission. No, I'm quite fine with my current chambermaid who comes in every-"

"Permission from the Bureaux," Milton said stoically.

"This is my home," Grodzak insisted. "Nobody will be doing anything here against my authority and knowledge." He looked off to the side, dulled by the prospect.

"It's already been performed," Milton declared. "The results from the scan are in. Follow me." Vigilantly, he ushered the man into the room, for he could not risk another escape attempt by the suspect.

Milton fiddled with the genomic polygraph, wirelessly linked to his phone. Multiple holocubes were projected, displaying electrical emissions. Looming beside him, was Grodzak in his hover chair. "No offense," he said, "but what am I missing? I don't see anything."

"It's encrypted in a grayscale, gradient z-buffer, creating a simple full cube effect."

"I don't know what this is about," Grodzak said, who was leaning to make out what Milton was supposedly looking at - a holocube of raining gray flyspecks emanating from a projector.

Milton, keeping his attention fixed on the graphical readouts on display, said, "The geometry of the focal surface is modified, embedded with distance information that jumbles the report. The patented algorithm simulates small displacements of the underlying object... the graphical data... hidden within a randomized, repeating-"

"No," Grodzak grated. "I'm not talking about your magical gold box. Forget that. I'm talking about this." His spindly arms articulated agitatedly. "All of this. You being here. Me wondering why this is happening. I don't recognize any of this."

Milton noted the suspect's palms out, frantically indicating the surrounds. "Trespassing. Conspiracy. Treason. Identity Theft. Surely, this sounds familiar."

"I don't know where you're getting at, but let's just drop this, whatever this is," Grodzak grumbled brusquely. "Just cut the posturing." He slanted over to one side. "Now, tell me. Does this by any chance have anything to do with the girl from today? I don't know what she told you, but it was consensual."

Milton produced a holocube on his phone, the dossier, which split off into numerous sub-holocubes. Presently, he scrolled through the documents. "It's not here," he said, "but I'll make a note." Making a memorandum of the fact, he minimized the dossier and brought forth the genograph. He approached the hover chair and circulated the golden gadget about him, first up and down, and then around the suspect, in a sideways figure eight motion.

Grodzak's eyes trailed the static projection with dubiety. "What's that?"

"It detects the presence of certain radical agents," Milton said. "Foreign environmental attributes conducive of anti-Ekonomic activities."

Grodzak stared incomprehensibly, getting a closeup of the pulsing visual, fizzing with golden bubbles. "The presence of radionuclides," Milton said, weaving the air.

"Radio-what?"

"Atoms with unstable nuclei. The genomic polygraph generates the energy spectrum by identifying and quantifying the gamma emitters that exist in a gamma source. Thereupon the elemental and isotopic report from the survey-" He paused then. "I don't mean to tax you with the details, but when-"

"You are. Frankly, I fail to give a shit."

"Excuse me," Milton said, tending to the readouts displayed on the phone's various holocubes and sub-holocubes, several of which buzzed with wiry meters alternating sideways, documenting oscillating patterns from the genograph beside it. He dipped down to conduct his orchestra of instruments and apparatus, gadgeting and adjusting, measuring and finalizing, projecting forensic significance.

"Why don't we reschedule?" Grodzak asked, squinting to make out the procedure. "Everything looks to be in order, and I'm actually quite busy right now."

Milton continued to go about his business, flickering with the neural control switches on the genograph and reviewing the presented data of electromagnetic nature. Finally, he said, "The departmental setup of the Bureaux, disallows postponement of public safety matters."

"Well, you should allow it. For someone like me," Grodzak stipulated, as if to convey his entitled status of seniority and handicap. "It's truly an inconvenience."

"I assure you, Mr. Grodzak, the service is being expedited with the utmost urgency," Milton said, extending professional courtesy. "But I'll pass that along."

The suspect pivoted around in his hover chair, dumbstruck. "I don't believe jadeites are real."

"It's not my job to convince you."

"You don't really believe it, do you?"

Milton finished his observations of the completed scan, revealing there was a 98.7% chance the man sitting across from him was a jadeite. Milton saved the log, and restored the genomic polygraph to a briefcase, and then, faced the pending jadeite. "I don't have a choice."

Grodzak noticed the inset safe door ajar. His hover chair steered in its direction. "If you're really who you say you are," he said, examining the desolate chest, "where is my money?"

"It's safe with me."

Grodzak looked into the empty container and turned to face the agent. "It was safe behind the lock before you pried it open."

"Mr. Grodzak, I possessed your pixels, because there were reasons to suspect they were funds raised for the Jade Association."

Grodzak chuckled dryly. "I didn't even know the Jade Association was an actual thing until you got here. My life was wonderful until you showed up."

"Mr. Grodzak, this is not a laughing matter. I've been sent here to clear you of any spurious claims linking you to anti-Ekonomic activity. May I safely presume that you are loyal to the planet of your genealogy, and thereby wish for nothing but its preservation and prominence?" Milton paused for objection, and then finished, "With your legal status in doubt, standard protocol mandates your willful participation in a quick survey to help discern your allegiance."

"I have nothing to hide," Grodzak protested. "It's just the timing." He grew quiet for a moment. "But you're here, and you haven't left yet. I don't know what to say, other than that I have nothing to do with anything you've brought up." He closed his eyes, and his head fell on his chest.

"Mr. Grodzak," Milton said, rousing the suspect by his shoulders.

"Mr. Grodzak."

"Mr. Grod-"

Grodzak unfurled and swung his head alertly, from side to side. "Where am I?"

"Mr. Grodzak, are you ready for the survey?"

"Oh, it's still you," he said in a soft whisper, deflating back into his seat.

"Can I start the survey?"

"You're here, aren't you? And it doesn't look like you're about to leave anytime soon. I- I'm willing to help the cause by entering whatever juridical review that will most certainly clear my name."

"Before I can commence with the survey, I wanted to confirm your name as Thomas Grodzak and straighten out the records."

"That's my name."

"Mr. Grodzak," Milton said, "what kind of work do you do? What's your occupation?"

"I've worked at many things," Grodzak said. "Mainly, I'm a forger."

"How long have you engaged in this profession?"

"It's hard to call it a profession. I kind of drifted into it, painting. I'm a forger now, and it's a very honorable profession, but when I started out actually-"

"Mr. Grodzak, answer the question."

"I have to explain that it really wasn't my profession. I picked up a little change in it."

"Did you practice your profession?" Milton asked.

"I painted for some publications, sure," Grodzak agreed.

Milton brought up the suspect's profile on the phone and browsed through his past history. "I'm looking at a compilation of announcements in newsletters, posters, and the black market organ Ivory Exchange, indicating you took part in numerous organizations that pushed certain agendas." Milton stopped to question the elderly man in the hover chair. "Was the Jade Agenda one of them?"

"I am not going to answer any questions as to my association, my philosophical or religious beliefs, or any political beliefs, or any of my private affairs," Grodzak said briskly. "I think these are improper questions, especially under such compulsion as this. I would be glad to tell you about my life if you'd want to hear it."

"That's not required," Milton said, with no inclination to stay any longer than he had to.

"I have never done anything of any conspiratorial nature in my life. And I'm deeply offended by the implications of this questioning, simply because my opinions may conflict from yours. That I'm less Ekonomical, or patriotic, or any less of a consumer or human than anybody else. This planet is where I was born and raised. It goes without saying I love the Ekonomy."

"Have you ever made contributions toward preserving Ekonomic institutions?" Milton asked.

"I feel that my whole life is a contribution," Grodzak said. "That is why I would like to tell you about it."

Somehow, Milton doubted his cause would advance from listening to Grodzak's hard luck narrative. Nevertheless, he was seeing a pattern. Everything was off the table. Everything, but his life. "That's not required."

"I will be glad to tell you about the artistic works that I have forged, because it's my profession," Grodzak offered, "But I decline to tell you whoever's seen them, or about the original artist. Or other forgers who have made them."

Works of art by themselves were subjective. What mattered was the intent. Milton had to make this clear. "During the enumeration of a certain jadeite who assumed the role of a forger just as yourself, it was testified that the art work that was commissioned by the Jade Association, was not art of a political character. It was said, however, that there were expectations to donate personal art work in order to raise money for the Jade Association. Now, did you, as the aforementioned jadeite confessed, produce art work in efforts to support the Jade Agenda?"

"Again," Grodzak said, "I would be glad to tell you anything about the works of art I've forged, because forging is my business, but not the whens and wheres and what-fors."

In view of the suspect's unwillingness to expose the details in question, Milton proceeded to read from the holocube. "According to the Ivory Exchange, Thomas Grodzak's *Manekin Collezione* headed the list of the items to be auctioned at a fundraiser picnic given by the Society of Aces, one of the Southwestern chapters of the Jade Association."

"My answer is the same," Grodzak said.

Milton glanced from the holocube. "I haven't asked anything in regards yet."

Grodzak stated, "I decline to discuss, under compulsion, where my work was hung, or who purchased it, or who I've known. I love the Ekonomy dearly, and I detest the implications. I will tell you about my life, but I am not interested in telling who drew the art work that I forged, or who viewed them."

The conflict of interest was apparent to Milton. It was not what he had hoped for. He was starting to get the sense this would not be an easy enumeration. Not that there ever was such a thing, he thought. But relatively speaking. "Mr. Grodzak, were you under Jade Association directive, or as what you considered to be the duty of the Jade Association?"

"I'll be glad to answer about the work," Grodzak answered, "but I'm

not interested in carrying on the line of questioning about where I have
sold my work."

"You may not be interested, but the Bureaux is, in whether or not
the Jade Association ever commissioned you for your services."

"I feel these questions are improper and immoral of any consumer
of the Ekonomy to be asked."

"It's a yes-no question," Milton said.

"My answer is the same."

"There's been no answer to your last question."

Deep grooves tugged at Grodzak's face. "I thought I had hitherto
answered all of them."

"You haven't been responsive."

"I didn't even know that was a question," Grodzak said.

"My question was-"

"How long is this survey?" Grodzak asked feebly.

"We haven't gone there," Milton said.

"Then what do you call this?"

"Fact checking," Milton said, "for documentation purposes."

Grodzak's distaste remained.

"Bureaucracy," Milton expounded.

Grodzak nodded. "What were you asking?"

Milton continued. "Whether or not you serviced the functions of the
Jade Association. You have answered inferentially, and if I understand
your answer, you're admitting that you have."

"Except for the answer I have already given you," Grodzak started,
"I have no answer. I'm proud to have forged art for consumers of every
political persuasion, and I have never turned down work for anybody
because I disagreed with their political opinion. And I am proud of the
fact that my work seems to cut across and find perhaps a unifying theme,
basic humanity. And that is why I would love to be able to tell you about

my life, because I feel that you would agree with […]"

Milton waited for the suspect to finish. "What you stated was not in response to the question."

Grodzak leaned back in his seat, self-contentedly. "I believe that a few questions ago, I gave my fullest answer to this whole line of questioning."

"You've beclouded your answer," Milton said. "I'd like to clarify what you meant. Did you make art promoting the Jade Agenda as duty to your membership with the Jade Association?"

"I've already indicated that I feel it's improper to say who solicited my services, especially under such compulsion as this."

Milton rephrased the question and pressed the suspect. "Was your art work created as Jade Agenda directive, or as what you considered to be a duty to the Jade Agenda?"

"I have already answered that," Grodzak said.

"Under what circumstances were your services acquired on those occasions?"

"I decline to discuss, under compulsion, why I did work, who the original artist was, and who else has done the same work, and the denizens I have known. I love the Ekonomy dearly, and I greatly resent this implication that some of the work that I've done or my associations, whether they are religious or philosophical, make me any less human. I will proceed to tell you about my life."

"That won't be necessary," Milton said swiftly. He referred back to one of the open holocubes projecting from his phone. "I have a newsletter entitled, *Two For Ninety-Nine Pixels*, showing a fundraiser at the Eko Motel, Jamboree Room sponsored by the Committee for Ekonomic Relief. It indicates that you were one of the artists furnishing the gallery of the event." Calmly, he lowered the holocube. "Did you design art for the site, one in particular entitled *Spoiled Milk*?"

"I don't know of a painting by that name," Grodzak said. "I do know of one called *Blue Milk*."

"Did you paint it?

"I can forge it for you," he said. "I don't know if you'd want to stick around until it's done."

"Have you painted it before?" Milton asked.

"Yes, I have."

"What inspired you to draw it?"

"You would have to ask the original artist," Grodzak said.

"You said you want to talk about your art work. Opportunity granted. Which of your art work has been hung at Jade Association functions?"

Grodzak said acerbically, "I will tell you about art work that's been hung any place!"

"The Bureaux is only inquiring about the ones at Jade Association functions." Milton referred again to the holocube. "Were you not a delegate to art exhibits under the auspices of the Jade Association?"

"My answer is the same." Grodzak fidgeted in his seat. "I take it that you are not interested at all of the different places that I have hung my work. Why don't you ask me about the churches and schools and other places?"

"That is laudable," Milton said. "Laudable, indeed, and the Bureaux only wishes that your body of work had been confined to those areas. If you were acting for the Jade Association at these functions, the Bureaux wants to know."

"I have forged for everybody." He smiled weakly.

Milton shifted his gaze, lowering the digital documents projecting in his hand to read the suspect's veneer. "Then it could be construed," he said, "you've forged for the locations cited earlier."

"I've forged paintings and dioramas of every political persuasion, and I am proud that I never refused work for any party seeking my skills, no matter who, or what, they are. That is the only answer I can append along that line." The suspect in the hover chair began to back away toward the center of the room.

Milton, fixated on phrasing the next question, paid little heed. He returned to the holocube, scrolling down. "Your admission of drawing for all parties at all sorts of functions, corroborates what I'm looking at in an issue of the Ivory Exchange. The Consumer's Artists presented the summer musical Babies for Champions on the 43rd floor of the City Park Building picnic grounds for the benefit of the Southwest chapter of the Jade Association, at which you were listed as a guest of honor." Milton stopped to stare at the elderly man. "Under what circumstances did you attend said function?"

"My answer is the same as before."

"Mr. Grodzak, just so we're clear, I'll ask you only once. Were you an illegal conspirator of the Jade Association at any time during the various art installations where your work was displayed?"

"My answer is the same as before."

"Are you a Jade Association member now?" Milton asked.

"Same answer."

"Refresh my mind," Milton said. "What was the answer?"

The suspect swiveled on his hover chair, making a full revolution. Milton caught a glimmer, the variety of glimmer that was often foreboding from his field experience.

"What do you say we skip to the survey?" Milton asked.

Purple striations emerged from Grodzak's right hand. Milton broke optical contact and sprung from the table before it went up in a steam of vapor. He circumambulated around the hover chair and hurried over to his briefcases and duffel bags.

It started with the faint hum of the nearby electromagnetic field. He broke into a sprint, shouldering the duffle bags and lugging the briefcases, as a white fog enveloped the room. A series of laser beams came gunning from the hover chair. His foot snarled in the frenzy of foam balls and crayons, and he tumbled to the ground, barely managing to dodge the lethal trajectory. His back was already beginning to flare from gamma ray exposure, the recurring effects of the phantom bullet phenomenon.

The hover chair pirouetted from the center of the room, building momentum. A beam sliced across the cabinets and the walls around it, morphing the linear flow into a radiating disc that neutralized everything in its circumference, the bags of money included. Milton was flat on his stomach when he watched it evaporate into the ether. He lamented it for one second, before laser beams came to perspective. He scrambled to his blast-proof briefcases and nudged it ahead, inching forward, slithering through the blender of plaster and paint plucking at him from all directions.

The emissions from the hover chair ceased. Milton hoped a piece of the ceiling fell on the jadeite's head and gifted him an enumeration, but it was unlikely. He considered assembling his plutonizer, but the entire place was shrouded in smoke and debris. He couldn't make anything out. Everything was compromised. It was better to get moving, than to sit idle for the dust to settle.

Up until that point, Milton had never come across a suspected jadeite of such age. There was perhaps the jadeite who posed as a 68-year-old woman. But she looked young for her age, and she exhibited faculty of all extremities. For that, it was an easier enumeration, even though he was almost killed. A jadeite on a hover chair had yielded an unforeseen learning curve. Why wasn't there a protocol for that, he wondered, except what boxes to check off on the administrative side of his work. It was all he gleaned from his basic training. The priority of documenting whatever happened between point A and Z. Data collection procedures he deemed insignificant outside the legal boundaries imposed by the bureaucratic scheme. After all, he thought, it's the enumeration of the individual in question, that's truly consequential to humanity's future. I should've stripped the senior of his hover chair and seated him on the floor, Milton thought belatedly, even though it was completely against policy. If so, he had been told, where do you draw the line? Not at 87 years, he thought, as he followed the trail of smoke escaping the room.

He pressed forward, clawing over the threshold, one elbow ahead of the other, blocking the back spasms, dragging along the floor like a maggot. The walk of shame of a failed assignment.

Milton was all too aware of the repercussions. This would be my second time, he said bitterly to himself. Second time in so many years. Enough to cost me my job. Milton had expected nothing less. He had come to terms with it. So why was he acting surprised? The thought of leaving the Bureaux was by no means a groundbreaking development. Just, for nebulous reasons, he had never got around to pulling the trigger. Unemployment was part of it. More than anything, he suspected it was his cowardice to state his case to Kyra. Now the issue's out of my hands, he thought vacantly. Maybe this was the only way. And yet he was mildly disappointed.

Anchoring one elbow on the floor, Milton looked back and glimpsed a bipedal silhouette emerging from the opaque screen of debris and particles in the air. Whoever it was, he thought- or, whatever it was, had abandoned the hover chair and regained the use of both feet. An eight-foot jadeite stepped into the clearing. Bulging out of its hand, was the bloated, purple tip distending from the shaft of a standard zap gun. A laser beam shot past Milton, into the hallway, and decapitated the head of an alabaster statue.

That should've been my head, he realized. Close calls served to remind him he was never really meant for this. But he paused to consider, neither was anybody else by that logic, especially when he looked around the headquarters each week, to see new faces replaced by newer faces. But goddamnit, he thought, if my lack of certification didn't affirm my intuition. Coupled with all the forms he had to fill out per enumeration, it got tiring fast. Why do I do this? he wondered. Was it really about planetary security? If not, this was no way to make a living.

Milton scrabbled to his feet and bolted out of the room. The hallway was lined with faceless white statues, groping forward with their arms, as if reaching out for him. He dropped and rolled behind one of them for cover. It was instantly pulverized by the jadeite's laser beam. He sprung back to his feet and repeated the drill, taking cover from one statue onto the other, until all the statues were pulverized and there were no more standing to keep him alive. Hide and seek and destroy was over. Or just the hiding part, he thought. Rapid discharges of the jadeite's zap gun thundered across the hall.

Milton hurtled toward the lobby, careening between laser beams and blowing past the flurry of domestic shrapnel. Straight ahead, he identified the door that would bail him out. Just several more yards, he thought. A laser beam beat him to it, punching a whole through the door. So much for that exit strategy, he said to himself. The only other way out was by an open window, if he could find one that proved authentic as opposed to ersatz. And even then, he wondered what he would get out of jumping from the 64th floor. Perhaps a journey to self-discovery, if not a crash course. Well, he thought, it beats being burned to death.

Getting away, he realized his world was covered in holes. Holes on the floor before his path, courtesy of the impending jadeite. The holes on the wall, indicating the time of day. For a while, the ersatz windows had him convinced he was at a beachfront property in the morning, but now he recalled entering the urban premises in the evening.

Milton turned left into the abutting wall in the lobby and crouched down, deliberating his next move. His options were nonexistent. Fleeing was out of the picture. The exit was visible from the hall. He would be gunned down if he tried. Suicide was a remote possibility. Fighting back was guaranteed, but surviving it was not.

Milton popped opened his briefcases, and referring to the diagram on his phone, forged together the plutonizer. Twisting around without exposing himself, he poked the plutonizer out into the open hall and squirted a generous blast.

Another beam of laser answered from the other side, shaving off the corner, inches from his head.

Milton pulled away and elected to lie in wait until he had the opportune moment to swing into the hall and blow away the jadeite in close quarters. But the jadeite seemed to have other ideas. A beam of laser exploded out of the hall and remained locked in a suspended state of discharge. Lightning filled the room. Everything in sight was being caramelized.

Milton retreated, stumbling into half-finished canvases and easels and hurled himself over a wide drawing table. He scrambled up to ready himself for the inescapable onslaught. Immediately, he was dragged back down by phantom bullets, shooting through his shoulder blades. His body petrified to stone, crippled by a spasmodic surge of lightning that zapped his neuromuscular network. With bated breath, his back contorted into a demonic arch, released, lurching him forward. The aftershock of the disarranged malady resonated through his nervous system, as he erected himself and braced his neck.

There was a cavity in the wall from the jadeite's extended laser beam. The last time plastic walls around him were dissolving into wax, he had reflected on life choices. But Milton realized now was not the best of time. Weakly, he angled his plutonizer on the drawing table.

The jadeite turned out of the hall and shot a laser beam in his direction. Milton narrowly rolled out of the way. The drawing table, as well as a chest of drawers that he left behind, molded into a lump. Milton returned fire to no avail. The jadeite shot back with a beam of laser that decomposed a nearby coffee table and its decorating chairs.

Before it was too late, Milton switched on his amplifier lens. The augmented view disproportionately multiplied the head size of the quarry by five times the normal surface area, creating an inflated target, affording him an unfair advantage that made head shots infinitely easier. He also checked to confirm the Aim Helper modification on his plutonizer was flipped to the ON position.

All at once, he could make out the green temples permeating from the abutting wall. It was the only surface area he needed. The crosshair automatically sunk into the target.

All Milton did was press a button.

The amplified head of the jadeite lit up. An orange and red inferno seared through the fissures. Rays of light emanated from the cranial cracks. The rinds on its skull rifted and ruptured, breaking off into a million fragments. It happened so quickly, Milton never even had a chance to blink. He stood there with his eyes peeled back, as chunks of slithery slugs and muculent grubs plopped down from the ceiling.

chapter 9

Eleanor Flutterby was monitoring the parkway that divided the streets between the shuffle of cookie-cutter houses, when she spotted it: a purple-colored beetle that was potentially askew. One of its corners was just off center from the demarcated zone by a fraction or two. Not a safety concern by any means, she thought, but an abuse of the code of fair parking practices nonetheless. So technically, a citable violation.

Eagerly, she landed her cart on the sidewalk and looked around to make sure the purple metabrid was still untagged and ripe for processing. As she had estimated from above, the preliminary indicators suggested it had not been bugged. No apparent treadmarks leading to and fro from it. Good, she thought, holding out yet that the automated sweepers had not tagged it.

Eleanor got out of her cart and scanned the vehicle through her phone for a popup of its complete history. License numbers and registration information emerged, along with past infractions. None dated for today. This is a gimme, she thought to herself, processing the license number and registration information.

Abrasive particles drizzled the vicinity. She veered her attention toward the patchwork of houses across from her, stitched together by interconnected conduits. Vaguely, she traced it to combustible activity from the upper crust, inconspicuous from her vantage point.

Incidentally to her left, two men dropped out of a black car, sporting tasseled hats and JERQS insignias pinned to their gowns. Syndics, she determined, moving closer. She had a feeling their arrival was connected to the source of the dust and debris settling around her. The men spoke to each other, unaware of her presence.

Clumps peppering down caused her to duck for cover beside her cart. Feeling the sizzle of grains on her shoulders, she squeezed her eyes and tucked her head. Larger dollops could be heard battering the streets. Car windshields were being smashed. Cobbles repetitively pattered the tops. I'm closing my eyes, she told herself as she did so. When I count to ten, it'll all go away. One... two...

Warily, she opened her eyes. A percussion went off, and her vision flustered. A boulder trundled away from her. It appeared to have glanced off the hood of her cart. She gathered her bearings and hoisted herself on the nerf bar of the beetle, from which she had ceased taking down information. Off the floor and nestled against the passenger side window, she watched the scene play out.

Her cart was not the only transport bent out of shape, resulting from the falling skies. Parked vehicles near her featured broken lights, cracked windows, and malformed hoods, resembling the aftermath of a multi-car pileup. Lordy, what just happened? she asked herself in disarray. Asteroids came to mind. But upon closer inspection, the bright, synthetic bits of colored rubble and loose bricks on the floor seemed less and less likely to have come by meteor shower. Her vision was still wobbling and rocking from the upheaval. Regaining her equilibrium, she traced it to particles of building blocks, as initially speculated. Maybe they were seismic waves that caused it, she thought.

She peered out through the windows of the beetle, disturbed by the spontaneous developments. The syndics appeared to be advancing through the network of conduit pipes. One of them hung back. She saw him talking to himself, possibly calling for backup.

There was a ringing in her ears that gradually worsened, transmuting into a distinct mechanical whizzing noise that made her look down. There were grooves beneath her feet. Tread marks. She stepped down from the nerf bar and followed the trail under the car and out, tracing it up to a rusted, triangle of squashed metal heap, whisking off with the coup. The momentary lapse amid the hubbub, had left an opening for the sweeper to capitalize on her claim. She noticed it was a duster, a late prototype. It was incapable of flight like the newer sweeper models, but it could still sniff out an asymmetrical car from miles away.

Eleanor dizzied with turmoil, as the duster scurried away with her commission. The AI unit lacked the capacity of social custom – a design that was advantageous for its purpose. There was no reasoning with it. No running it over, she thought. It was durable, tough, roadkill-proof. After all these years, its silver hull had developed a hearty, burgundy patina and a protective layer of dirt, and it maneuvered without a glitch.

She returned her gaze north before the house, where a man holding dual briefcases stood surrounded by three tasseled hats. She could not hear what they were saying to each other, but she could tell there was some friction by the way the three men extended their weapons.

Eleanor's hand foraged the side of her waist and grasped for a handle. Drawing out her regulation-issue laser pistol to aim, her concentration wandered clockwise, further down the road. There, she locked onto her metal target, fired and hit it perfectly. The laser beam deflected off the corroded hull clangorously and went jetting in another trajectory. The unharmed sweeper continued roaming as if nothing had happened.

She adjusted her crosshair, when her visor cap flew off her head. Hey! she thought. Laser beams scattered her senses, prompting her to distance herself from the pandemonium. She glimpsed her cart, which was in no condition to be driven; the hood had been flattened to the floor. She would have to call it in. And what random disaster would transpire in the span it took for help to arrive? she wondered.

She sailed to the ground and squeezed a peak between the hexapodic appendages of the beetle. If I can only close my eyes, she thought, as a pair of sneakers advanced, thudding to the pitter-patter of her heart. If I can only count to ten.

Instead, she pushed herself off the ground, squatted on her haunches and identified the outline of the approaching figure. Briefcases dangled from both arms. He was closing in, to her alarm, and the purple door butterflied open. The car, it turned out, was his. He heaved himself inside.

As she stood there in the brief instant of stunned silence, the passenger door on her side also rose up. Brooding from the interior, sat the dubious profile of a man in a pale green jacket, uncombed. He turned to her, and she saw a big pie face. "Get within," he said.

chapter 10

The door lowered automatically and locked shut after the blonde safeguard of the DPM. Even in the dimness of the interior, he could make out the familiar pink uniform: fat red buttons and sharp collars, double-breasted and short-sleeved, red stripes running down the obliques, and the pink shorts. She looked like the doll that accompanied each Trufflehard action figure and featured leg-clinging action. Seat straps mechanically went to work on her, as Milton fired up the ignition.

The top of his car unhinged to sprout metallic wings and propelled above the light show of laser beams, joining the minimum driving altitude of the holoway. Milton activated forward thrust and ran into the inevitable wall of cars wedged bumper to bumper. The first and second tiers, public and toll-free, were always congested, regardless of the time and day. These are the times we live in, he thought. No matter where you are. Every city was overpopulated, teeming abundantly with denizens, unsuspecting targets for jadeites.

Sirens were catching up behind them.

"Why were they shooting at me for?" the safeguard beside him asked over the cacophony. "Do they think I'm affiliated with you?" She paused at her own suggestion. "No offense, I don't even know who you are."

"None taken," he said stoically, barely managing to squish his beetle into traffic. "My name is Milton Grainjar."

"Am I supposed to know that name from somewhere?"

"I'm afraid not," he said, keeping his eyes on the road. "I work for an agency." He checked his rear view. Multiple boxes, radiating dull, monochromatic undulations, elbowed through the lanes, scraping metal, sideswiping all the other vehicles obstructing the path to the purple beetle.

"Which one?" she asked. "There're like a hundred out there."

"You wouldn't have heard of it," he told her, giving up his spot, barrel rolling the car away from the ranks and pulling back his joysticks to rocket upward.

"Tell me. I may know."

He was reluctant to comment, his eyes remaining fixed on the ascent.

She said indignantly, "For pity's sake, I work in law enforcement."

"XYZ."

"What does it stand for?" she asked.

"It's just a pseudonym for the Bureaux." He bypassed the honking motorcade, employing several complex maneuvers, illegal as they were, looping around the shoulders. He raged free, unconcerned with violating various merging laws in the process.

"You know I can finish you for that."

Milton wondered what she meant by those words, but he did not doubt it. Most of the fines he had accrued came by violations he had never committed. But it made no matter to him, taking credit for something that was not his doing. He had been told by a trusted source that civic citations and fees were how the Ekonomy built its capital. By that method, he had decided to contribute his patriotic part by collecting a magnanimous share of fines. Making the payments on the other hand, seemed to require an altogether disparate area of commitment from him, a financial aptitude that he had not achieved but aspired to reach someday.

"Don't ask," she appended. "Part of the new traffic lexicon."

That much, he had figured, but he decided to leave it at that. With both hands on the dual sticks, he had enough to do for now. The car's rearview flashed with alternating strobe lights. Blue laser beams darted past them.

Eleanor turned to look over her seat. "Why is this happening?"

"I never paid interest to the politics of it," he said flatly. "I let the Bureaux take care of that. I'm just their errand boy."

"You must know why they're attacking us. Syndics don't just go after denizens for no reasons."

"They're jadeites," he said matter-of-factly, "and that's sort of their agenda."

They continued to rise, penetrating ceilings of clouds delineating restricted levels reserved for toll-paying consumers of the Ekonomy. Tier after tier, the purple beetle climbed the traffic hierarchy, despite lacking special clearance. He dodged corporate vehicles and the occasional luxury brands, until holographic lanes stretched as far as the eyes can see with virtually nobody else. The upper tiers were practically unused, reserved mostly for Execs. And still below, was the gridlock pattern of immobilized neon lights and cars crisscrossing at intersections, in and around the Ekonomic empire. He checked his rearview again and counted three cars encroaching. The purple beetle ascended further, merging up to the tier called no man's land; dubbed so, as minimal air supply permitted only specific cars that could handle the altitude.

"Do you mean that colloquially?" she asked.

He had trouble making her out over his buzzing ears, the aftereffects of the piercing whirr of sirens. On their faraway tails was the trio of crimson dots; they blinked out one at a time.

As the airspeed indicator maxed out at the red zone, the skyline swept beneath the palpitating beetle. Milton turned to meet the woman who had caused the distraction on the ground, creating him the diversion to circumvent three jadeites. Before that, he had observed them arguing over who would get to vaporize him. In all likelihood, he thought, she had saved his life.

"Colloquially?" he repeated, wondering if he had heard her correctly.

Her face was hard to read, pulsating with charcoal colors of the trailing aurora. All he picked up was the electronic name tag emitting from her left breast - Safeguard Eleanor Flutterby. His overall impression was limited to the intensity of her eyes, emoting a multitude of thoughts flickering against the synthesized nocturnal sky. "I get called a jadeite all the time for falling short of behavior befitting a model denizen. Almost as often as wompous miscreants. We get that a lot."

He consoled her, "Kids can be the worst, Miss Flutterby."

"Kids are sweet, innocent. No, these were fully grown adults."

"I'm sorry to hear that," he said, gripping the joysticks, adding distance between his beetle and the tasseled hats helming modified muscle cars of yore; they were a symbol of size and power in the public tiers. At elevations higher, they handled clumsily, due to the clunky design and lower maximum altitude rating. The sirens were starting to abate, the pulsing gray lights dwindling. Milton's gamble was paying off.

"Don't be," she said. "After a while, you imagine them as compliments." She broke off. "Hold on, what the blue blazes did you mean then? You don't actually mean a twelve-eyed oddity that gravitates on tentacles."

"No," he said, bewildered by the visual of such chimera, "where did you get that from?"

"The Ekonomicopia," she said. "It was on the front cover today at the Mart."

The development was acknowledged grimly. Milton had yet to encounter such a variant. "No, I mean the eight-foot tall, feline-eyed shape shifters."

"Oh," she said, elevating her pitch with epiphany, and then dropping off, "you're one of those…"

"One of what?" he asked, confused by the undertone.

"Those denizens who think illegal aliens are about to take over the world."

"It sounds zany when you say it like that," he admitted.

She manifested a freshly mirrored hundred-pixel coin from her pocket and motioned above the console box. "Which one do you recommend?"

"The original. It's made with real marshmallows. But it's out of order."

She fed the vending machine and made her selection, heeding neither of his suggestions. A moment later, the printer squeaked, after which she reached for the takeout port. "It worked," she said, peanut butter crisp in hand. "Would you like to share it with me?"

"Sure," he said dully. She offered him the broken half of the Health Bar, and he accepted it. "Thanks." The moment the chocolate-covered peanut crisp hit Milton's palate, he felt magically replenished.

The GPS utility informed him they had reached their destination. He circled the perimeter and initiated descent.

"Do you have a solar-powered underground shelter stocked full of laser guns, reverse osmosis water filters, and self-sustaining stock of ersatz food like those denizens on TV?" she asked unseriously. "To prepare for the invasion."

"Those denizens are end-of-the-world zealots," he said dismissively. "Post-apocalyptic enthusiasts begging for a reason to wear gas masks."

She chewed nonchalantly. "Then you agree."

The car shot through an artificial waterfall and swooped beneath a rainbow in the dark. Turbulence commenced. The interior started to rumble. Trees came to life. Leaves bristled and forked limbs cracked all around them, as the purple beetle plunged through the umbrella of foliage. The ground jolted them to a stop, the hexapod stand of the vehicle digging into the hump of dirt.

Milton cut off the car lights to avoid macroscopic detection, and they got out. The air up at the 99th level of the local inner-city park was thin, misty, crispy, and scented of botany. "We should be safe here," he said.

During the evening, hardly anything was visible at such elevations but the deciduous backdrop of two-dimensional silhouettes.

"Where've you brought me?" Eleanor asked rigidly. She seemed lost, disoriented by the thick expanse of trees. Every direction looked the same.

"This is where I work," he said. "We should be safe here."

Milton watched Eleanor glancing for direction, as though she was in search of a luminescent building with signage. Instead, her eyes faintly spotted a rectangular shed, black on black in the darkness.

"I feel practically blindfolded," Eleanor said, caressing herself. "I can't see anything."

Neither can I, Milton thought. It's all muscle memory from here. "The area of the park is off the grid and restricted," he said. "Ready for initiation?"

Eleanor treaded shrewdly, straining to distinguish the outline of angular construction. "It looks like a ramshackle shack."

"The unassuming exterior is the optimal screen for a multi-tasking, highly advanced monitoring facility," Milton said. "Your eyes may need to adjust to the bright lights, Miss Flutterby. Kyra's gonna be in there. When you see her, say hi. Don't mind her nature. Step right up and welcome to the Bureaux." He slid the door open for her. "Oh, and no matter what," he said, following her in, "you can't tell anybody about what you're about to-"

Three-dimensional posters and placards infringed on the crammed, moth-eaten space. Trufflehard ads and Anti-Jade Agenda brochures waylaid him. The walls scratched and screeched with scribble marks. Formulas and equations incoherently scrolled across. Plotted maps of the cities and news articles plastered him, alongside posters strewn of nude women, completely unrelated. He ceased swaying round and round, as he steadied himself.

Eleanor stood at the center of the creaky interior, underneath a light bulb dangling on a wire. "Is this what you do in your spare time?"

Milton walked up to the holographic posters and started raking at them. He ran his fingers across the walls, groped it and proceeded to bang and pound with his fists. "No, it's a mirage. There should be a conveyer chute right here, where we're standing," he said, pointing to the rotting floor boards, "and it should lead us to the automatic doors of the entrance."

Eleanor shuffled nervously. "Are you sure we came to the right place?"

"Yes, I've been coming to these coordinates for over a decade," he said, which prompting her to take a step back.

Goddamnit, he cursed to himself, what a mean trick. A sleazy illusion, triggered by my invitation of Miss Flutterby. Denizen non grata in their view. They didn't let in just anybody, what with the policy about unauthorized personnel. But after everything I've been through, you would think they'd trust me. By "they," he meant Kyra.

Milton tilted his head back to address the ceiling. "Kyra, I know you're there, watching from the air-conditioned, state-of-the-art headquarters." He spun around. "This is Miss Flutterby. She's with me. Make this go away. We're being pursued by jadeites." Milton hung his head, hands on his hips. "Kyra…" He trailed off, overcome with a blank look on his face. "Well, there's no use standing around here."

"Don't tell me that's Kyra," she said, pointing at the discovery of a silhouette leaning against the darkest corner.

Milton confirmed the shadow of swollen body, comatose and sagging, bundled in a flannel shirt and overalls. He shuffled toward the baffling gestalt, tilting his head to perceive a close-up. The bottom of the pant legs, as well as the flannel cuffs, stuck out with hay and grass clippings. The collar was duct-taped to the head of a plush pony adorning a red wig.

"Why don't you go on without me," Eleanor suggested from the doorway. She shivered, burnishing her arms. "I can find my own way back."

"What will you do?" Milton asked, trailing after her.

She turned to step outside. "I can call the Depart-" Instantly, the surrounding trees lit up, and she crashed to one knee. An aerial raid of laser beams seared the sky. Sirens started back up.

"They must've detected our thermal radiation!" he relayed, as they ducked down and scuttled to the beetle, clamoring inside. The rickety engine generated a roar. They shot forward, dodging the sporadic trajectory of laser beams, weaving through gaps in the wooded terrain. Milton turned the car sideways, narrowly slipping through the dense population of lumber. A broad barricade of tree trunks ambushed them. Milton pulled the dual sticks, accelerating up into the air, and rocketed through the verdant coverage.

The GPS utility activated, opening a search field on the top-left corner of the interior.

"Where are we going this time?" Eleanor asked, panting, gripping the handles of her seat.

"Remember that place with all the amenities you talked about back there?"

chapter 11

Eldridge Kane was at the top of the world. He was at the 515th floor of the Kokiri House, erected on the Pacific coast. His office was not an inner-office. It did not have four walls like most other rooms, but eight. Walls that were not mere partitions, but walls to the outside world. The entire floor was his office. If it became too isolated, he had only to look under his feet. He could see from the elevated vantage point, the divisions and subdivisions of overcrowded rooms through a one-way looking glass.

Bird's-eye surveillance of all the levels was viewable from the uppermost floor. At the cellar levels, rows of red-faced grunts cultivated a monotonous landscape of productivity, men and women bumping elbows, squished together on a long bench, addressing callers, each of them working hard as ever for the elusive promotion. These were the hardest workers, who made the gears turn, first ones in, last ones out, crunching numbers, auditing data, addressing calls, all the necessary travails in the interim of waiting for the prospective upswing that would superbly evade them.

At the mid levels, secretaries of some rank were situated among cubicles. Entry-level Execs shimmered in wrinkle-free, five-piece suits and hats, posing to appear self-important in their shared offices. Eldridge remembered when he had to play dress-up, an abhorrent memory of squalid times, when he was young, working in the preceding floors, before taking over his father's company.

The Exec culture at the top levels had not changed since. Often they sat around, appearing in deep thought, staring out an ersatz window, pipe in one hand, swirling rocks in a glass of intoxicants in the other, likely wondering how they would spend the evening after work. There was always a fool in a powdered wig snoozing on a sofa, and an Exec and a bikini model making out beside. A mariachi band dressed in furry costumes played in another room. It was a wonder how anything can get done amid the distraction of commotion, or of sleep for that matter.

The assistants here used to be secretaries. Now they were pegged the up-and-coming go-getters, some of whom strutted with purpose, browsing holocubic documents on their all-in-one phones, answering the calls, cracked out on gurgle, losing hair, running in circles, doing whatever they had to do to earn a wig; some of them were peddling carts of office supplies. They yielded to fairy tale princesses walking toward the pool party at the center of the outer-office, wielding trays of amuse-bouches and fruity-colored margaritas.

Eldridge averted his gaze from the work environment and lifted his head, appealing horizontally to the roaring surfs opening on the western hemisphere of the octagonal room. And he thought, What a relief I don't have to look far to wash away any jarring sense of productivity.

He walked back to his desk and stood before the view of the city. The glass walls were made of a durable diamond structure that was perfectly transparent. Beneath him, he could make out the perimeter of eight smaller structures that flanked the octagonal skyscraper. These multi-faceted buildings were an extension of the lower levels. Fanning out from the Kokiri House, comprised the buildings of the downtown capitol, exhibiting various forms. The Rainbow Towers - popular with the 14-and-under demographic - were a quartet of tubular, rainbow-colored arches. It stood next to the largest urban park, 300 levels of genetically modified greenery and benches and hiking trails. The Upside Down Pyramid stood on a single block that rotated at the base, gradually changing positions throughout the hour. The Corkscrew Building housed the largest Eko Gym in the world, each of its 200 floors containing fancy weightlifting equipment, gymnasiums, running tracks, swimming pools, soccer fields, basketball courts, etc. Distinctly spinning above the industrial structures was the largest Ferris wheel in the world. Seating over a thousand passengers, its axle was mounted 3,500-feet high atop a pole. It looked like a giant baby's swirly lollipop from afar, and you had to take the conveyer chute to the top before getting on the ride.

The holoway intersected the expanse of architecture, spanning across the pink and purple horizon. The upper tiers of the holographic lanes projected high above the cities, unperturbed, restricted to Execs of the Ekonomy and toll subscribers; occasionally, a luxury sports brand would zoom by. Down by the lower tiers, traffic was stuck as usual. It always improved Eldridge's spirits to see that. Hideous cars suspended in the air, dawdling in radioactive exhaust fumes.

A thought occurred to him. Monte Cristos, strawberry preserves, fried pistachio ice cream - deep fried. He returned to his seat and added to the list he had been compiling for the Executive Chef.

BURGER WITH 1 LB GROUND KOBE BEEF, EXTRA RARE, BLUE CHEESE, PEPPERJACK CHEESE,

CARAMELIZED ONIONS, FRIED JALAPENO POPPERS, ONION RINGS, GRILLED PEACH, DEVILS ON HORSEBACK, BUFFALO WINGS (GENETICALLY ENGINEERED BUFFALO, NOT CHICKEN), FILET OF NEPTUNE GROUPER, GOLD SHAVINGS ON TOASTED, ULTRA PREMIUM SESAME SEED BRIOCHE - NO "SECRET SAUCE"

BISCUIT STUFFED WITH BUTTERMILK FRIED SQUIRREL, VEAL MEDALLIONS, SMOKED BACON FROM PRIZE PIG, BLUE FIN TUNA, MOOSE MILK CHEESE, FOIE GRAS, BELUGA CAVIAR, PLATINUM AROWANA GRAVY

PIZZA WITH SICILIAN SAUCE, PULE CHEESE, LOBSTER TAIL, MOONSTONE OYSTER, GRILLED RABBIT MEDALLIONS, BABY KOALA, WHOLE WHITE TRUFFLES, SUNNY SIDE EMU EGGS

Hydraulic footsteps came to Eldridge's auditory awareness. He stared up from his list to see a tall robotic shape. It powered toward him, smiling and swinging a tubular phone in one hand, before pulling up at the desk.

"Good day to you, Lord," said the bantam assistant crammed inside the bionic torso. He manipulated a metal arm to situate the phone within range, whereby he referred to one of the holocubes. "As you were likely informed," he said, "an impromptu meeting was held at 3 p.m. this afternoon to examine the state of Ekonomic affairs. But first, new reports have come in, concerning the man identified as Milton Grainjar, on file for chronic linkage to property damage and tenant disappearances."

Eldridge had heard the name before. More than once, in fact, over the past years. Intel was limited to mere sightings in and around the area of residential disturbances. Frankly, it was a matter of domestic affairs. He failed to imitate interest. "Unless your reports concern concrete, investigative progress, I'm occupied."

Reggie Johnson rearranged the display of holocubes. The ekosuit swiveled left, arms swayed up as if to commence marching, froze, withdrew its arms back to its side, and swiveled forward to address the LCEO. "I come bearing notes from today's conference, in the aftermath of the six arrested members of the Wakeup Group petitioning before the building earlier in the morning. They were arrested and detained for questioning, the sidewalk of their activities being a neutral zone. They await trial at the moment. CEOs from multiple subsidiaries of Ekonomy Ink were present. Your vacant stead at the conference table was sorely felt."

Eldridge cleared his throat. "The scheduled activities of my morning ran longer than usual." Following the prompt finish of the spectacular burlesque program, the shapely masseuses had stayed overtime at his insistence, obediently obliging to the opportunity to assuage the LCEO of his surplus tension. Rubbing down all his kinks demanded extra tending from the ambrosial figures, leading to an exultant experience that left him charged and depleted all at once. "You may regurgitate what was discussed in my absence, but keep it brief. I'm rather ragged from thrusting a most intense physicality."

"I beseech you to temper the rigors of your daily upkeep," Johnson said, "if I may be so saccharine."

"You may not," Eldridge said. "Proceed with the condensed report."

"In light of the arrests, the gathering of the CEOs was coordinated to gauge prevailing winds of the Wakeup movement," Johnson said.

"However, a consensus could not be reached. Missing from the record, was your enlightened insight."

Eldridge was well aware of the global demonstrations credited to the Wakeup group. Some of them walked the streets of neutral zones, carrying signs insisting that businesses pay taxes. New adults driven by the mercurial ideals of reckless youth. Their naivety would not discount the minimum sentencing for such an offense: twelve years of forced labor in a rehabilitation factory. "They're familiar with my take," he said. "A new faction premieres every year in the protest industrial complex. This year, it's the Attention All Shoppers. Last year, it was the Now or Never. Before that, Rise Above. And something new will be ready to fill in for the subsequent years."

"I sense you're considerably unalarmed by these proximate developments," Johnson said.

"We have laws in place," Eldridge said. "Laws that classify any form of permitless protesting as a first class felony."

Expressing a skeptical leer from his jejunal station, Johnson said, "It is not beyond the capabilities of the Wakeup group to dodge said political hazard and manage to come out with a permit, as did movements past."

"A bridge that we won't have to cross for another six years at soonest," Eldridge said, "not to mention dozens of megapixels in legal fees paid to firms owned by the Ekonomy."

"Cupcakes compared to the social ramifications of these movements," Johnson said, hesitating. "Perhaps I speak out of oblivion, but why even let it stand the opportunity to acquire a permit? The disruptions that would be all but eliminated by banishing any form of protest."

"Protesting is a form of free speech. It's essential in our free world. And as long as it's conducted under the regulations circumscribed by protest zones, no damage is posed to the Ekonomy. If anything, the residual effect of their costly efforts serve a vital function."

"The nonpartisan documentaries reflect poorly on the Ekonomy," Johnson said, observing carefully. "Truly, you haven't misjudged the political climate that badly."

"No matter the degree of sanction over the masses," Eldridge said, turning the seat away to face the view of the city, "a nagging minority persists on the fringe, somewhat privy to the guiding mechanisms, fancying themselves immune to our network of influence. Attempting to convince them contrary would only lead to further resistance."

Johnson advanced the ekosuit and rode up beside the LCEO. "Oppositely, you pander to them."

"In turn," Eldridge explained, peering at the skyline, "the documentaries make up a meager but viable sector of the cinema industry. Worldwide, six hundred thousand megapixels are generated from marketing these annual movements. All the while showing the number of jobs the Ekonomy creates and supplies on an annual basis. Unemployment is at an all-time low."

"On the counter end of the spectrum, the detractors presented in the anti-Ekonomy documentaries criticize the scarcity of jobs that pay livable wages." Johnson paused to contemplate his suspicions. "But you are well aware of that fact. My hunch portends the conflict of interest reaps dividends."

"These documentaries offer many things to many denizens," Eldridge said. "Outsiders on the sidelines who pray for change, are offered a certain hope from the activities to expose the alleged corruption. That there's someone out there on behalf of the homebodies, protesting against the hyped-up, subliminal evils of the Ekonomy. Protestors relegated to designated partisan zones of uninhabited volcanic islands and sand dunes, somehow fabricate within their being a sense of purpose."

Johnson nodded with impish lucidity. "The self-righteous pretext only belies the vanity of their anarchical claims, ultimately invalidating their efforts."

"The Ekonomy is non-profit, but it is not a charity," Eldridge said. "Instead of climbing up the Ekonomic ladder through hard work, there they are, preferring to hold up signs in the Himalayas."

Johnson ascertained, "Meager fanfare is observed in the media of the leaders of the movement who are almost always scouted by the antipodic establishment they swore against."

"Creative differences aside, their stalwart resolve and intestinal gumption does not go unrecognized."

Johnson added, "Just as they're overcome by the sobriety of a crumbling membership base with fruitless demands, skeletal and battered by the harsh environmental conditions of their legal jurisdiction."

"Hypocritical as it may seem," Eldridge said, "they're more than happy to reform into healthy, contributing consumers of the Ekonomy." In fact, the former leaders of past movements were now under the payroll of the Ekonomy, operating within the lower levels of the Kokiri House, where their dynamic skillsets were being groomed for future administrative positions."

Perceptively, Johnson annotated, "With the principal leadership plundered, the group loses its centralized voice…"

"Civilization wins," concluded Eldridge. But let the mouth of the wigs rabble dissent among themselves, he thought. Impudent wraiths. Yawning, he gyrated back to his desk and asked, "Anything else that was covered by the adjournment of the gabfest?"

Johnson hauled the ekosuit away from the glass. "A stipend hearing, resulting in a unanimous vote to reward each other a seasonal bonus."

Eldridge's eyes drifted past him, beyond the mechanical outline. Johnson maneuvered the synthetic suit around to see two women dressed in silken hanbok garment with spectacular shades of pastel, centered by a pink bow below their breasts. Fixed on their heads were light blue ayams. They gravitated forward.

Johnson studied closely as the Executive Grapers took a moment to salute him with a bow: they knelt down, balancing with both hands, a platter of blooming dark, purple grapes. Seedless concord – the LCEO's favorite variety.

Eldridge nodded, signaling his blessing, and the grapers converged to his side. Thereafter, they alternately popped orbs of pulp into his kisser in exchange for the wizened skins. "Next order of business," he said, with juice streaking down his chin. The red-haired graper drew the tip of one horizontally-striped sleeve and delicately blotted at the trickle of nectar.

Johnson observed reticently, fidgeting the collar of his dress shirt. "I have bestowed upon me, headlines for news, awaiting your signoff."

These were the sensationalized articles, commercial works of yellow journalism to boost readership and market products. They were planted innocuously beside actual news, which were prosaic in contrast.

Urged Eldridge, "Go on."

A circuited arm angled the phone, focusing the corresponding holocube to Johnson's field of vision. "Jadeite Spaceship Sighted Over Ekonomy Promenade."

The classic Armageddon ploy. It boosted sales of everything from canned goods, solar-powered refrigerators, hydroponic equipment, water recycling systems, laser guns, etc. Eldridge exhibited no objection.

"Trufflehard Magnet Sells Out in Minutes."

Fixing demand, in response to the gross overproduction of the mediocre refrigerator magnet set featuring the patriotic icon. They had to move the backlog of products somehow.

Citing no objection, Johnson went down the list. "Eko Ink LCEO Appears on Pavement Pizza."

Symbolic of his appointment of worship among members of Executivism. Trite, Eldridge thought. Just what they wanted.

He saw his assistant waiting patiently for a response. He opened his mouth. The woman with the lustrous brown hair, plugged it with a grape. The red-haired woman went n ext, and back and forth, grape, grape, and grape. Before he could take another breath, it seemed, the women in hanbok inserted more grapes than his mouth could hold.

Johnson shifted in the cabled belly and continued anyway. "Studies Show Eko News Readers Are Smarter Than Non-Readers."

Eldridge was busy bursting immense grapes in his mouth. His lips were bruised, his teeth blackened, his cheeks puffy, his chin sticky with splotches of purple pigmentation. He smacked his lips furiously, hulling a multitude of grapes inside his mouth, and spitting out the desiccated hides in the direction of the daintily cupped hands. "Keep going," he sputtered. "Don't stop until I tell you."

chapter 12

The purple beetle was descending onto a vacant lot, next to a large glowing down-arrow circumscribing the words "Ekonomy Mall." The vehicle planted itself on level ground, and Milton hopped down from his respective side, with his dual briefcases. Eleanor followed, and together, they proceeded toward the conveyer chute.

"But I thought they were just in the movies and…" Eleanor trailed off, examining what she was saying.

"In the news," Milton finished for her.

"You're fooling, right?" Eleanor asked. "Just because it's in the news, doesn't mean it's true."

The ground sizzled, inches from their feet. They looked up and saw above, the square vehicles rippling dreary currents and the syndics inside with their zap guns drawn.

Running toward the opening of the conveyer chute, Milton asked, "Is that true enough for you?" He gained access with his ubiquitous passcode utility.

"That's different. That's a laser blast." She encapsulated herself within the cylindrical chute and plunged ahead.

Milton went after her and came out of the other end, remarking, "From a jadeite."

A carousel of multiple conduit pipes, ordered from floors one to fifty presented itself at the main directory of the subsurface mall. "There," he said, guiding her to one of the chutes.

She turned to argue. "But those aren't jadeites. Those are just… syndics." She shook her head with incredulity.

"Go on." Milton gestured her to step over the pipe and take the dive. She hopped over the lip and disappeared. He went next.

"I'm calling this off," Eleanor said, as he joined her on the 48th atrium. She manifested a phone and started dialing with her mind.

"Who are you calling?" he asked.

"The DPM," she answered.

"Of Public Mobilization?" Even if they weren't already in cahoots together, he said to himself, what good would the DPM be against the jadeites? "To issue them a fine?" he wondered aloud, puzzled by her purpose.

She stared at her phone intently. "We have a working relationship with the syndics. The director of the DPM can call them off."

"They've infiltrated every sector of law enforcement," he told her.

"I know the denizens I work with. Good-for-nothing despots and trilobite food, perhaps," she said laconically. "Eight-foot tall and cat-eyed?" She looked up from her phone, sent him a rhetorical look. "I'll call my superior."

"You don't know your co-workers as well as you think you do."

"But everyone thinks we're scallywagging goosesteppers and statutory racketeers," she said. "We get no respect from anyone."

"I don't mean that part," he said, "although I can commiserate."

"What do you have, if you can't trust your intuition?" she asked.
"Your life."

She lowered the phone indignantly. "What do you suggest then?"
"Run."

They began running across the vast, empty interior of the shopping mall, surrounded by the jumble of closed retail shops crammed together. Milton tried to pick one as hideout, but it was hard to decide. The wide array of storefronts marketed themselves with what was configured as unique and tailored and researched, be it bold and obnoxious displays, or more regal and mature in setting with golden trimmings, each one vying for the attention of passersby. But after a while, they all started to look the same.

Between the stores facing across each other, from the center of the atrium, were the tortured tracks of a rollercoaster that resembled a metallic beanstalk, growing out of the lowest depths of the subsurface complex.

"Is there someone more suitable for this?" she asked, loping alongside. "Someone we can call."

"Someone who specializes in the numerical handling of such preeminent planetary affairs?"

She hastened the momentum of her feet. "Whatever you wanna call this."

"That would be me," he said.

"You?" she asked, her voice wavering.

He exhaled, "Yes."

"We're done for," she said.

He gandered over to her, panting and straining to keep pace with her.

"You're welcome to disagree," she added.

Taking sporadic breaths, he found it hard to assure her.

"I want to believe you," she said after a while. "No, I don't want what you're saying to be true. But if you're serious, prove it. Call for help."

"I can't," he said.

She spun around to see him swallow large gulps of the atmosphere. "What do you mean you can't?" she asked.

"In my field," he said, refilling his lungs, "we're responsible for saving our own hides." He took another wallop. "The Bureaux needs to maintain plausible deniability." He started walking.

"How convenient," she said.

"Quite the contrary," he said. Despite the Bureaux's emphasis on functioning as a team, he thought, you flew solo in these missions. It did not matter that you had twenty-four hour live support or that they provided you with a flashy car. All the pep talks and comprehensive background details on suspects could not save you from oncoming death rays.

"You've come up with patches to support your conspiracy theory. Tell me, what is it that you do exactly? How do you even know anybody is an illegal?"

"Calling them 'illegal' is pejorative. It's considered offensive to jadeites." He paused. "Kyra told me. But we have a whole protocol in place. If all goes as planned, they undergo enumeration for-"

"Melty Crux!!!" she exclaimed, gaping gaily.

Milton traced her gaze to a sweet shop. It was, as she had intoned, Melty Crux, followed by three exclamation points to drive the memo-randum. Well, he thought, how could you not yield to that? Turning to see they had lost the JERQS, he acquiesced. "In and out."

He stood guard, as she walked inside and browsed through the selections. "What should I get?" she asked.

"Whatever you want."

"Something sour," she said.

Rarely straying from the classics, he recommended the modest belts and straws. Eventually, she manifested with a cotton candy that evanesced different colors, snow globe candies, and a bottle of some multi-flavored soda pop, layered by their density levels. She turned to him abruptly, and perhaps Milton saw her truly for the first time when she blushed and her moist lips formed into a pink crescent. "I used to love these when I was a kid."

Her selections weren't sour at all, he observed. And then she offered it up to him earnestly, the iridescent, color-changing cotton candy, as though the whole store was not for the taking. "It's mystery-flavored," she said. "Trying to guess is half the fun."

He detached a wad and shoved it in his mouth. Without exerting a ton of thought, he wound up with a piece of cake.

Eleanor seemed slightly more invested in the activity of solving the mystery flavor of sugary fibers. She pawed at the polychromatic puff and fluttered her lashes prettily, and then extended another helping toward him. He accepted, regarding the refined, cosmopolitan quality of her approach. How she covered the length of her palate and chewed it over with an analytical squiggle drawing above the nomadic movement of her eyes.

"On the nose," she ventured, "the aromatic bouquet of mango blossom, passion fruit compote, and fig molasses are obvious. But I'm also getting a lot of florals. What do you get?"

She angled it toward him, and he whiffed. It smelled like cotton candy. "Everything you said," he bumbled. "The florals," he amended, nodding. "Intense."

Milton trailed Eleanor out of the art gallery. She seemed the more inspired of the two. He did not remember much. There was the depiction of bipedal cows, strolling a shimmering shopping district, dressed in Jaxon Napoleana mink coats, carrying Manfred & Mulaney bags, wearing Zeus Henry pumps, with lipstick and blonde wigs, to which Eleanor had said, "That's cute."

And he remembered standing before a tableau of consumers, browsing through a space-savers farmers market, displaying watermelons, cantaloupes, and honeydews, efficiently stacked beside each other, made possible by the genetic modification that gave them their cubic properties. There were also pineapples, and other fruits, pink and wrinkled, too. Eleanor appreciated the eye-popping colors of that one.

As they dallied by the top franchises, the ground tremored and steamed before them. Beams of laser danced around their shoes, prompting them to set off. Eleanor stumbled and fell on her hands. The cotton candy rolled hayward, and the bottle of pop clattered to the floor, its contents bubbling into a light blue color. Milton stopped and turned to look back. Behind her, four tasseled hats were taking aim, shooting their zap guns. More shapes materialized from the pipe behind them.

"Let's go," Milton urged. He put down a briefcase to grab her by the hand and yank her back to her feet. As she propped up, she motioned to lift the other briefcase, but he swiftly moved to reprise his grasp. Avoiding further misstep, they scuttled together into the dark and vacuous void of the Family Arcade. An enticing gallery of luminous pinball tables chirped and chimed, tempting them to stop and play.

Laser beams chased after them, one of which shriveled a nearby vending machine into a heap of coal. Milton and Eleanor stopped and collapsed together, pumping their lungs, behind a beefy barricade of sparkling machines.

Milton was on his hands and knees, scrounging for oxygen. Instead, helium seemed to fill his head. Without further thought or consideration, he found himself laughing. When he glanced up from his senseless, feeble fit to see that Eleanor was not nearly as enthused, the dire reality crept back in. Her eyes were closed, and when she opened them, sober concern blanched her expression. He adjusted himself accordingly and peered away.

The symphony of clattering bells and howling whistles rang in his ears, soothing him, drawing him back to the nostalgic milieu of the pinball cornucopia. Across from him was the vintage Trufflehard Forever pinball machine, with its aggrandized playing field, taking up the whole wall. He had the urge to play it again, smacking his flippers, timing his dexterity at crucial junctures to keep the ball alive, as though he was the pinball, hysterically crashing into jadeite-themed spinners and bumpers, maneuvering between tight aisles, gliding down the rails, smacking awake, accelerating to keep the momentum rolling, tallying points, ricocheting faster, to counteract the inevitable.

The game was aptly titled in that sense. It took forever. A game of pinball never ended, and whatever world was saved became unsaved by its self-governing nature. The numerical points indicated progress, or at least the appearance of it. Everything that was worked for, built up to, would eventually reset, he thought. Like the time I had played for twelve consecutive hours. I was well over on my way to setting a new national record. But there was a glitch. The pinball got trapped behind an animated jadeite prop. The machine locked up, and the tech had to shut it down for repairs. I didn't even get to record my score for the public to see. My score, he reflected, would've been the highest, and I would've registered my initials to be displayed: TRU - the first three letters of the man I wanted to become. And when other denizens came along afterward, they would see the initials gliding across the marquee. And they would wonder who TRU was. For everybody initialed their handle as TRU.

Eleanor scrutinized him. "What do you keep laughing about?"

The lethal barrage had ceased. He craned his neck out around a pinball table that stood in the way of the offensive, scanning the mall to face what they were running from.

Around a remote conduit pipe hung about a cluster of hatted figures. One of them was noticeably taller than the rest: a woman in a pink coat and visor.

Milton leaned in to Eleanor, questioningly. "What's the DPM doing here?"

She came over to confirm the sighting. "They're here to help."

He resented the revelation. She had sent out a distress call. "Why would you do that?"

A woeful expression crossed her face, foreboding gloom. "Because we need help."

The help she was insisting upon, he realized, had nothing to do with saving the world. It seemed he was watching his hopes and dreams dwindle away in an instant, while a web of debacle ensnared over him.

"There are no illegal aliens," she said woefully. "Or jadeites."

"Answer me why they're shooting at us." It was the only reasonable response that came to his mind at the moment.

"You probably did something to attract their attention," she said uneasily. "Can you try to remember?"

"How pathetic do I have to be to make this all up?" he asked her.

A synthesized voice boomed from the public address system. "You are surrounded. Come out with your hands where we could see them, or you will be forcibly dealt."

"Don't do it," Milton said.

"Let me try calling first." Eleanor produced her phone.

A woman's voice, deep and assertive, boomed out of Eleanor's loudspeaker. "This is Director Claudette Bauzer. Who is this?"

"It's Eleanor."

"Eleanor, is he holding you hostage?"

Eleanor clarified, "No, he's not holding me hostage. It's all just a big misunderstanding." She broke into a rapid squall. "I was going through my usual route, when I pulled over for a standard parking violation. As I was processing everything, I realized I was in the vicinity of an investigation. I didn't know for what, but anyway, there was this sweeper nearby-"

"Eleanor," interjected the voice of the director, "it's okay."

"-laser beams were coming out of nowhere, and the next thing I know-"

"It's okay," the director repeated calmly over the flurried speech.

"I thought they were shooting at me. My laser gun went off, but I swear I did not shoot any of-"

"Calm the fuck down, Eleanor," the speaker blistered. The director, exerting authority, had silenced the line at once. In a softer tone, she said, "Everything will be fine."

Eleanor could be seen nodding obediently, while Milton remained unconvinced.

"Yes, ma'am," she said.

"I've been informed of the events," the director said. "You're not in any trouble."

"Glory," she gasped gratefully. "Yes, ma'am."

The director continued, "The syndics were unclear of your involvement during the attempt to apprehend the man beside you." A pause. "He is beside you, isn't he?"

Eleanor straightened up. "Yes, ma'am."

Milton intervened. "Do you actually believe that?" He was preparing for the worst, unclasping his briefcases in preparation. Behind the popped cover, he swiftly and quietly began the drawn-out assembly process of the plutonizer.

"Can I ask you a question?" Eleanor said into the phone.

"Eleanor, I promise you'll get all your answers in good time," the director said, enunciating sharply. "I have questions too, and as your supervisor, you have my word we will hold our own investigation into the matter and get to the bottom of what took place today. We need both of you to come out with your hands in the air."

"Yes ma'am."

"Can we expect both of you to follow simple instructions and come out peacefully with your hands up?"

Milton was without expression.

"He says he's not coming," Eleanor said.

"What's the issue?" the director asked.

"He thinks that you're jadeites," Eleanor said nervously. "That the syndics beside you are jadeites."

"He has an extensive history," the director said.

Milton stolidly shook his head. To which she said into the phone, "He's shaking his head."

"The man beside you is a nutter," the director said. "Do you hear me, Eleanor?"

"Affirmative, ma'am."

"Is he armed?"

"No, I don't think he is," she said, staring in Milton's direction. "He does have with him brief-"

"Are you armed?" the director asked.

"Yes ma'am."

"Make the arrest," she ordered.

"What? You want me to-"

"If he doesn't voluntarily surrender, facilitate the application of force. Do it."

"He's right here," Eleanor said with uncertainty and anxiety in her voice. "He can… hear you. You're on speaker."

"You said he's not armed, and you are," the director said. "Just do as I say and execute the order. Afterward, everything will be explained. Do I make myself clear, Safeguard Eleanor Flutterby?"

"Yes ma'am. Loud and clear." Eleanor rang off, whereby she and Milton sprung to their feet at the same time. She reached for her laser pistol. Milton's plutonizer was already drawn.

Eleanor froze in her tracks, dread infiltrating her face. She closed her eyes and opened them slowly, incrementally, burdened by the turn of events. "How does it feel to be the hero?"

Milton, cradling his plutonizer, answered, "It's not what it's cracked up to be."

"Evidently not," Eleanor said, the color drained from her voice. "Why are you doing this?"

"I won't shoot you," he said. "But I won't let you out of my sight either."

"What are you doing?" she said, appealing to him. "What are you really trying to accomplish?"

Ten years ago, he would have given her an idealistic, patriotic response. These days, he wondered. "I don't even know, anymore."

She looked off to the side. "I hate denizens who say that. That they don't know. They're just not thinking hard enough."

"It's just that I'm sleep-deprived." To say the least, he thought.

"I hate denizens who say that, too," she said morosely. "Denizens are always tired. It's not an excuse."

"You must really hate me," he concluded.

"Don't try to put words in my mouth," she quipped. "I would never expose myself that way."

Milton slackened the grip on his plutonizer, his chest rising and falling. "I haven't thought about it."

"Well now you have."

"It's common sense."

"Common to you."

"To me," he agreed. "I don't even know what I'm doing half the time. The other half, I'm not doing anything."

"Obviously, there's a reason."

"I think there are voices," he said. "But after a while, we lose the ability to discern the difference. What's good and what's bad…"

She appealed to him, probing desolately into his eyes. "Is that the voice that tells you to do bad things?"

"It prompts me to follow directions," he said.

She posed, "If it asked you to jump off a ledge, would you?"

He stepped toward her. "Probably."

She stepped backward insecurely, keeping her distance with eyes that gauged him guardedly. "You know how buggy that sounds, right?"

"So is love." He approached her slowly, and she did not move away. Nearing her, he calmly lowered his plutonizer to the floor. "And it doesn't just tell me to jump," he said. "It's always a combination like left, right, left, left, down, up, up-" He leaned in, up close, striving blindly for her.

He felt something.

A substance, hard and metallic, hindering further progress to his bliss. Before even looking, he already knew what prodded the front of his head. He had misread the signals. He blinked once, twice, thrice. The laser pistol came to focus, poking him in his third eye. He followed the front sight of the gun, tracing it to the frame and the trigger guard and the handle, held by the lady fingers of its possessor.

Without design, he pushed against the muzzle of the gun, driven by an obscene impulse. Eleanor stumbled back, apparently startled by his foolhardy persistence. But she kept the gun glued on him, showing no signs whatsoever of ever withdrawing. He charged again. And she retreated accordingly, with the gun still projected at arm's length, as if to say it was as close as he would ever get to her. It took a while for him to realize, he was going against the grain of reason. But he tried. And tried. Until his head throbbed more than ever. "Well," he said with eventuality, "you get the idea."

Milton faltered and sidestepped, pitching a hand up toward the barrel of the gun, latching onto it. She fired at him, but the beam missed, gusting past his ear. He heard the sound of destruction behind him.

With his free hand, he chopped her wrist, making it go limp, in an effort to disarm her. Somehow, she was able to maintain her grip on the laser pistol. He attributed it to his poor technique. Struggle ensued. Milton wrestled for control of the gun, keeping the hollow end far away from himself, as laser beams launched out of it. The ceiling broke out in spastic sparks, precipitating a monsoon of golden glitter.

Milton could not relinquish the gun from her. He had both hands around her wrist, but she managed to pry one off and clasp it; their mirror-opposite hands fell into each other's, and their fingers fastened. He stretched her out against a holographic poster of Trufflehard on the wall and faced her. He pinched her wrist, cutting off circulation to the armed fist. She sunk her nails into his opposite hand, tearing into his flesh. But he hardly felt it; he was numb to it. They were tied up, and no matter what, it seemed to him she was not dropping the gun. It was a stalemate.

Eleanor looked up at him. "Why would you do that?"

"You tried to shoot me," he said.

"Before that," she said.

It was a demonstration, he wanted to say, of what he thought of her and what he wanted. "I find you deeply fascinating."

"We're worlds apart," she said, revolving away from the wall and firing another laser beam from her pistol. A claw machine went out of order.

Milton kept pace with her methodical, box step in the moonlit game room. "I'm not going out there with you."

"You have to," she said, freeing her opposite hand and breaking off in the other direction.

Their arms extended and locked out. She fired the gun, and a laser beam went through glass. Milton maintained a tight grip around her pistol-toting right wrist, keeping the crosshair of the pistol aimed away from him. He yanked her back, guiding her into an underarm turn.

Eleanor took her available left hand and raised it toward him, leading Milton to take his available right hand and do the same. They merged palms, her left to his right, for a moment and let go, spinning away from each other, standing back to back, about-facing to their previous position, merging palms again. Another flash, another beam attempted on his life.

Milton was losing his grip to sweaty palms. He transferred her armed, right wrist, diagonally to his right hand, as he patted his left hand on the side of his pants and went to grip her wrist again. She intercepted it with *her* left, intersecting their arms. He unwound their pretzeled limbs, twisting her around, exposing her back to him. He fanned her arms out, holding her in the crucifix position, and she tapped her nimble feet to the left, followed by a sequence of traversing steps to the right, and he trailed her close behind.

She crossed over with her left leg, and then raised her arms over her head, twirling back around to encounter him. He released her vacant, left hand, and raised her armed, right wrist overhead and turned with her, dodging her laser beams in the process.

He switched grips again, holding her right wrist with his left hand, and intertwining the fingers of her left hand into his right, assuming mirror-opposite domains. He took three progressive steps, raised her arms above her head and gyrated her, causing her to face away from him again, a permutation that snagged her arms in embrace. Shots fired from each other's left.

He released her left hand and tugged her right wrist. She unraveled leftward, making a revolution and three quarters, halting sideways from him with her right arm trapped behind her back. Laser beams whizzed by his vital organs. He drew her in, and she spun rightward, whereby he raised her wrist and twirled her again. They met amid the ballroom of demolished pinball tables.

In that moment, his eyes washed over with vertigo. His left foot smoldered. He looked down to notice a heel skewering his big twinkle toe, grounding it like a cigarette.

Milton lost his balance. Eleanor tore her wrist free and spun away from him. Milton dove and rolled for his plutonizer in a crouch. Simultaneously, they were zeroed into each other.

"You're coming with me," she said sharply, threatening him behind her laser pistol.

"I can't," he said, steadily rising to his feet, nursing the plutonizer. "I have expectations to live up to. An obligation to defend the world from jadeite invasion." He felt chock-full of crud, saying what he said. Sometimes, he wondered if his heart was still in it, when nobody else did believe in him. Hell, even he was starting to doubt himself.

"Milton," she said.

His own name sounded foreign to him, borderline exotic when she said it.

"That's your name, isn't it?" She rubbed her right wrist, letting blood back in. "We all justify our lives and tend to dignify what we're doing. We all want to believe that we're serving a higher function. It's not your fault. We're cultured from an early age to strive for greatness, and that anything short of that is unacceptable. So we end up believing anything to convince ourselves that we're important." She fell silent. "I'm not saying you don't matter. I'm sure you're of great importance." She paused with uncertainty. "Perhaps to your mother."

"I don't have a Mother."

"Your father, then."

"No Father."

"Whoever. You must mean something to someone."

Or some thing, he thought. My work, if anything. But I'm disposable to the Bureaux. Amber Blacklight came to mind. "I have a Friend."

"Your Friend," she obliged, "there you go."

"When I have the money," he said. "To meet her."

"The fact of the matter is, you're special," she said. "But you're not a special agent. You've done nothing to prove it or show it. Do you have any evidence for what you believe in? Any physical proof?"

"Don't you read the news?" he asked.

"Times have changed," Eleanor said. "Nobody buys into that eiderdown unless they're bugged out." She reassigned the gun to her left hand, and flexed her right hand, closing and opening it. "I'm not calling you a bugger."

"You just did," Milton said.

"I used to think jadeites were real too," she said. "That didn't make me a bugger."

Milton limped to a briefcase and drew out the genograph. He slid it toward her.

Eleanor crouched down discreetly, without averting her eyes from him, keeping the pistol aimed high. With her other hand, she picked up the golden gadget by the handle. "Is this the protocol you were talking about? A modified Geiger counter." She assessed the genograph, unaffected. If anything, she looked relieved. "Some sort of oscillator.

Garden variety props that you see from a self-professed jadeite tracker."
She bounced back to her feet. "Did you make these yourself?"

"It was provided by the Bureaux."

"The one with the acronym that doesn't stand for anything." Her
tone was doubtful.

She was challenging the fundamental principle of a cryptic
enterprise. He expounded, "It's the same bureaucratic agency that
commissioned Trufflehard."

"You know Trufflehard isn't real."

He figured she would say that, ever the skeptic. "His character is
based off a real denizen."

"Then where is he right now?" she asked. "Why hasn't anybody ever
seen him?"

"Because Trufflehard works undercover," he explained. "There
would be no cover if you could see him."

"Have you ever seen him?"

"No," he said truthfully, "not that I would know it if I did." He
hesitated. "There's a shelf life with what I do," he said with minor
reluctance. "Every enumerator drops off the face of the planet at one
point or another. It's just the nature of how it works."

"You've really thought this out, but look out there." She tilted her
head toward the atrium. He counted a dozen hats waiting in the wings.
"There's no talking a way out of this," she said. "What do you see?"

"Jadeites," Milton said attentively.

"You see a panorama of 8-foot-tall aliens and a mammoth retail
outlet. Whereas I see denizens in polka-dotted uniforms, performing
their civic duty. And you wanna know what kind of voices I hear?"

"What kind?" he asked.

"The ghostly sing-alongs of humming birds inebriated on nectar,"
she said.

She dropped the genograph to the floor and dismissed it to the wayside with a sweeping motion of her foot. "Does that at all sound like relatable viewpoints to you?"

Even he had to admit, she had a point. "Miss Flutterby, you have me confused."

"Milton," she said, echoing his name for the second time.

And under such bleak circumstances, he thought, her voice spelled it with warmth, the kind he wanted in his life, a warmth that portended optimism for the future.

Eleanor said, "You seem like a really semi-decent guy. I mean, considering…" She advanced backward, stepping further away from the plutonizer targeting her. "But you don't even trust yourself. It's not too late to get help. It's not too late for either of us to get help. I'll make you a deal. I'll hold your hand. We'll walk out together, disarmed. Just be true to yourself."

"Those things out there are not what you think they are," Milton said. His words came out scratchy and hoarse. "They're jadeites."

"Yeah, I heard you the last couple times." She kept backing up. "I don't know what you had to endure in the past, but let everything go. You've been brainwashed. There are no jadeites. At least not in the physical sense. Jadeites are fantastic metaphors, Milton. Dramatic portrayals from journalists and illustrators. Did you flunk out of school?"

"Yes," he said. His concession was not as bad as it sounded. He had excelled in particular, Intro to Masonry, Fractions, and Sexual Education. But save for that one class, he thought, it was more or less the truth.

She said cheerlessly, "If I didn't know any better, I'd say this was eventful in a kind of lively manner. Almost to the point of fun."

In a moment's fragment, a polyglot of conveyances filled his head.

Not enough time to analyze what it all meant. Just the way she looked at him. Perhaps wishing him the best. And perhaps glad, it seemed. To have made up her mind.

Wait, he started to say. Don't go any further, he was trying to say.

But he lurched forward, and the words failed to declare from his mouth. He stared up, his gaze following her. He staggered, in her direction, before his body seized, from the phantom on his back. The plutonizer hung flaccidly to one side as he reached for the nearest support. She caught the lapse. Her expression wavered. She could have ended him then and there, but she retracted her aim, opting to merge with the brightness of the atrium. Her face warmed with a spirited glow. He slid impotently to the floor, while she twirled off.

Milton crawled behind the base of an air hockey table and sat leaning against it. He cranked his head, watching her loping across the floor to the solidarity of uniforms. With her backside turned to him, she appeared to be answering to an immense, coated figure, which had emerged from the assembly. Probably the director of the DPM, Milton thought, noting the pink visor, discrete from the rest. Other than that, he could not make out the collared face; it was cloaked in obscurity.

He swapped on his amplifier lens for better visibility. Instantly, everything above the shoulders ballooned up. The director turned the brim of her visor toward Milton's general vicinity. He was prompted to pivot away. When he leaned in again to see what was happening, the director's long arms were snaked around Eleanor in embrace. A dozen syndics stood there, waiting, watching the ceremony unfolding. Something glimmered from the director's hand. It slithered up Eleanor's spine and positioned at the base of her skull. The visor swiveled again in Milton's direction. He opened his mouth to warn, but what sound that traveled out of his mouth was preceded by the speed of light.

A rainbow shone from the top of her head. Milton felt the air crushed out of his lungs, as her body bashed the floor. Miss Flutterby, he thought. He clamped his eyes and looked away, refusing to believe the reality he had witnessed. His head tilted up and knocked on the arcade's anterior pixel scanner. He gradually opened his eyes by degrees and impatiently twisted around to take another look.

Graduation hats were being chucked high above, evoking a strange atmosphere of celebration. The slim figures had clearly outgrown the length of their gowns. The jadeites marched forward, stepping on the mangled body on the floor, led by the director.

Milton receded into the darkness.

He shuffled toward the backend, bypassing rows of pinball tables, wriggling between their legs, eventually settling at a spot providing a strategic overview of the entrance.

Footsteps scraped against the floor. A swollen green face appeared in the plutonizer's crosshairs and shortly erupted with lava: lucky customer number one.

The second stormed in after the first. It shared the same fate. In walked a set of jade twins, side by side. They surveyed the floor, scanning for heat signatures with their exaggerated heads swaying. He aimed too low, capping one, causing a shriek. The effect on the jadeite was apparent. The zap gun flew out and its stance buckled, reflexively reaching down to brace its damaged knee. The jadeite adjacent to it, went flapping for cover, but did not get far, before it joined the body count.

The wounded jadeite was immobilized, stooped over, applying pressure with both hands to the damaged knee, which was spraying the floor with a swamp of mucus. More jadeites trickled in, scattering throughout. One of them slipped on the plasmic surface, the zap gun flailing out of its grip and spinning across the checkered floor.

At that point, he came out of concealment without reservations. He walked briskly between the aisles. From his leftmost periphery, an alien bobblehead manifested behind a pinball table. The plutonizer went off: headshot.

He kept going, swinging the plutonizer, detecting the earliest movement of via jadeite. It was in the act of springing from its cover, before it went down in flames. Something rolled out before him, unraveled to point its zap gun: it never had a chance.

Electrical striations pulsed violently from the magma chamber of the plutonizer, casting his face with a radiant blood orange. He continued down the aisles of pinball tables and arcade machines, blasting jadeites out of their hiding places. Some of them opted to make loud splashes, telegraphing their presence by exclaiming their arrival. They went flopping just as soon with their innards on display. Others employed a stealthier approach, keeping still, dormant from the other side of the table, ready to pull up at close range. Little did they know he could see the rough outline of their heads hiding in plain sight through his optical augmentation. He came up behind their blind side. The last thing they would see would be the approaching phantom.

More jadeites came through the portal, as if they had some kind of agenda. They probably did. One of them was a death wish. And he was not patient for them to bleed out and tip over, as he walked past their lobotomized physiques, somehow with their motor functions intact; they would run into each other and the walls, confused and beheaded, shooting their zap guns aimlessly in the air.

He came across the capped jadeite on the floor, floundering in its own blood. One hand held its gushing knee, the other was outstretched, grasping for the nearest zap gun from fallen company. As it fastened its narrow, bony fingers through the loop of the weapon, he crunched his foot down on the wrist, tilted his plutonizer, and ended its suffering.

Laser beams greeted him when he surfaced from the mouth of the Family Arcade. Opposing him were five jadeites armed with zap guns. They circulated around an imposing twelve-eyed monster with a great pink visor atop its dome, sweeping about in countless tentacles.

He, wasting little time, pulled the trigger. A geothermal stream knocked one of the jadeites out of orbit and overboard the glass guard rail. But it did not plummet; it swayed over the edge on one arm, clinging to a neighboring jadeite that had reached out and extended itself. More jadeites joined the collective effort, necessitating another volcanic release from the plutonizer that volleyed all of them down the central exposure of the 48th floor.

The surviving jadeites jockeyed for position and took aim. They spurted their zap guns, taking swings at him with protracted beams. He eluded the variegated raids of focused energy and hosed them down with a single torrent of tangerine current, setting off a pyrotechnical showcase that filled the air with blossoming cortical matter.

Bits of green rained on the tentacled jadeite's parade, provoking it to berserk with steam and shrill the atmosphere with an aimless raid of beams from its six zap guns. Beneath the pink visor, featured eight hyperspectral eyes mounted on stalks that protruded out of its head. The amorphous body was a lustrous green, mottled with darker flecks. A number of its countless limbs coiled around a zap gun each, while the rest dictated its gliding locomotion.

The Mother of all jadeites composed a sextet of zap guns, simultaneously maximizing the power source and wielding fixed rays of concentrated photons. The intense and overreaching wavelengths sliced through the mall, converging on the human target.

He launched into a fantasia of impossible geometric transfigurations, over the erratic onslaught of flashes. He returned flux of his own at every turn, tracking the mutant aberration over a series of bursts, plucking off its optical stalks. Meanwhile, the lasik beams projecting out of the zap guns started blinking out, batteries drained. He kept the trigger depressed to crank open the reactor gate of his plutonizer, unleashing everything he had, the demons and the damnation that they plagued. The battle-scarred jadeite thrashed its tentacles with malevolent finality and slouched in a cough of smoke.

chapter 13

"Deliver me a white bark raspberry pie, Dolores," Eldridge Kane said to the new private secretary he handselected from the cellar levels. "The real stuff. None of that ersatz shit."

"My name is Barbara," she said.

He rang off and signaled for his apprentice to continue reading him the weekly sales figures.

"Subscriptions to the Ekonomicana are up three percent and Ekonomicopia, two-point-seven percent, November-wise," Johnson said. "Single-issue purchases, including but not limited to browsing time, partial, and whole-issue purchases, are up by twelve percent."

The double-digit increase was in light of limiting the access of the digital copies to just the front page and the table of contents, in addition to all of the ads. This, in contrast to the past, where scanning the 3D barcode of the cover at newsstands brought about the entire issue on the corresponding holocube for as long as customer idled within the vicinity, was devised to discourage penniless moochers. Eldridge had determined that the cover page and the table of contents were enough to hook passersby. If they wanted to read on about the jadeite invasion, he thought, they would have to purchase it like normal paying customers. "Twelve percent in one week. Marginally passable," he deemed.

Johnson continued with the statistics. "Eko Mart and Eko Mall report for a combined 18% increase in just the last quarter."

The phone on Eldridge's desk tinted the room a stimulating blue with its incandescent pulsing. The LCEO reclined in his executive chair, drinking his third customary mid-afternoon cocktail. He declined the call.

His apprentice continued, "The best sellers include emergency water filtration kits, solar-powered refrigerators, ersatz food, laser guns, containers, surveillance cameras, alarms, automated security, locks, shutters-"

Blue lights emitted from his desk again.

Eldridge accepted remotely, setting down the glass of multi-layered, quintuple sherbet colada. "Surely, you've been instructed to never interfere with my sales review. I accept no calls."

"Yes, Lord," said his new secretary. "I just thought you should know there's been a report of a safeguard in repose at one of the Ekonomy Malls."

There's nothing I could do to bring her back to life, he thought. So why consult my expertise? I don't have to be assaulted by grisly mental photos to enjoy my motherfuckin colada. "This could have waited," he said, tense with contempt.

"The mall has been shut down for investigation and repairs."

A mixture of confusion and dread grated his temperament. "On whose watch?"

"I'll obtain an official with more information. But until then, coverage of the reports are being wired to the central directory as more details emerge. "

Eldridge broke the circuit. "Log on to the central directory," he ordered his assistant. As a large holocube blinked open from a light source, the LCEO was assailed by an unsightly intuition. Of denizens losing jobs, even losing lives, and not much else beyond that.

chapter 14

Bruleed aromatics from the plutonizer engulfed Milton's senses. Zapped to the marrows, he fell back and blearily scanned the atrium. Activity had ceased, and peace was restored, damage to the mall notwithstanding. The inert bodies, all but one, evanesced without a trace.

He rose from his slouch and trotted over to the safeguard crumpled on the floor, expecting the worst. He slowed down, plodding as he came near, reluctant to examine the degree of casualty. He faced her, blinking. He wondered if he could still kiss her, but it seemed impossible. He shut off his amp lens, zooming out the fuzzy and unrecognizable. She looked empty and misshapen and adrift, lifeless as a one eyed marionette, orphaned to a scarlet puddle.

What happened? he said to himself. Who cut her strings? There used to be life in those steps. All that vivacity and zing. Her movement and build were more efficient than mine. She was healthier and prettier. She was better, he realized. I should've been the one who died.

It was hard for him to believe how quickly one's whole state of being could change. You could own the convertible and the dream house, he said to himself. You could be the doll whose dreams were dashed in a blinding light. Milton wanted to believe she was in a better place. Anywhere else but here, he thought. Where we're in no more control than ants whose limbs get picked apart for no reason at all by giant powers too nefarious for us to comprehend.

The time on the phone indicated dawn. And fourteen missed calls to boot. Eko Mall would be open soon. He had to get moving before the morning shift. As he stirred into motion, a weary voice broke through: "Don't leave."

Miss Flutterby, he thought.

Milton turned and stooped his head. "You're alive?" It was a stupid question. He referred to the translucent rod he held in his hand. "Let me call the medics for you."

"No," she said weakly. "Please." She seemed adamant. "Don't go."

Milton came close, and closer, kneeling to face her.

"I know you have to go somewhere," she said in a crestfallen whisper, "but please. Just stay."

He submitted. "I'm sorry," he muttered. He did not know what else to say.

"What for?" she asked. "You were right. I saw them, Milton." Despite the trauma, she still remembered his name. "Eight feet tall and all. You tried to tell me. They were just like the movies. But they were real, and they were terrifically green. You saw them too, don't lie."

"Yes," he said admittedly.

"Well," she said, wheezing, "what'd you think?"

It was nothing new for him. And somewhere along the way, it stopped being fun and started being work. Pests, they were, and he was the exterminator. "Not much," he said dispassionately.

"I'm not looking too great, am I?" Her formerly, forested blonde hair was mostly scalped. What irregular clumps remained were torched and ashen and sodden.

"You're an eyeful," he said, ravaged by fever and fatigue.

She scoffed gently. "Is there something you want to tell me?"

"I don't know." He felt an abysmal liability for the shape she was in. "I just wish… I could've handled everything differently."

"I should've believed you," she squeaked softly. "But there was nothing that could've been done. I have no regrets. Because I met you."

"Wait until you get to know me."

"No," she murmured. "This is the perfect… ending…"

He felt her slip away and he heard her name spoken. It was his own voice. He scarfed gravel down his throat, and he looked up in a surreal haze. His eyes scanned the horizontal ascension of atrium layers from the 48th floor, drinking it all in. What a scenery it was. Just him and her, stranded in the great desert island of food and water and high fashion and everything else but a bookstore. This was the omphalos, promising the world on the half shell. Was this what gods were made of? he wondered. Where heroes were forged? Surrounded by walls bursting with the ultimate trinkets. Everything that could ever be had and needed. Everything that could ever be wished for. It was all here, he thought, in tangible form. And yet when he went to clutch her hand, to feel her, he was mildly disappointed. There was nothing there. And he felt nothing. Almost nothing.

chapter 15

"Is he still talking to himself?" Eldridge asked, viewing the large-sized holocube projecting what he deemed was the assailant and the victim. He had been informed about an incident at the 703rd Ekonomy Mall in St. Frank. Presently, the details were unavailable.

Reggie Johnson helmed the neural controls, streaming surveillance footage from a secure terminal. "The supine woman appears unresponsive."

"By Gawd," Eldridge uttered under his breath with twisted curiosity, "what has he done to her?"

Shades of blue strobe lights pulsed from the phone. "Speak," he said.

"I've expedited your request for the follow-up," the new secretary said. "I'm patching you through to one of the members of the investigation team."

A male voice came through. "Permission to speak, Lord."

"Granted," Eldridge said.

"Good afternoon, this is Inspector Robert Rhodes speaking. I was instructed to provide you with the damage assessment. As you might already know, an automaton from the 703rd Ekonomy Mall found the body of a DPM safeguard an hour ago. She's been identified as Eleanor Flutterby, age 36. Preliminary reports indicate a homicide."

"Yes," he said, "I'm watching it on the cube. Is that all? Call cleanup and get her out of there, you get me? Don't scare the kids away."

"Her body's been taken care of, but there's also damage to parts of the floor, resultant from some kind of donnybrook." He stopped, unable to elaborate. "I haven't been briefed on it, since I had to flee the scene to tend to private affairs."

"Then why do you wax philosophical?" Eldridge disconnected and called his secretary. "Dolores darling, send in personage in charge of this carnage. The previous referral was a bust."

"I can try to get a hold of the Lead Inspector," she said, "but the investigation is still in the middle of-"

"Deliver him to my office, if it means teleporting him. This is a direct order." He walked away from the desk with a higher blood pressure from the aimless interchange.

"Johnson!" Eldridge said. "Did any harm befall on the business?"

As they awaited the arrival of the Lead Inspector, Reggie Johnson was scanning the latest notes. "From what I'm gathering, there are fissures and craters on the marble floors. Some storefronts are missing their displays, and the Family Arcade will require significant repairs."

Is there anybody who can make informed decisions around here? Eldridge wondered to himself. "Tape up those sections, and let the consumers pass to the unaffected areas."

"Apparently," Johnson said, reading from his phone, "the entire floor has been declared a safety hazard."

"Precipitate Defcon 1," Eldridge said. "We can't afford to lose business. Especially not during the holiday season."

A skinny male in a gray suit, approached the LCEO. He had on formal headwear with antennae on his head and white-framed glasses. "Forgive me for entering unannounced, Lord. My name is Anil Magney."

Rather young for his rank, Eldridge gathered. "Mr. Magney, so you're the man with all the answers."

"Only to the questions I know," he said.

"You have much explaining to do," Eldridge said.

"That's Milton Grainjar," Magney said, indicating male in the holocube. A scene with him kneeled over the casualty was being played back on a loop. "It's the only footage of him recovered."

"He was the suspect in connection with the series of missing consumers and property destruction," Reggie Johnson said, seeming to recognize the name instantly. "The notes indicate our in-house team has been delving into the matter for the better part of a year, by various surveillance methods, phone taps, and advanced record searches."

Eldridge remembered, vague as always, the sporadic mentions of the name over an undetermined period. "So at last, we caught him in the act."

"It's inconclusive at best," Magney said. "Anything before this footage was surgically removed."

"Likely his bidding," Eldridge said. "To abolish the evidence, we can safely presume."

"It crossed our minds, but there's no reason to keep this portion of the tape intact. He would've erased everything."

"Precisely that," Eldridge said. "To cause doubt in judgment, throw off suspicion."

"It just seems like a lot of work to thwart off suspicion when he could evade traces of record altogether."

Milton Grainjar was overheard from the holocube, saying, "Wait until you get to know me."

"Look at him," Eldridge said. "He talks to corpses. Nothing is beyond him."

They watched Milton, hunched over the DPM safeguard, whispering, "Miss Flutterby…"

"Spawn of a fungus," Eldridge uttered under his breath.

Magney added, "He would also need to have obtained an authorized clearance code to access secure files."

"Someone with access," Eldridge said.

"Correct, I'm unaware of the full details, but the team was arriving at an inkling it was somebody else working from inside this building, when I was prematurely whisked away to come here at the cusp of a breakthrough in the investigation."

Eldridge tore away from the holocube and panned over to Anil Magney. "Why would any toiler inside this build-"

Blue flashes issued from the phone. Without turning to look, his eyes moving to one corner, Eldridge said, "Speak."

"Lord," the secretary said, "I just wanted to inform you that Inspector Amelia Pillowspoon has checked into the building. She should be coming up the chute and arriving any minute into your office."

"Who's Inspector Amelia Pillowspoon?" Eldridge asked.

"The one you requested," she said. "The one in charge."

He turned to Magney. "I thought you were leading this."

"Oh God no," Magney said. "I'm just an intern. I was told Inspector Pillowspoon wouldn't be able to make it, so I was sent as a proxy to explain the excavations thus far."

"Disperse," Eldridge said.

"I'm sorry?" Magney asked, with a confused stare.

"The Lead Inspector is here."

"Understood," Magney said. "I'll reserve from delving further-"

"Reserve your face and just-" He broke off, the complexion of his demeanor suffused with the pink color of exasperation. He appealed to Reggie Johnson. "Tell him."

"Please go," Johnson said.

"No problem," the intern said, backing up with his palms up, disappearing without resistance.

Eldridge looked to Johnson. "Do you see the disappointment I suffer every day?" He marched back to his chair to cool down.

"Lord," Johnson said, swiveling the ekosuit to face him, "my faculties cannot compute how you do it."

Eldridge was prostrated over the desk. He was made weary by the wasted energy, the futile hoopla, general incompetence that governed the staff. Like we're paying denizens just for the perception of having a job, he thought. Nevermind the estimated cost of damages to the mall and closure of a whole level. Lost profits were guaranteed to tally in the hundreds of megas. The sooner he knew what was going on, the sooner he could expect when everything would be back to peak business levels, up and running again.

"Let this be a lesson, if you ever supposed reversing roles with mine. It's not as glamorous as it looks. Mayhaps now you're besieged by secondary and tertiary thoughts."

"Not in the least," Johnson said. "There's nothing in the world I strive after more than your supremacy. My job here is done if I could emulate even a fraction of-"

"Find another role model," Eldridge said, gnarling half his face. "The hardest part of your job is fetching me gurgle."

"Does the Lord CEO scorn my attempts to be worthy of command? My imperative instructs me to learn as much as I can before you're retired," Johnson said.

Eldridge looked up from his desk. "Retire? Who speaks anything of retirement?"

"I was in the faithful act of reciting my shiver at the thought of sudden depart-"

"Save me the life insurance pitch," Eldridge interjected, "because I'm not buying it. There is no plan B. I am the LCEO. Remember this and remember well. If it is my disposition, I can get new bones and organs for the rest of my life, as well as other regenerative treatments. I am theoretically immortal. I can even get a new apprentice. Better yet, I'll task you the honor to choose your successor."

"Lord," Johnson said, "my faith in you is supreme. I defer to you for all important decision-making. And with all due respect, there is much doubt anybody is worthy of this honor."

Eldridge let him know, "There are more than enough candidates waiting in line to fill your diminutive shoes."

Strolling in their direction was a petite woman with a trim and delectable face. Her straight brown hair was tied neatly in a pony tail, and she had on a navy blue jacket, white jeans, and sneakers. Business casual.

Meanwhile, Johnson was going on, "Please overlook my sincere lack of perspective. I am humbled to bask in your astral presence and serve you-"

Eldridge cut him off with a sideways glance. "Why do you still blather?" He shifted to the lady. "To what do I merit this pleasure?"

"Inspector Amelia Pillowspoon," she said. "You called for me."

Eldridge had not been expecting a woman. Instead, he had expected the Lead Inspector to be a sallow-faced crone, smelling of cheap cologne. He estimated Pillowspoon was older than she probably looked. Indeed, he thought, she doesn't look much older than the intern who recently soiled us with his presence. She had a natural youth about her demeanor, an alluring innocence without even trying.

"You're the one in charge," Eldridge said. "Make it good."

"In the past couple years," she said, "we've been receiving reports from housing reps of a man named Milton Grainjar claiming to work for the Census Bureaux, an agency set up to survey denizens to fine-tune market projections. During the time Milton Grainjar has come under our surveillance, his visits to residences have coincided with missing denizen reports and destruction of property."

"What kind of training program have they instituted down there?" Eldridge asked. "I order you to contact the agency about this."

"We already have," she said. "The Census Bureaux did not recognize anybody in their department under the name of Milton Grainjar."

"But then again," Johnson said, "we can never know for certain, for that is what is expected of them to say."

Eldridge determined gruffly, "They refuse to claim responsibility for the damage, fine. Snuff him."

"We've tried, apparently, and suffice to say, the plan backfired, as you will see in a moment." She paused the holocube, accessed a video log file. "We authorized the JERQS to go ahead and make the arrest, and well, at the risk of sounding spooky, they were never to be seen again."

"What happened to them?" Eldridge asked.

She turned to Eldridge. "All related footages falling within the perimeter of the collateral damage to the mall, were expertly deleted from the system. Whoever did it however, was unaware of the following surveillance footage, which operates independently of the central directory." The holocube tuned into a dark room, monitoring an array of blinking images. It was installed with the intent to keep an eye on security personnel." The unresponsive security official with the head drooping on his chest, was duly noted. Behind him, was what appeared to be a mosaic of a thousand holographic tiles, scanning the floor. "But it also contains in the background, holocubes of all surveillance in the mall. We can zoom into each zone at the specific time. Our techs were able to manually hone in on several active locations on the floor. Milton Grainjar was captured on 184 streams. Some of them feature him and the defunct party Eleanor Flutterby exhibiting behavior commensurate of acquaintanceship. However, the majority of the crucial footages were fritzed out, possibly due to the exchange of crossfire that ensued."

"She was lulled by Grainjar into letting her guard down," Eldridge conjectured, making his fingers into a gun, "and just when she would least expect it, pew."

"Grainjar was not the trigger man." Pillowspoon hesitated. "At least not when it comes to Flutterby. We tracked the climactic portion missing from the earlier footage, revealing she suffered a laser fire to the skull at close range by the director of the DPM."

Eldridge scrutinized the inspector. "You're positive."

"Yes," she said, "if we're going off appearances. The director's face cannot be seen underneath her outerwear. But upon asking around, the look is usual for her."

"Are you saying it could've been an impostor?"

"It's the circumstances under which the victim Flutterby was shot and killed. From what we observed, she was in the act of relinquishing herself and lacked any body language warranting such an extreme response."

"Was she armed?" Eldridge asked.

"Yes," she answered, "but her laser pistol was still holstered, and her body language indicated no abrupt movements or hints of threat. At least not from the angle available to us."

Eldridge intoned gravely. "You seem to be implying a certain kind of coverup."

"The videos displayed an utter disregard for standard protocol, and the JERQS and DPM have yet to issue any official word on the incident. We're on standby."

Eldridge scoffed boorishly. "Standard protocol has failed to yield any amount of success, considering Grainjar has eluded indictment and arraignment for the umpteenth time."

"Grainjar is not who we're after," Pillowspoon said.

Eldridge's expression rumpled with incredulity. "He speaks to corpses."

"You'd want to see this footage yourself for context easier exhibited than explained." Pillowspoon tended to the big holocube, navigating the options. She leafed through a sequence of images, pausing at a stream of Milton Grainjar holding two large briefcases, standing outside of a candy store. More frames skipped by before the inspector chose to magnify a video footage scanning a recreational setting with checkered floors. The visual quality was murky and dark, save for the rows of fluorescent pinball machines and neon trailers blaring from arcade games. "Keep in mind the corruption of resolution, as the images you're about to see is a recording of a recording of a dimly lit environment."

Orange slashes of light darted throughout the scene, as bodies crumpled to the floor. The proprietor of the laser beams warped in and out of focus. His movement was erratic, hard to trace.

"Why is he nictitating from place to place?" Johnson questioned. "What's the frame rate on this?"

"All surveillance cameras are regulation issue - three trillion FPS," Pillowspoon said.

A willowy physique in a waist-length gown, resembling an undersized JERQS uniform, manifested from behind a pinball table, whereby the scene froze. The inspector acquired a close-up of the figure. Even under low visibility caused by the twilight fixtures, the face was salient and striking, distorted to take on mutant characteristics.

"What's the first thing that comes to your mind?" she asked.

"The lighting and angle certainly lends an elongated appearance," Johnson said.

"My what large head he has," she said, leading in a trajectory of foreboding. "My what green skin he has. My what vacuous, black eyes he has. My what weird-"

"We get it," Eldridge piped in. "He's no heartthrob, and his clothes are too small on him."

"As well," Johnson said, "I struggle to see the productivity of this judgmental examination."

"These traits are not occluded to the face of just one individual." Amelia Pillowspoon panned the footage and zoomed in on various other baldheaded, zap-gun-toting gowns to denote their startling semblance. "The same misshapen manner of facade is observable on every syndic in these videos, almost as if they're clones."

"Let there be an end to this physiognomic debauchery," Eldridge said with profound distaste.

"It could simply be the aggregate of a projection anomaly," Pillowspoon said, "although the consistency of the characteristics, when juxtaposed to the background for frame of reference, seems to suggest otherwise. Unlike the compromised holographic entries from the central directory, tampering in the case of this autonomous entry was not evidenced by our tech advisors."

"Your point being."

"We suspect our worst fears have been confirmed," the inspector said. "The Jade Association has contaminated the Judicial Enforcement and Regulations Quadrant of Syndics, and possibly other sectors of law enforcement as well."

"What is the meaning of this japery?" Eldridge asked.

"The jadeites have been exposed."

"How is that even remotely plausible?"

"Our team tested a number of explanations, all of which have been thrown out as unlikely. There was one exception, but it's too soon to tell. The parities and ramifications of the theory are still being worked out."

"Just what are you trying to say?"

"Milton Grainjar is Barret Trufflehard."

chapter 16

Milton reverted back to the girl of his dreams. Funny how long ago it seemed I knew her, he thought. But it isn't that funny. It's actually pretty pathetic, when I really think about it. A certain girl I knew or thought I knew, when I thought I knew it all. What do I know about her, anyway? he asked himself.

Following another dreary day of work, he had asked her how she handled all the disrespect, the lack of cooperation, the attitude, the bureaucratic side of it.

She told him she had no idea what he was talking about.

But she told him, sometimes, when she was feeling tired, she would fall on her bed and lie around. Just lie there, without thinking or doing anything. For some reason, that image stuck with him. Her in all her professional gear, fully suited, lazing around in bed. And the image of blackened toast, because that was how she liked her slice of bread, besides cruelty-free. Burnt to a crisp. He had asked for elaboration, and she told him she liked it charred, utterly cauterized. In turn, he had told her her preferences could predispose her to cancer. Something to the lame effect.

I wonder where she is, what she's doing right now? he asked himself. Probably married with a family, with a spacious, multi-room unit at one of the upper floors of a downtown residential complex. Good for her, he thought, picturing a successful husband, three daughters, and an arthropodic fido. Ain't that the Ekonomic dream. Eldridge Kane seemed to preach it. And I can't seem to follow it. Here I am on the far side of the moon, sleepy but still awake, wondering and wandering about, the way of the world. Stumbling through, was more like it.

Goowi Dara, he thought. How I never spoke a real word to her. She never even knew me, and perhaps she preferred it that way. And I've been thinking about her all this time.

Milton opened the door to the concrete shack. The enclosed conveyer chute took him sublevel, whereby a helical escalator unfolded before him. Steadying himself on the banister, he let it take him down, until he reached the entry point, a circular aperture. It swished open and presented five access conduit pipes. He lurched over the third one and dove in, appearing into the anteroom with a second aperture. He stepped through, entering a dim, synthetic cavern. The dark blue setting was immersed by a high-tech conglomeration of monitoring gadgetry corresponding to satellite surveillance of jadeite activity. Electronic maps and radars connected suspects all over the world. Above him, was the domed ceiling composed of blurred circuitry. And not too far away, with a knee bent, sole affixed to the side of the CPU rack, leaned Kyra McVeronica, welcoming him with arms folded in her trademark leather jacket, no buttons.

"What are you doing here?" she asked.

"You wanted to see me," he said, taking leaden steps toward her.

"Should I go first," she asked, "or do you wanna?"

Before he could answer, she bound from the rack and swooped up to him.

"You couldn't just let me slide once, Kyra?"

"Are you talking about the part where you led a random stranger to a top secret bunker?" she said, circling him.

And so you had to make me out to look like a zany, he was about to blurt. But it never escaped his lips, with prudence. Why go there with her? "Forget it." Too late to do anything about it, he thought.

"My turn," she said into his left ear, strolling around him. "Let me start off by saying you just never cease to amaze me, Trufflehard. You did all the things I told you to, not do." Her voice emerged in his right ear. "And yet, you still managed to come out of it unscathed."

Milton was not sure if she meant that as a compliment. "Is that good?" he asked, looking straight ahead.

"No, it's not good. You did great."

He treaded with caution. "Really?"

She walked counter-clockwise into his field of vision, appraising him. "Great enough to get everybody else killed."

He had walked right into her trap. It always happened. Yet he was mildly disappointed. "So what's changed?"

She faded from his periphery. "Not much, evidently. Maybe you're just having a long day." She stroked his upper arms from behind. "A long, excruciating day."

He hardly slept a wink in the last forty-eight, if that was what she meant, and the forty-eight preceding that. "Maybe," he agreed.

"Still," she pressed, "it's no excuse. There's no margin for tomfoolery."

She let go of him and rotated around, showing herself again, as though she was studying him on a slide. He glanced at the floor despondently.

She took off and tended to a black cooler, drawing chilled flutes, a bottle of ebullition, and a squirt bottle of dragon fruit Indoctrin-Aid. She poured equal parts of each into the pair of glasses, and when she set the ebullition down, Milton read the lettering, unmistakably. Dom Esperanza. 25,000 pixels a pop. She returned and passed a glass to him. "What gives?" he asked, receiving gratefully. "Am I finally getting certification?"

She raised the glass to him. He clinked it with his own without much thought and led the vessel to his lips. She placed a hand on his wrist, stopping him from irrigating his mouth at the last second. "Don't look away when we engage glasses."

She tipped the glass up. Again he clinked it, making sure to delve into her eyes this time. And she drew closer, weaving her glass around his arm to link elbows. He swallowed the green effervescence, chained to her this way.

After which Kyra asked, swirling the glass in front of her before setting it down, "How long have we known each other?"

Milton approximated ten years in his head, though it felt more like twenty.

"Thirteen years," she said. "We're practically married, if you consider the turnover rate in our field."

"Even though we've kept our relationship strictly professional," he appended.

"Up to this point." She came forward, pushing herself onto Milton, backing him up against the rack.

Milton zagged away from her.

"You murder for a living," Kyra lashed out. "Since when did you become a born-again virgin?"

Milton's energy levels waned with impotence. The adrenaline from his recent altercation was wearing off. He felt physically depleted from the rush of retreating from his last mission to the detour to Eko Mall and back. He searched his mind, and it felt barren. "There's something I've been meaning to ask you."

She smoothed herself and looked to him. "Anything."

"Miss Dara, an ex-enumerator."

"Dara what?" she asked, puzzled. "Goo?"

"Yes."

"She had potential," Kyra said passively. "Shame she's no more."

"Do you know what she does these days?" he asked.

She took a swig. "Other than being dead?"

"What do you mean?"

"Death is the one thing you can't multi-task. Barret, it's been over ten years. Do yourself a favor and move on."

This was news to him. "I didn't even know that she died," he said. "You told me she retired."

"They all do, Barret. Anyway, why are you bringing her up out of nowhere? Don't tell me you and Goo…" She paused.

"Was this before or after she left this gig?" Milton asked.

"You don't wanna know."

Milton walked several steps and turned in her direction. "Goddamnit Kyra, why didn't you tell me?"

She came up to him. "Didn't I? What'd you think I meant?"

"You said she left on her own terms."

Kyra shoved his chest. "She did leave on her own terms."

"A laser beam passing through you is not exactly dying of natural causes."

"Blunt force trauma," she said passively.

"How?"

"She got thwacked in the head."

"That's self-explanatory," he said. "But how? With what?" as if it mattered, and immediately admonished the futility of such an inquiry. Who cared with what? Perhaps the pith of his inquiry had not much to do with the voyeuristic interest of *How?* and *What?* but more precisely, *Why?* Why of all denizens, he wondered, did it have to be her? She had too much going for her.

"With too-much-information. What more do you need to know?" She placed a hand on his shoulder, as if to reassure him. "She died. Give it a rest."

It occurred to him that his superfluous curiosity could be taken the wrong way. "I'm the guy that's going out everyday and directly dealing with these jadeites. Not you. Not anybody above you. I have a right to know anything and everything that helps me discern the enemy and the environment."

"You're in over your head. But," she said, considering the circumstances, "you do have a right to know whatever'll help you carry out your task as cost-effectively as possible, and there is nothing you don't already know that'll be of any support. If anything from my experience, knowing too much is a performance hindrance."

More than somebody trying to blow your head off? Milton asked himself, as he walked over to the cooler, above which Kyra's glass sat idly. She had hardly touched it. The door immaterialized, and he retrieved the respective bottles of champagne and Indoctrin-Aid.

"Refills are coming out of your own pocket," she warned him.

Throw it on the tab, he thought. What's another 25,000 pixels? He poured the contents as high as the glass permitted, drained it, and proceeded to pour himself another. Kyra came and scooped the bottle out of his grasp. He reached for her glass on the cooler, but accidentally knocked it over. Itty-bitty crystals radiated on the floor. Things fall apart, he said to himself, as he squatted down. To become pieces for me to pick up.

She took hold of his wrist, pulled him back to his feet, and dragged him from the cooler. Clumsily, he went along. Kyra ushered him ahead, driving him toward the servers. When Milton stopped and turned around, she decelerated on him. "We function on a need-to-know basis, and it's best if you only know your part." She formed the side of her head on his chest. "We lost track of her when she failed to enumerate a jadeite. We hoped for the best, but expected the worst. Officially, she was MIA. That is until… you found her."

His nose tickled, taking respite on the crown of her copious, auburn bob. "Found her where?" he asked dully.

"You exhumed her remains," she said. "'Member the bones you dropped off last week?"

He could feel the barbed belt around Kyra's waist squishing against his pants. "The bones I discovered at Melano-something."

"Coincidentally, some of the relics matched the bone and dental of Goo," she said, giving pause. "You know what that means."

Milton emerged from the tangles of her hair, and reflected half-aloud, "That Goowi Dara is probably not married, with a successful husband, three kids, and an arthropodic fido."

"That, and there's a jadeite posing as Goo somewhere out there." Kyra lifted her head, examined his face. "Pay attention."

Milton took control of the bottle and brushed her aside. "Why didn't you tell me sooner, Kyra?"

"What do you want me to say?" she asked. "Good morning, Trufflehard. PS, y'member someone named Goo? Guess what, she died." Following Milton to the cooler, she swiped the bottle away. "What good does any of that do, but affect employee morale? If I kept it from you, it was only for your own protection." She skipped to the work station projecting multiple holocubes and turned the corner.

Milton trailed after her. "I dodge alien death rays for a living. What protection?"

"Oh quit your *wah*," she said with her back toward him, approaching the labyrinth of CPU racks and losing him around the bend.

Milton wobbled to one of the aisles in vain and put out a hand to catch himself. "Kyra, I've gone my entire life without feeling anything. If you thought that I was gonna feel feelings, then let me feel."

Kyra's voice came from the other side. "I did what was in the best interest of all parties involved. And if I made the wrong decision, it's mine to live." She paused momentarily. "But I didn't. Your numbers speak for themselves. I didn't want you to react this way. Right now is exactly why I avoided telling you."

Leaning against the rack, Milton sagged to the floor. "I'm reacting to you covering it up."

"You want a telegram every time something goes wrong?" she said from the opposite end.

"She used to ask me how I did," he said. "Like she cared. And then, without a word, she was gone. Story of my life, I thought, but apparently not."

"Well, what do you know?"

"I know she liked to read," he croaked, half to himself. "She was always reading. Something. Always had her nose in a holobook." It came to mind she had been reading the Trufflehard biography, when he saw her last. I wonder if she ever got to read it to the end, he thought.

"Whoopteedo."

"I do. I admired her for it, even though the platform is superannuated to me." And that's what got her, he thought. She was booksmart.

"Say zippity-flying-doodle," urged the invisible voice.

"Zippity-flying-doodle," he said dejectedly.

"Get up and say it."

Milton picked himself off the ground and lurched against the adjacent rack. He rested his forehead there and closed his eyes. "Zippity-flying-day," he mumbled.

"There, don't you feel better already?"

He turned to see Kyra standing before him. The bottle was gone. "I can't go any further," he said.

"Zippity-flying-doodle means shit happens and you get over it. It works, Barret. You just need to believe it when you say it."

"I don't believe zip."

"What do you need me to do then?" she demanded. "Blow you?"

"If you insist," he said.

She started to unbutton his rumpled green jacket and peel it off his shoulders, and then stopped. Woefully shaking her head, she retracted her gaze. "You're bereaved and drunk."

Milton felt the gradual decline of the handprint on his biceps, curtailing to his forearms and abating.

She said, "I refuse to take advantage of your feeble state."

"I've never felt better," he said, launching himself off the rack and almost tripping over his own shoes. Kyra took hold of him and propped him back up.

"Now you do." She draped the jacket back on him and buttoned it, swept his collar, straightened his head with her hands. "You won't start feeling exploited until much later."

In a low volume, he assured her, "I won't hold it against you even if I do."

Kyra clutched his neck and dragged him close, scorching his ears with a whisper of breath. "How do I know it's not the ethanol talking?"

"In case you haven't noticed, I'm desperate."

"I didn't before, but now that you mention it-" She rescinded abruptly. "What's the matter with you? Shape up and have some self-worth."

She turned briskly and retreated from him. He went his separate way, retracing his steps, cutting the corner and back across the multiplex workstation. He returned to the cooler and grabbed the squirt bottle of Indoctrin-Aid. As he brought the nipple up to his mouth, Kyra reached from behind and groped it away.

"Is this what your parents foresaw in you? God Trufflehard, I can't imagine being your real father."

"What are you talking about?" he asked, rubbing the base of his neck.

"To have sacrificed everything just to have you throw it all away."

"Good thing you're not my real father."

"You're not my son, either," she said. "But do I have to fuck your mother and pass a paternity test to care?"

"Relief I don't have parents," he said drably.

"You have to have come from somewhere. Try to remember."

"False memories at best, even if I did."

"You need rest, Barret. Go home," she advised him, "right after you make one final house call for the day."

Milton took his phone out to locate the new assignment.

"Where's your genograph?" she asked.

It was as if she had a sixth sense. He had lost it and was in need of a replacement. "It's all somewhere back where," he started to say, gesturing behind himself ambiguously, before conceding, "I don't have my hardware anymore."

"Looks like you'll have to do it the oldfashioned way."

"What's the oldfashioned way?"

"Going 'graphless."

Milton accepted, even though he knew they had always used equipment. But then again, perhaps it was a crutch after all.

"Then you can go resurrect yourself," she said. "You probably just need a good shave, not to mention a prayer or two."

"The last time I prayed, I almost got killed."

She rubbed his arm. "Well, you're still here. You ever think about that?"

"No."

"Well, you are," she said, briskly turning to her side, "and there must be a reason why."

"Step away from the pulpit, Kyra. There's no place for God in this world. Not after everything I've seen."

"The porno of exploding body parts and flying dicks and jack-all," Kyra said, glancing at him. "When did you get gunshy?"

"Not physical things," he clarified. "Psychological. After a while, you realize you're all alone, and there's nobody else to blame."

"The world is depending on you."

"Let them depend on somebody else," he said. "I'm not right for it, anymore. Not that I ever was. I'm not who they think I am."

"Of course you're not. If they did, your cover would be blown."

Milton took a couple steps. "There were great expectations of me, weren't there?" he asked, vacantly. "I was supposed to live up to a legacy. To be Trufflehard. But I have nothing to offer. I'm sorry I didn't turn out the way I was supposed to."

"I know how you can get when you're drunk," she said from behind. "This isn't you. Because I know you."

"Maybe you did." He turned around slowly to face her. "But he you knew is now the chitin that I've shed."

She pivoted on her heels, folded her arms and looked over her shoulder. "I respected that chitin."

"It's just exoskeleton," Milton said.

"I've known you for over a decade now, Barret," she said, turning to glance reprovingly at him, "and I swear to God the one thing you're not is a quitter."

In a quiet, despondent tone, he said, "You're not a quitter until you are."

"Do you admit you're a quitter?" she asked, her voice piquing with contempt.

"Sure," he admitted numbly.

"You are?"

A redundant sense of fatigue settled over him. "A thousand times yes."

She leaned close. "Then say it." She passed a mirthless smile. "I want to hear it come from your heart." Her glacial hot sigh evaporated against his neck. "Straight out of your oh-so-great mouth."

Milton resisted the glare of her blue-green eyes. "I'm a quitter, a dropout, a giver-upper, a punker-outer, a softminded refug-"

Kyra muffled his mouth with the palm of her hand and threw it back. "Stop talking about yourself. This is not about you. This is much bigger than you."

"Then pick on someone of commensurate size," he said.

"You were never my pick."

The frost stuck. "Then don't try to talk me out of walking away." He started moving toward the aperture that led to the conduit pipe.

"Enumerators have wanted out in the past, but they always come back," she said. "You'll see, Barret. This bloody job is your only salvation. It's what's become of you. Or at least, what's left of you. And I can tell you from where I'm standing, it's not much."

Milton halted his feet and panned around to see Kyra's haunted comportment. "Thanks Kyra, it means a big deal coming from you."

She was strutting over now, piercing the polished floor with every deliberate step of her jagged heels. "Our scouts chose you because you were meant to handle this. What you're feeling right now, I get it.

Honest, been there, done that. I know where you're coming from." She stopped in front of him. "Actually, I don't." She delivered a flying knee to his gut and stood over him as he keeled, his body rippling grievously. "What the fuck, Trufflehard? You were selected for a reason."

Hunched over, the pang in his stomach squeezed the air out of him. Pain impulses dominated his limbic system. He covered the bruise with his arm, gasping, "What about Goowi Dara? What was her reason?"

"Who? Goo?" asked the frigid voice from above. "She died for a cause. Don't be such a gravedigger."

"She was put to rest before she could even count to one," he grunted.

"I'm not the grim reaper, Trufflehard."

Milton rose to latch onto Kyra's arm for support, but she swatted it away. "And I'm not Trufflehard," he heaved, hands on his knees, huffing down at the grubby straps of his velcro sneakers, "so stop calling me that, because the self-fulfilling prophecy trick won't work on me." He panted. "I'll never be him." He jerked himself up wearily. "I'm leaving, Kyra." For good, he told himself.

"Go ahead then. Leave already." Kyra smirked, waving her fingers. "Nobody's stopping you. Actually, I wouldn't mind it if I never heard back from you again. Go on. Get retired by a drive-by laser. You're not what you used to be anymore, anyway. Your prime years are behind you. God, look at you. I can't reiterate how awful you look."

"Didn't need much convincing anyway." He turned to leave.

"There was a Trufflehard before you, and there'll be a Trufflehard after you."

"There'll never be another Trufflehard, Kyra," he said, without turning around, limping to the exit.

"Fine, but you know what they say in our line of business. You never retire from enumeration. Enumeration retires you."

He stopped to face her again. "Why does it have to be like this?" he asked. "And in thirteen years, I've never heard that."

"I'm sorry things have gotten this way," Kyra said, getting a hold of herself, softening her stance. "I won't mean any of this by tomorrow."

"Don't set a deadline you can't make," Milton said. Besides, he thought, I won't be around by then. "I'll carry out this last assignment, and then I'm out of here."

"We'll talk about this when you get back."

Suppressing the cloud of remorse billowing from within, he said, "It's all over, Kyra."

"See you in a jiffy," she quipped.

Milton about-faced and double-backed, gesturing with his arms out to his side, appealing to her, "Can't you just honorably discharge me and arrange some form of severance?"

"Go to hell," she suggested.

Already here, he said to himself, and inevitably turned back to leave. "It was nice knowing you too," he grumbled under his breath.

"You asked me what changed about you," she yelled to him. "I remember when you used to be thankful for a job!"

So do I, he thought, as he walked through the aperture.

chapter 17

Eldridge Kane constricted his countenance. "Truffle-hwat?"

Reggie Johnson pointed out, "The patriotic poster boy against the war on the Jade Agenda, and the protagonist of the Trufflehard franchise."

The apprentice's annotation went without warrant. Eldridge knew better who and what Trufflehard stood for. But why was the household name coming up in a corporate investigation? "A wannabe, you mean. He suffers from delusions of grandeur."

"The one and only Trufflehard," Amelia Pillowspoon said.

How? Eldridge asked himself. "Trufflehard is a movie."

"He was based on a real denizen," Pillowspoon said. "The movies are categorized as a biopic."

She was partially right.

"Sure it's based on a real denizen," Eldridge said. "The character is a representation of the inspirational source."

"But the veracity of the representation still holds," she said.

This was a common misconception about the media department. That stories based on truth, were necessarily true. How cloistered she was from the industry's proclivity to exaggerate the ordinary, Eldridge said to himself. "Don't take everything for face value. All the material distributed is filtered through nine stages for commercial purposes. Our content adheres to strict standards of verisimilitude, because market research has proven the general demographic is most receptive to credible portrayals. Most of the population is unaware of this, so your susceptibilities are not unique. Having said that, yo

u're out of your depth. I regret the fantasy must be ruined for you. We mean to maintain credibility with as great an audience as possible, but full disclosure seemed necessary."

"I was fully aware of that, Lord," Pillowspoon said, her voice lacking epiphany.

Eldridge let her know, "Nescience to privity, you can attest as foremost inspector, has steered your investigation to erroneous conclusions."

"It still doesn't change anything," she said steadfastly. "We will continue to pursue this lead."

What deviltry is this? Eldridge wondered to himself. Defiance! Despite rendering any basis of her case obsolete, a form of blatant neglect persists to disregard the verity of my words. Clearly, she's under some kind of spell, he thought. Some kind of influence. Watched too many movies. Read too much news. Lost the ability to distinguish fact from fiction, through no severe fault of her own. And yet, she should've known better. "Amelia," he said huskily, stern in his reasoning, "I don't know you well, but I trust your high rank is a reflection of your intelligence and capabilities. How can you and your associates ever deduce that the Trufflehard mythos could be relied on as an authoritative source, when most personages of your distinction possess enough wherewithal to dispute the events in the story from ever happening?"

"My colleagues and I include ourselves in that group," she said firmly.

"Then we're in agreement," Eldridge said, returning to his seat, now that the miscommunication was settled. "That Trufflehard is just another character invented to engender a broader meaning for political and commercial ends. A symbol of patriotic pride." He stopped midway, cheapened to find himself in the middle of spelling out the alphabet of the media, prerequisite knowledge that should have come with her title. Too often, he found himself needlessly laboring to break in subordinates on subjects he had to figure out all on his own. But these are the top stars, supposedly, he thought. Amelia Pillowspoon. Even Reggie Johnson. Crème de la crème of graduates. Through affirmative action, he conjectured, based on their gender and physical disability. He wanted to gag. "Even if he was a real denizen, you can't ignore the chronology of events. The legend was written before that madcap in the video was ever born. Economics allow us to forecast inflation, employment, projected earnings, but it hardly makes us prophets. No pun intended."

"Lord," Pillowspoon said, "are you familiar with the bleeding edge research by Dr. Silverfish?"

Eldridge squinted doubtfully. He turned to his apprentice, acceding, "Elucidate me, Johnson."

"Yes," Johnson said. "I came across Dr. Silverfish in my studies. The obscure product of some city college in Carmel-By-The-Sea."

"I said 'Elucidate me,' not 'Humor me.'"

"I address you in earnest," Johnson said.

"Impeccable," Eldridge said with mock regard. "What about him?"

"Dr. Silverfish is a woman," Johnson corrected. "She never graduated and thus died without acknowledgement from the academic field."

"So she's not even a real doctor," Eldridge said, growing impatient.

Johnson continued. "She withdrew from collegiate pursuits partway into the first semester due to differences with the professor. What eventually followed was her institutionalization for clinical paranoia and hallucinations. One of her noteworthy symptoms was her refusal to eat, upon claims of seeing zeroes and ones in her food. After she was admitted for electroshock therapy, she subsisted on dough injections in a vegetative stup-"

Eldridge interrupted, "Spare me the life story."

"She proposed the Latency Paradox," Pillowspoon said.

Eldridge pulled up his schedule on the transparent band on his wrist. "I already have a different all-nighter appointed."

"I can resist delving into the mathematical breakdown of the principles," Pillowspoon said. "The abridged version will suffice."

Eldridge agreed with reluctance. "Commence the slumber party."

"Dr. Silverfish goes on to quantify how the conscious world experiences time. She purports that it takes time for our actions to resolve. Fundamentally, time is fiction. But it's how we denote the degree of change. And the changes occur for us at different rates, based on various factors, such as synchronicity, processing capabilities-"

Eldridge cut her off, shaking his head. "What are you going on about?"

"Somehow," Pillowspoon said, "Milton Grainjar exists in our collective memories as Barret Trufflehard, before the occurrence of the antecedent events."

"The effect, superseded by the cause," Johnson mused. "That explains how his legend came prior to the originating factors that inspired it."

Eldridge sat up. "How could that be? It violates everything we understand about natural order."

"Dr. Silverfish posits that somewhere among us in space," Pillowspoon said, "there exists an invisible force whose effects are evident by its influence on time-space perception, our reality construct."

Eldridge made a profane, snorting sound. "An imperceptible ersatz god."

"She calls it the Virtual Protocol Network, and it's responsible for processing everything that happens in the world. Any action that you trigger, moments and thoughts, must be pinged to the VPN to be ponged back to our planetary consciousness. This round trip of transmission and reception requires an interval of time that cannot be quantified, due to our limited nature."

Eldridge closed his eyes and took a deep breath, pondering the significance of what it all meant. Abracadabra and other magic words. Watching Amelia Pillowspoon get sawed in half and put back together, would have prompted a more preferable reaction.

"Lord," Johnson said, taking a stab, "allow me to abbreviate - while reality appears congruous and sequential, technically, there's an immeasurable lapse that constitutes a period of consignment. But this gap of time that we perceive is really just an illusion created by our rate of processing information."

Johnson's explanation was equally vexing.

Pillowspoon expounded, "There lie variances between all matter, due to deviation in configuration. Among humans, it's been largely indiscernible. The professional runners that Dr. Silverfish conducted her tests on - when she was lucid - for example, transmitted data that bounced back in rapidfire bursts, detecting irregularities by up to a few nanoseconds. A span considered trivial to human consciousness, but the theoretical implications are infinite notwithstanding."

As delicately pleasant as her pixie, little voice was, Eldridge thought, she was just as well damn talkative. Every time he thought she was finished, she would keep going, at which point he would pick up slippery scraps of ideas here and there to formulate an incomplete impression. Perhaps the only part he truly grasped came by way of the provided study, runners having to do with dynamics and speed. And when he got up to take a closer look at the subject campaigning the action on the big holocube, he drew the connection. "Is that the reason for his movement?" Milton Grainjar's holographic construct flitted about across the holocube in a hectic, wayward motion, appearing, disappearing, and reappearing with mercurial expedition. "When he gets stirring, he looks like a blur out there. Hopping all over the place like a grasshopper on a pogo stick in a flipbook, despite the advanced motion capturing capacities of high resolution surveillance."

"Milton Grainjar is an outlier, yes," Pillowspoon confirmed. "His ping is simply off the charts. However, the interval circuit measurement for his transmission of data to boomerang back is multiple times the standard deviation. The command has been executed. The signal has not returned for sensory input."

"In other words," Eldridge said.

"He's slow," Johnson said.

"Imperceptibly slow," Pillowspoon said.

Presently, the footage on the holocube showed Milton Grainjar stalking a slender silhouette, striking from behind.

Eldridge observed impassively, arms folded. "That's his problem. I'm unclear as to how this applies to us. Are you exonerating him based on some obscure mental condition that he has?"

"A mental condition is circumscribed to the personal experience of the individual," Johnson said. "From what Inspector Pillowspoon seems to be suggesting, this is not an isolated phenomenon."

Eldridge turned to the Lead Inspector. "What is it now?"

Pillowspoon faced him with immense, grievous eyes. "We're all feeling the Latency Paradox of Milton Grainjar."

Eldridge drooped of exasperation. He had no idea what it meant.

"Dr. Silverfish uses the analogy of a star," Pillowspoon said.

"A star," Eldridge repeated ponderously.

"It's a glowing, celestial body," Johnson said.

The description warranted a tiresome glance from Eldridge. "Now I know." Obviously, he had known before that. It was just, he could not remember the last time he had seen a star in person. Not since all the light pollution, he thought.

"It takes light years for stars to reach us," Pillowspoon said. "When we stargaze, we look into the past. The effect of latency is attributed to the distance the visual emission travels to project unto us. We know that the star looks different in its most present incarnation, possibly even burned out. The Milton Grainjar you saw today, was the Barret Trufflehard of yesterday."

"You mean-" Eldridge hesitated, still apprehending. "The information hasn't reached…" He broke off in concentration.

"The sensory input of Grainjar's consciousness," Pillowspoon said.

Grainjar, Eldridge estimated, was experiencing life from a far away place, if it was even conceivable. Like a star, he thought. A million miles away. Essentially a million years away. Infinity for that matter. And he wondered, Is he experiencing us from afar, or are we experiencing him? What does it matter? He felt parched.

He shot a dehydrated glower toward the refreshment wall, beckoning irritably. Arising from the back was a snap-crackle-pop. A radiant woman in a coconut brassiere and grassy mini skirt manifested gliding toward the LCEO, gyrating her hips. Moments later, Eldridge sat rimmed in shades, draped in a lei of orchids, newly crowned by a laurel wreath, siphoning a green coconut cauldron garnished with peppermint sprigs, a wedge of pineapple, a wheel of lime, a slice of watermelon, a seahorse, and cherries and strawberries and kiwis kabobbed by a tan plaid umbrella.

"And what happens if the individual in question sees himself?" Johnson asked. "Is that even credible? For him to mingle with his temporal analogue?

"You mean watch his own biopic," Pillowspoon said. "Most likely, he would draw allegories with his eventual identity, but considering the liberties taken by the entertainment industry, as the good Lord corroborated, the individual might connect some dots. No more than the average viewer who could just as well relate to anything. Hardly there'll be a realization that he's gazing into a crystal ball, witnessing his whole life unfolding before his eyes. And when you account for the perceived time gap, he'd attribute the figure in the movie to be a lot older than him."

Who cares? Eldridge said to himself, sipping cool coconut juice. He's probably already dead, little does he know. Imagine finding out your life is merely memory in progress, he thought, waiting to be computed. Sucks to be him, boohoo. But that takes care of itself. I can't have a would-be hoagie running around disrupting businesses for nothing at all, jadeites or not.

A premier service of trained professionals - such as the JERQS - procured by none other than Ekonomy Ink would be contracted, even if there really was a fictional party of members that adhered to the Jade Agenda. Lone vigilante operating independent of the Ekonomic system need not apply. Alas, he determined, nonsensical hypotheticals I've no obsession to tolerate.

His thoughts rallied back to the inspector's earlier assertions. That the JERQS subsidiary had been infiltrated by jadeites. Baseless accusations, he thought. Jadeites were ersatz. *Is* ersatz. Thereby rendering this chronic deconstruction as imperfect logic. Barret Trufflehard was a byproduct of an ersatz premise. You could not have him without the other.

Eldridge waved away the emptied shell, and a new coconut with all its tropical decorations, was presented. "You still haven't accounted for the jadeites. The Jade Agenda and its associated party is make-believe. It's a political cartoon engineered by the creative team."

"Then it should come as no surprise to you," Pillowspoon said, "that an extensive investigation was just launched into the media department."

The coconut girl had just leaned in to dab the perspiration under Eldridge's chin, when he ejected a mouthful of fluid. Heedless of her freshly glistening hair, he asked "When?"

"Just before I walked in," she said. "I was able to make it here in the first place because you were in the same area of our focal radius."

By the time Reggie Johnson had turned his ekosuit to the refreshment station to flag down assistance, scantily-clad women were already on it, rushing over to tend to the spill. They swarmed the LCEO all at once, rabidly applying towels and drying his face. Eldridge slapped about in an indignant fit, thwarted them away. Then he leaned in, snapping off his tilted sunglasses to reveal a boggled groove above his brow. "You're investigating my department?"

"We suspect the creative team has been penetrated by the Jade Association," Pillowspoon informed him. "Perhaps other staff members as well. All of the Kokiri House is effectively under lockdown."

Eldridge ejected from his seat and declared, "This futile inquisition desists immediately! The only coverup here, is your flagrant mismanagement of corporately funded resources. Your reckless role in this fiasco has sufficiently demonstrated an overall lack of objective aptitude befitting Lead Inspector status."

"Lord," Pillowspoon started, "our team believes that there are-"

"Your team had to believe in something," he interjected. "The alternative to that was admitting folly. So you've introduced fanatical explanations to accommodate for your crummy fieldwork. Your entire team will be dishonorably discharged. As for you-"

"Lord," she said adamantly, "I assume ownership of all credit for results arrived by the team. If you would please just take a moment to reconsider Dr. Silverfish's theory-"

"Ah," Eldridge said, cutting in, "why yes, I almost forgot about Dr. Charlatan. Or was it Silverfish? More like Silverduck. A glorified excuse to circumvent responsibility for a profitless outcome. Go peddle that quackery elsewhere." He moved away from his desk and met the inspector upfront. "Consider yourself stripped of rank and removed from active duty. You will wait until further instructions."

"But Lord -"

"What say you?"

"Thank you," she muttered, glancing away in wilted rejection.

"Now disperse."

She padded away morosely, without further protest.

When the conveyer chute sounded, Johnson said, "Your patience is formidable."

Eldridge sauntered past his desk and stared at zooming cars. "Where do you find these denizens?" Eldridge asked.

Johnson joined him, guiding his mechanical augmentation to the glass overlooking the city. "In the Investigation Field."

"You would think we had more discriminating processes."

"Yet you've demonstrated mercy both formidable and, to some degree, unforeseen, by favoring suspension over termination."

"On the contrary, I portend a bright future for her. A longterm investment that will cultivate her untapped potential. The position of

Lead Inspector was underutilizing her strengths. She deserves advanced placement."

He returned to his seat. Two women approached him timidly and citing no objection, proceeded to wipe him down in a circular motion. He crossed his fingers behind his head and reclined, as they polished him underneath his arms. Afterward, one of them drew a cigar, snipped one end, and jammed the other end into his mouth. The other woman produced the spark.

"You took pity on her," Johnson said. "Otherwise, your optimistic regard for her defies the manner in which she was dismissed."

"You undermine my generosity," Eldridge said, puffing. "I'm always in search of fresh faces to nurse me back to health. I'm transferring her to Private Domestic Services, where her best assets will not be squandered away." He paused to wonder how she would look in a milkmaid uniform. "You can't disagree she has a rare allure that is hard to come by. Nevermind all that squawking." He took another puff. "Her and her paradox business, though I do recall having the impression that you put stock in it."

The hefty head of the ekosuit lowered dutifully. Johnson said, "I've continually endeavored to maintain a neutral disposition in the interest of serving you."

"She was purporting that we created our own enemies," Eldridge said. "That somehow, an imaginary party of abstract, alien memes, no more palpable to the touch than a thought bubble, had corrupted our world and infiltrated the JERQS - a civil force we commission to serve and uphold our purpose, not conspire to war against us." And for a while, he thought, she caught me off guard. She had me going.

Eldridge smooched the cigar in rumination. "All of this, based off circumstantial evidence of a defunct DPM safeguard and a holographic aberration that could be more easily explained with a smidgen of rationale. Instead, an overcomplicated alternative to preordinance was devised to justify the debacle of apprehending the mischief maker. It was beyond reason, nonsensical lunacy I've spent far too long tolerating." His usual, introspective aplomb was offset by restless compulsion. He put away the cigar and put a palm to his nape and flexed his neck around, shaking off the chilled swell of discomfort, allusions that seemed to cling to him, despite the halfhearted efforts to regain his composure. Enough already, he told himself. "Better not to pretend to understand the depths that some denizens will dig to vindicate their failures."

Johnson chimed, "It certainly deviated from the dogmatic boundaries of hypotheticals that dictate cause and effect."

Eldridge jolted from his seat and swiveled to face Johnson. "Johnson, are you still here?"

"I gathered you required my attention," Johnson said.

"You mistook my soliloquy for a monologue," Eldridge said. "Don't elevate yourself. I have nothing to say to you."

"Is there any service I can render?" Johnson asked, his face stoic as always.

It was the same cross-eyed and pug-like countenance, to the disdain of the LCEO. Well, he determined, no more. Eldridge made up his mind then and there. "Consider yourself discharged in T-minus... one minute."

"One minute?"

"However long it takes to check with the secretary on my food. Now cease to offend my senses and disperse. Go scuttle along with your toy robot. The grownups have to do grownup things."

Eldridge's eyes wandered lustily to the refreshment wall. Johnson, getting the memo, said, "It's been an honor," and clunked across the room, disappearing in his prosthetic underneath the conveyer chute.

Shortly thereafter, Eldridge scanned the lineup of potential suitors at his service. Just what I need to get my mind off what had just happened, he said to himself. Something to sooth my pent-up nerves. And also, he noticed just then, replenish my fuel tank. Visceral hunger gnawed at his jowls. The crisis will not avert itself, he thought, but it will have to wait. My electrolytes and glycogen have been depleted from the thriftless brouhaha.

chapter 18

The Zwylx Q-Ten gurgle machine flickered on, building pressure. The mechanical brush swept and the blower blustered, discarding any oxidized sediments and remnants left over from the last cycle. The cherries were depulped and washed sextuple times over. The lasik burrs of the grinder proceeded to cut the pits down to microscopically identical size and dimension for equal extraction. The grounds fell into a thoroughly pre-wet leaf filter, whereby boiling hot water, the optimal solvent, sprinkled gently from the shower screen. It took less than two minutes for all the water to filter through the finely ground seeds and dispense into the flask. The grounds to water ratio was 1:17, and the total run time was about par. Kyra removed the flask, and decanted two mugs with freshly brewed gurgle.

She handed a vessel of the hot beverage to Nelson Wattlecup, who had been waiting at a nearby table, drumming his fingers. He received the steaming mug eagerly, and started guzzling the solution.

Kyra observed remotely, the reckless abandonment of measured discretion. Wattlecup, a self-proclaimed connoisseur of gurgle - upon attending a three-day course one weekend - preferred the drink to reach room temperature, before touching it to his lips, having to do with the development of taste and tactile sensations. Presently however, it became apparent he was disinterested in taking the time to critically evaluate the subtle nuances of the cup. She witnessed him burn down his esophagus before his palate could register flavors besides extreme heat.

A waste on him, she thought, considering the gurgle hailed from the highest elevations - 40,000 feet and above on a cherry farm inside a greenhouse skyscraper. A three-ounce bag of handpicked and pre-cleaned gurgle cherries was 200,000 pixels. And that was due to it being wholesale. This was the world's best secret, tiny tropical seeds, yielding to a clean, effervescent profile, zero defect, black market grade, not the bitter and oily, titanic embers from Ekonomy Cafe that brought on global warming.

"Look who has a callused tongue," Kyra remarked, when the reflexive jerk never came.

"I'd rather you didn't put it that way," Wattlecup said, sloppily wiping his chin with the chevron kerchief and stuffing it haphazardly into his breast pocket. "There's urgent business that needs taking care of."

"You wanted to discuss Trufflehard's contract." Kyra hoisted herself on the counter across from him. She sat there, legs crossed, fingers wrapped around the humongous mug, waiting for the gurgle to cool. Beside her, the self-sanitation procedure of the gurgle machine kicked into gear. "Considering our shortage on staff, I thought we agreed to fine him for his incompetence. Dock from his pay. As it stands, he owes us work for at least the next several lifetimes."

Wattlecup's brows adjusted with grim austerity. "That was before what happened today," he said. "Have you spoken with him yet?"

"A little while ago."

"And how'd that work out for you?"

"I think I really got through to him this time," she said, enveloped by the fog of aromatic trails dissipating from the mug.

Nelson Wattlecup did not have to know the only enumerator on the active roster had just signed off on the Bureaux. Or sort of signed off, Kyra thought. Nothing was set in stone. He was still obligated to one more assignment, providing enough time and distance from this morning's altercation. Give or take a day or two, passions cooler, Kyra expected him to come crawling back for more assignments in no time. He always does, she said to herself. What else would he do to pay back what he owed the bureaucratic agency? He couldn't hold a normal job, not that anybody would hire him in the first place.

She weighed the implausibility of him actually following through on his short notice. Worse in the dubious event that somebody took a chance on him: no degree of any kind, no public record of any work history, over the hill, with his chubby cheeks and bulbous nose and sparse hair, she could go on and on. Fortuitous forces would need to come to play for the alignment of these hypothetical scenarios. But given no other option, she was prepared to make the call to his future employer and volunteer scintillating information.

Wattlecup interrupted her judicious cogitation. "If that pinhead got you all riled up again. I don't have to remind you you're his superior," he said, chiding her with empowerment. "You can fire him for insubordination."

"That won't accomplish anything. We've used that card already, and it had the inverse effect of what you conjectured."

His expression twisted. "Why not? You are more than authorized to do with him as you see fit. I trust your judgment."

"And I don't take that for granted," she said, sliding down from the edge of the counter and approaching the table, gurgle in hand. "Having made that clear, I don't think he's responsive to any scare tactics. He's just not programmed that way." She found a white stool and sat adjacent to Wattlecup. "If anything, it deals more damage."

Wattlecup defined the lines on his face. "What are you implying?"

"The unique ID diagram of his cephalic activity, mapped out via recording the electrical potential energy transmitted by the global neurological enterprise in his brain - including but not exclusive to propagation, frequency range, and spatial distribution of his cognitive functioning - revealed abnormal voltage charge fluctuations from each intracranial current source."

"So?" he asked.

"He's scored over 30,000-odd enumerations, and he's still managed to stay in one piece." Her eyes settled on the glassy surface in the cup. "I'm just saying, he's different."

"Then why argue with results?"

She looked up, moistened by the emanation of fragrant warmth. "I'm not."

"You think we're holding him back."

"How long could we deny him certification?"

Wattlecup shot out of his seat. "Is that what he asked of you outright? Small wonder you're upset. The effrontery of that kid!" He balled his hands into fists, pacing himself. "Kyra, I swear I don't know what you see in him. I never liked the way he looked from day one."

"You're the one who hired him and advised me to practice patience. You convinced me to keep him around for this long." If anything, she thought, I was the prejudiced one from the outset, not you. Transmogrified, how our perceptions shift.

What was more, Wattlecup appeared visibly rattled, as though something inscrutable had taken hold of him. He composed himself with effort. "I should've followed my instincts and done this much sooner," he said, screwing up with repugnance, "because he's not worth the hassle. Give me ten enumerators with no enumerations but possess the capacity to listen to basic instructions, follow simple rules, and prove their competence by passing our universal measure of skill and proficiency, than have one Trufflehard with 30,000-plus enumerations but can't run a six-minute mile to save his life."

"He doesn't need to run a six-minute mile to save his life," Kyra said, reservedly observing Wattlecup straightening himself once more and sitting back down.

"Or finish an obstacle course inside of sixty minutes for that matter," Wattlecup countered, speaking from one side of his mouth. "There's no point in agonizing over a trainee who can't cut full certification because he can't pass the physicals or written exams. Cut him loose."

Kyra took a sip of gurgle. "It's a bureaucratic loophole."

"Only the strongest survive out here." Wattlecup's voice came out low and abrasive, guttural. "The system is in place to filter out the weak."

"He has over 30K enumerations."

"Numbers lie, Kyra."

"Statistics can certainly skew interpretations, but he's amassed the most enumerations of anybody under my command of influence. A fully certified enumerator in Joanne Bonnar, a distant runner-up has eight. Excuse me, had eight. She was retired some odd days ago. Most of our trainees acquire full certification by their first enumeration. Nobody has ever bucked that trend. And we've never had anybody surpass 30 enumerations, let alone-"

"So what are you suggesting?" Wattlecup interjected, disfiguring his face. "That he's entitled to a break? Because if you are, we've entitled him break after break. Cut him loose or cut him a break, is that it?

Ungrateful bastard."

"I don't suggest cutting anything. On the contrary, I believe you should earn your break."

He relaxed his shoulders, smoothed his sleeves, toyed with his cuffs. He looked serious. "Good, it would set a bad precedent. You start making exceptions for him, and the next thing you know, everyone's a fully certified enumerator."

"Among the fifteen new recruits we just padded to our roster, none of them have any enumerations. I have one prospective trainee who seems somewhat promising. He registered a perfect score on his timed essays and a near-perfect score on his mathematical evaluations. But if history's any indication, it's usually the ones who demonstrate outstanding performance in the standardized tests and systematically voted most likely to succeed, who end up retiring without quite hitting their potential."

Wattlecup leaned over the table. "There's simply no way we're giving him full certification. It's just not happening."

"You said you trust my judgment," Kyra said. "Then trust me on this."

His eyes darkened. "I'll veto it and fire him myself."

"Until recently, you've been his staunchest advocate." Kyra smiled scarcely. "Must I remind you, you're the one who rehired him after I fired him."

He wrenched his forehead. "A decision I regret to this day."

Kyra lowered the lipstick-stained mug. "It's only been twenty-four hours, if that."

Wattlecup slammed the table as if to lay down the gavel. "Which is why I'm exacting the annulment of my premature ruling."

She rose to her feet, aroused by the unfolding drama. "I was thinking the complete opposite. To give him full certification. Yet you want him gone. Have we ever been at further odds?"

Wattlecup postured out of his chair, squaring off with her. "His cute little stunt at the Eko Mall this morning caused damages racking up in the thousands of megas... ultras."

"Most of the damage was caused by the haphazard jadeites. Not to make excuses for him, but the circumstances sort of called for it. Besides, what's it to you?"

"An innocent safeguard was killed because of his reckless actions today."

"Collateral damage comes with the territory."

"His consummate miscalculations cost us a lot of grief. He's not balanced."

A visceral bucket of slime was tilting over her head. Clammy tendrils plucked at her. "No, he isn't," she conceded slowly. "That was why he was scouted."

"There's something deeply irregular and jagged about that kid." Wattlecup's countenance twisted miserably. "I don't like it, Kyra. I don't like it one iota. Call him off."

"What have you suddenly got against him?" What's gotten into you? she wondered, dawned by a cumbersome premonition. "This is unlike you," she said, retreating against her heels. In fact, she decided, this isn't you at all.

Guns whipped out in sync. The room lit up in a frenzied burst of photogenic energy. It was Wattlecup whose shot went off before the other. But his vector was off. Kyra bored a hole through the center of his face. He made several more attempts in vain, depressing his trigger in spontaneous trajectories. Finally he wavered and collapsed.

Kyra withdrew her laser gun, holstering it behind her. The green sludge erupting out of the donut head confirmed her instincts: the jadeites had gotten to Nelson Wattlecup. Probably they had gotten to the others, and they were about to get her as well.

It started to make sense. Wattlecup's characteristically monotonous demeanor, operating with recurrent formalities, substituted by a bellicose imitation. Even before, she knew something was off when he threw back the gurgle like a cheap shot of admixtures. Nevermind that he exhibited a lack of sensitivity to heat. Maybe he took up the pipe or mouthwashed for too long, she thought sullenly. But to lap it all up like it was some darkly generic tar pit from Eko Cafe was troglodytic.

She deliberated her next move. I can't make any calls, she thought. It might draw unwanted attention. Nobody could be trusted from now on. Nobody but Trufflehard. Why else would the jadeite have expressed interest in his contractual release, by appealing to her under the guise of Wattlecup? A plan that evidently blew up in its face.

When did we lose our agency? Kyra wondered, as her heels clicked toward the mutilated aftermath. She bent over, examining her supervisor laid flat on the floor, oozing glow-in-the-dark monster blood. It made her glad in a way seeing that. The enumerated jadeite. The boss was avenged. Imagine it had turned out she had executed the real Wattlecup, a mentor of sorts to her. Nothing feel-good about that. Warranted yet, if he was about to start micromanaging her affairs. Fortunately, that was not the case.

Quickly, she turned her attention to Trufflehard. If the jadeites tried to get to him through her and failed, they would most certainly resort to a direct approach. She straightened up, upgraded her weapon, finished the rest of her gurgle with much appreciation, and dashed for her souped-up, lime green trike. If she was fast enough, maybe she could make it in time.

chapter 19

Eldridge phoned his secretary. "Lord," she answered timidly.

"How's the job so far, Dolores?" Eldridge asked. "Comfortable much?"

"I'm a little held up at the moment," she said. "But your food has arrived."

"Good," he said tiredly, "would it delude me to expect its arrival on my desk before the invasion? Or must I onerously peel away from my stately responsibilities for the picayune task of procuring my own food?"

"I'm unable to step away at the moment. I pray that you'll understand."

You can pray all you want, he said to himself. You'll still be discharged. He got up from his seat and made his way across the room and jumped into the conveyer chute. "Goddamnit," he grumbled underneath his breath, barging out on the corresponding side. "Do I have to do every-"

Something snagged his foot, and his body went plunging to the floor.

Gnashing his teeth, he sat up to see what it was that had caused him to fall and froze at the discovery beside him - the former lead inspector, face down, inert and twisted grotesquely, the lethal recipient of a laser beam. He realized she was not the only one, as he returned groggily to his feet. All around, more employees - Execs and assistants and secretaries and supermodels alike - covered the floor, sprawled out and unmoving. The pool in the middle of the room was tainted of carmine; levitating on its surface were bodies prone.

Blurry shapes, long and green merged in and out of focus. Anthropomorphic figures with domed scalps warped into view. They held out glass tubes, zap guns upon further study. Something told Eldridge they were not the life of the party.

Sitting across in the corner, his secretary was petrified and breathless. Eldridge considered using her as a potential shield. He wondered if he could inch his way toward her. She was the closer of the two surviving. Johnson was situated further along his right. He was equipped with his own zap gun through the extension of the robotic arm.

Oppositely, the three alien figures started to speak at once. "We are the Jade Association," they said without opening their mouths. "This is the revolution."

Jadeites were real. How that was so, Eldridge did not care to ponder. A moot point as far as he was concerned. Here they are. They got Amelia, he realized with bereavement. She would've made a great chambermaid. What more did he need to base his next directive, than her death and the zap guns aimed at him? "Johnson," he rasped, "what are you waiting for? Shoot them and save me!"

Johnson pulled the trigger, twice. The beams shot up in the air, blasting open the ceiling above them – warning shots. The three jadeites did not even stir.

"How hard is it to shoot straight?!" Eldridge cried, stumbling toward the pregnant robot. "They're right in front of you. Hand it over here."

Johnson pivoted and shot a laser beam that darted by the LCEO. Behind him, the secretary slumped over the desk.

Eldridge patted himself, checking furiously to make sure his limbs were still intact. "Friendly fire, you two-bit brat! You almost got me killed! Quickly, pitch me the gun before we're all doomed! You heard them! They're here to depose of me!"

Johnson did not relinquish the zap gun.

But why? Eldridge wondered with blasted animosity. Because I ended his employment, he realized. He was under no professional obligation to defer. After the golden opportunity I gave him, he thought. "You can have your job back!" Eldridge exclaimed. "I'll even throw in a promotion."

Johnson sat still in the ekosuit, his beady eyes unblinking.

"You can have your own office!" Eldridge negotiated, waiting with outstretched hands. Seconds felt like minutes, minutes he did not have. "You can have your own company car and chauffeur!"

Johnson, his face slack, exhibited no alterations to his demeanor.

He's relentless, Eldridge thought. "Buster, now you're pushing it!" After some hesitation, he stopped to wonder, What am I haggling for? It's not as if I mean any of what I'm offering. I'll have him in a labor camp, he swore to himself. "I hand over my office!"

That did it. That got Johnson budging.

Cringeworthy invertebrate, Eldridge thought to himself. I'll have him digging tunnels beside exuberant automatons.

Johnson squirmed orgasmically from the wired stomach cavity and poked his foot out.

"Where are you going?" Eldridge wailed. "Just hand over the dastardly gun. You don't need to get-"

Johnson's foot exploded.

The effect of it left mutilated toes swollen out of the shoe. It swayed from the rubbery leg that stretched and traveled down to reach the floor. Arms furled out, spindly and long. Eldridge stared, speechless and stunned at the limbs garnering length, writhing and combing the air, as though a plant was maturing before his eyes at 3,000 times the speed. The domelike head popped out, turning vast and sprouting like a bud. It peered up at Eldridge with eyes devoid of meaning and direction. The rest of his body contorted away, outgrowing the dress attire, launching buttons in myriad directions and bursting open seams, dwarfen garment fragmenting and giving way to glowing green flesh. Creeping fingers latched onto the periphery of the synthetic host, posturing for leverage to flop its other leg out, whereby the flaccid figure freed itself, wobbled around and filled out, taking shape to crane above the Lord CEO.

Eldridge was rendered immobile. How had I seen what I had just seen? he wondered. He tried to retreat now, but could not. He was twined by the inhuman clasp of the jadeite. This is me paralyzed by the prodigy of my own endowment, Eldridge divined with quiet revulsion. I'm only as helpless as any of this is real.

"No," he started to bray, quaking his cheeks at the looming eclipse. "I am not your enemy. I'm Eldridge Kane. And I-" I created you, he thought, thrust by the realization of it all. "You're in my mind," he said, revealing to himself, coming to understand. "Why, look at you - my living testimony. An inadvertent manifestation of my vision. I'm the material god. Ruler of the Ekonomic Utopia. Fathom that."

When nothing happened, he was undeterred. He visualized another angle.

"This whole building is crawling with security guards," he said, concentrating on transcribing his words to substance. "My knights in shining armor are coming after you. They're on their way as I speak. They're already here, on the other side of that wall, waiting to converge at my expressed desire." Snickering preceded fullblown guffaw. "Even if they weren't, I can make them appear with naught but a thought. In fact, the JERQS will be here any moment, spilling out of the conveyer chute. And you'll rue the day you laid your grubby hands on your almighty maker. You have my word."

Even as he gazed into the gaping abyss, he thought, It's working. I'm starting to break through. His temporal arteries surged, meditating intensely on the jadeite, thrusting his mental everything to reprise control, levying the full gravity of his words upon it. "I have the power to pardon your sins or condemn you to hell. I have the power to christen you with fame or cast you to the eternal thralls of mediocrity. I have the power to mold you with my mind or combust you into a cloud of vapor, because you are an externalization of my imagination, a role player in the fabric of the reality that I dream. I wrought you from the fiction that drew you, and I can recall you with the same intellect that inspired you!" A visceral wheeze issued from total exertion, his breath constricted. "Unless you obey my command and put me down. Whereupon, fortune awaits you with the power vested in me. A golden key to the world. Humans abound. To take captive, sacrifice, experiment on and torture, whatever you glee. Not out of fear. I fear nothing but my own ingenuity. Nor do I bluster, when it is easier done than said."

He faltered, lest his words betray his stream of consciousness. What green he could still see at the edge, receded to his blind spot. "Your destiny will be fulfilled at my whim. A blessing that is yet subject to change, if you do not respect my instant wish and release me. Do not render me bankrupt..." His vision darkened, his focus waning with the bodily shift. He felt weightless, coalescing with space, incorporating into the greater conglomerate. Almost there, he thought. Almost over. Just a little more… flexing of the mind… pushing wind through these unflappable lips. "There is nothing I ask of you. Hearken, I am too proud to beg-" After which everything came out garbled. He heard the echoes of his speech diffuse to thoughts.

I am worth too much to die. I possess too much power to surrender. Too vain to look dead. Too big to fail. I order you to take heart my testament and bend at my will.

At last, he thought. I did it. It's gone. Falling away, tumbling deeper, he was relieved to know.

chapter 20

Milton Grainjar appeared from the corresponding conveyer chute to the glittery streets, briefcase and briefcase in hand. He took a couple pedestrian steps in a haze, glancing back momentarily at the 62-floor parking structure. Towering above him, an equal exchange of cars could be counted entering and exiting through the rooftop portal. The noon sky was a brilliant blue, spinning clouds reminiscent of the cotton candy he had shared with Eleanor Flutterby. He squinted weakly and shielded his eyes from the pervasive brightness with his hands.

The boardwalk promenade was surrounded by a billowing amalgamation of stores, clamoring on top of each other. Interconnected bridges zigzagged among the upper levels. The center of the path was filled with illusionists, dancers on stilts, mimes, a bikini-clad woman entombed in a block of ice, and other street performers. Behind glass walls, shoppers were seen escorted via conveyer belt from one store to the next, holding on to overflowing bags.

High-powered holographic signs merged between neighboring

brands. From past experience, Milton had learned that going inside the stores was simple and straightforward, even accommodating. Entrances swung wide open at the slightest detection of foot traffic, extending onto the walkway to receive absentminded guests. Exiting required more involvement, due to a layout that encouraged patrons to flow through conjoining stores. It was easy to return to the same store twice or more, without paying careful attention to the ad-based directions.

Knowing this, Milton had no impulsion of committing to the fractals of businesses. Wisely, he stuck to the curb, passing up the lateral domino of conduit pipes that led to the subsurface levels. The food gallery archway emerged overhead.

A loud combustion sounded out of view. Immediately, he looked around. Vibrant plumes of smoke gave way to a gathering of cheers and applause. Some sort of grand opening for a mattress store, Milton abstracted. Echoes and trails of alarm and pretty colors bombarded his sensory receptors. An upside-down pole dancer pointed toward him, attracting his gaze. She was fingering him to come inside. Behind her was a baby registry.

Every store featured its own set of costumed mascots and promotional models, smiling, waving, striking poses, blowing whistles, anything to maximize exposure.

Milton, momentarily distracted by the race car models waving large checkered flags before a perfume shop, almost stumbled into a street vendor who was constructing caricature masks. Malformed faces of celebrities and famous figures were part of his setup, exhibiting his work. Presently, a little girl was having her face molded. Her brothers, mother, and father were already wearing their masks, plastered with surrealistic expressions.

There was a long line of customers waiting outside of a phone store, with a news crew interviewing them. The quasi-annual launch of the latest and greatest model was merely months away. A similar line was also apparent, across from him at an athletic footwear store. Milton watched his feet, making sure not to trip on any of the consumers sitting on the floor.

The seats at the food gallery were filled to capacity with loved ones polishing off the globs and crumbs from their trays. A raucous crowd centered around a platform of purple-faced individuals choking down food. A flashing banner above them read Bi-Monthly Fried Locust Eating Grand Prix. All of the nationally ranked food eating contestants were there, competing for the grand prize trophy: recognition and a full stomach. A man in a star-spangled top hat was spitting fast on a megaphone, providing play-by-play commentary of the action.

Over the years, it was much easier for Milton to lose himself and get swept up in the festivities. But his head was running through a fever swamp. He waded one foot over the other. The side effects of sleep deprivation and the adrenaline dump were starting to build up. Dehydration exacerbated matters. It had also been a while since ingesting any sustenance for him.

He made it to the automats with minimal delay, considering the circumstances. He took shallow breaths, mutely browsing the menu of instant food items. The options were overwhelming. From stir-fried panda and lobster on a stick, there was something for everybody. Milton was not persnickety, but he was selective for another reason. He had on him all of 4,000 pixels, which could only hold him over for a duration. Hence, he sought out something cheap, preferably 600 pixels or below. The funnel cake sliders and ice-cream-filled donuts seemed particularly interesting, but both items registered outside of his designated price range.

His innermost meditation was disrupted by the advancement of two girls. He gathered they were twins, amid adolescence. One of them handled a phone, readily displaying a form on the holocube, presumably to collect tidings. Milton glanced around stiffly, roughly estimating a million and a half shoppers in the entire complex. He was probably the last of them to have anything to give.

He expedited his deliberation, settling on the cheapest item, which was 900 pixels: a grilled cheese sandwich with fifty different ingredients. As he brought out his phone to transfer the funds from his account, one of the twins finally broached the subject. "Have you accepted Eldridge Kane as your Lord and Savior?"

"I'm really sorry," Milton said, glancing momentarily, "but I have nothing to spare." He idled for the automat to ID his preference.

The other twin started speaking. "Is that what you'll say supposing one day you find yourself face to face with God? What'll you say then? That you have nothing to spare?"

"That's blasphemous!" the other exclaimed.

Milton turned to the doppelgangers out of reflexive curiosity, and then peered beyond to meet the eye contact of onlookers. The outburst had been loud enough to attract the scrutiny of nearby shoppers lunching in the cafeteria. They viewed him critically, amid speculation of the heresy uttered to have riled such upstanding children. The twins, he noticed, both wore matching white suits, mini skirts, and heels, resembling future Execs of the Ekonomy. How old were they? he wondered. Twelve? Thirteen? Kids these days were in such a hurry.

The automat finished performing its neurological scan and printed out the ersatz sandwich. Milton grabbed the food to go. "He doesn't care," he said sluggishly, moving away from them, searching for an empty seat.

A twin crept up to his right. "Why should He?"

"He's the LCEO," said her sister, alternately appearing to his left.

"How would you feel if He had nothing to spare you?" the right twin asked.

Milton picked up his pace. "He doesn't owe me anything."

"God can survive your opinion," the left twin said.

"But can you survive His?" the other said.

"He seems needy," Milton said.

They continued to stride alongside him, side by side. "Why are you doing this to yourself?" the sister to his left asked.

"I'm not doing anything," he said, halting and spinning his axis to scan the cafeteria for any chair unoccupied by shoppers and shopping bags.

"No," the other sister said, "you're most definitely not."

"But you definitely are," hissed the counterpart.

Milton had heard enough. "Save the patronizing for the kids." He realized as he said this, they were kids themselves."

"It takes more muscle to deny God than to accept him into your heart."

Where the hell did you get that fun fact? he asked himself, as he broke away from them and remarked, "I don't have any muscle."

"That explains your weak brain," he heard from behind.

A variant of the same voice appended, "She said we'll keep you in our prayers."

You're only kids, Milton said to himself in an orthodox daze, swimming through the sea of shoppers. Be kids. Go play. Have fun. Fall in love. Do all the things you'll never do as an adult, he thought. The righteous panhandling can wait.

It became apparent he would not find any place to sit in the cafeteria. Especially not with the pandemonious atmosphere frenzying the center stage. Droves of fans screamed motivational chants. Others just screamed. And then there were those who stood agog with awesome apprehension. Milton weaved through the back-to-back crowd, filtering through the sticky cluster impinging his knuckled briefcases, warily stepping on the unstable surface of stagnant toeboxes. It was the only way to maneuver out of there. None of them seemed to mind. Their concerns were restricted to the rotating platform of juiced-up, gastronomic athletes, whose bellies were bulging with lean protein.

It took strenuous effort to break away from the assembly, but Milton managed to make it across to the opposite extension of the promenade. For a moment, he lost track. His undershirt and jacket clung to him. A layer of moisture accumulated above his brows. Wiping his forehead with his sleeves, he took a couple steps forward and turned back. He recognized the looming archway that he had seen earlier. The food gallery was the central body of the promenade. From it, branched off eight other directions. He was already disarranged by the likeness of each extension, almost a mirror image. The material complex repeated more or less identically, with spanning rows of asymmetrical stores piled on top of each other. The shoppers milling about, were similarly happy-go-lucky, equivalent and inseparable. They all looked content and gratified.

Locating an available bench, Milton proceeded. Music and laughter overlapped, creating a mishmash of strange noises that rattled his ears. Another explosion went off somewhere, followed by loud screams and clapping. When he was not adjusting to the visual fantasia bending and tilting his orientation, he was seeing stars. He retired his gaze to the floor, where tiles changed colors and warped to emit holographic gnomes who corresponded as guides that led guests to various franchises.

A boy sat unattended, his face waxen of tears. The wrinkled collars of his red shirt were stained from the outpour, dribbling from his chin.

Milton settled on the converse corner of the bench, placing the briefcases beside his feet. The boy stared at him, as Milton drew out his grilled cheese sandwich and popped open the clear casing.

He brought the sandwich up to his mouth, wavered, set it back down. He could not banquet in good conscience with the way the boy was rubbing his eyes at him.

His lips quivered, about to speak. "My m-mother," the boy managed to stammer.

"It's okay to tell me," Milton said. "Is she in any trouble? Where did you last see her?"

"At th-the to-toy store," the boy started, indicating the store front at the far side. Barret Trufflehard, shimmering in heavy armor, was signing autographs and posing for the cameras. A line of families waited their turn.

Milton determined the boy was just lost. "Your mother is fine," he assured the boy. "Wait a while. She'll come back looking for you." He raised the sandwich to his mouth.

"Sh-she w-won't," the boy blubbered. "Not af-after telling her I-I wish-wished she wasn't m-my mother."

Milton set the sandwich back down. "What could she have done to you?" he asked somberly. "Deny you of the newest version of the Trufflehard foam dart blaster? There's a directory around here. Just follow one of the gnomes, and you'll see it. Tell them you lost your mother. They'll know the rigmarole."

The boy did not answer, ogling what was inside Milton's hands.

Milton leaned back and offered the kid a wedge of his sandwich. "You want?"

The boy scooted over sheepishly and accepted it.

Milton popped the remaining half into his mouth and let it dissolve. "If it's any consolation," he told the boy, dusting off his hands, "I didn't get any toys when I was your age."

"I hate being a kid," the boy grumbled, wiping his face with the soiled palm of his right hand. "I wanna be old and do whatever I want."

"And what's that?" Milton asked, looking at the boy who was sniffling, hitching, and chewing. "Buy up all the toys in the world?" He turned to the excitement at the toy store. "That's what I figured. Until I grew older, and I was busy just trying to get through another day without getting myself killed."

"No, I wanna smoke a pipe and drink libations like my father." The boy spoke clearly now, articulating himself without stutter. The breaking of bread had temporarily remedied his worriment and doubts.

Milton inquired about the boy's age.

The boy looked up. "Seven."

Across the street, a costumed Barret Trufflehard genuflected, swinging an arm around a mushroom-headed little girl, who held an ersatz plutonizer. They beamed for the cameras. The girl's father watched on proudly, sincerely delighted for his progeny. The bundle pack for 11,999 pix included an autographed photo and an animated reel.

Milton was moderately bemused. He had always seen families like this, families who spent money to buy pleasant memories, souvenirs and keepsakes. And he thought, Whoever said money could not buy love and happiness… "I remember my father say I could never amount to anything or become great." He took in the parents who were willing to wait in line with their children. "And I wanted to prove him wrong. God did I want to do that."

The boy stared at him blankly, eyes rimmed pink. His face was mottled with dirt and the residue of dried tears.

It was the first time Milton had disclosed to anyone about the Father he never had. He had retreated into a latent repository. Perhaps, he reflected, Trufflehard had the better upbringing. He certainly displayed the mental strength to attribute for it. Parents who instilled in him confidence and purpose, the intellectual maturity to understand who he was, and furthermore his role in defending humanity. Whereas for the longest time, he realized, it wasn't patriotism that compelled me to pursue my call of duty, but survival in the most single-minded sense of the organism.

Milton turned to the boy. "You really wanna be like your father? Do you want to end up like me? Or that guy?" He indicated the ersatz Trufflehard etching a neural trademark on the little girl's phone. "There's no future once you grow old. You either accept you're not who you wanted to be, or you accept that you are, and realize, they're not who you thought they were." Milton observed the tall, beefy model with the platinum blonde flat top. "Or you stay innocent and keep hoping until you die."

The boy was quiet. Then, something registered. His brown eyes lit up. "I wanna be like Trufflehard. I wanna join the war on the Jade Agenda."

The boyhood dream, innit? Milton mused to himself. Survive life-threatening altercations and travel the globe. But it's not a vacation. It's a business trip. "You think Trufflehard became Trufflehard because he wanted to be like someone else?"

"The commercials said I could be-"

"They're selling you a fairy tale," Milton said. "Let up trying to be like Trufflehard, and learn to live with yourself, not the standards of other consumers. You can be someone all of your own. Maybe then, you won't be wishing one day you were a kid again just for the sensation of wanting to become something, to know you're still alive and act like you can make a difference and do something to be remembered by, to believe you can change the world by saving it, and that in itself will make everything right." He was just getting started, when a strident caterwaul dispersed his pontification.

"Tommy! Tommy! Get away from that man, and come to Mommy!"

The boy, Tommy, hopped off the bench and hurried over to a plump woman in a furry moomoo. "Get your grungy hands off my child!" she whinnied.

Milton studied his palms and started to mutter, "I wasn't even touching-"

"What did he do to you, Tommy?" she asked, clutching the boy by the shoulders. "Tell Mommy what the strange man did to you!" She grimaced, squeezing him tight. The smudged-up boy started to weep, seemingly in discomfort. Some passersby reached out and consoled the Mother.

Another shopper, this time a gaunt male, got involved. "You stay away from her child!" He made it a point to shake his fist. "Fruitcake!"

Was that last part necessary? Milton wondered, as he gathered up his briefcases and left.

The short pit stop to grab a bite at the outdoor promenade was developing to be a squalid decision. Between the process of ambling for half an hour just to binge on half a grilled cheese and somehow raising the ire of several institutions, a mile or two separated Milton from his vehicle. The energy he had expended to get to his current juncture, outbalanced the fuel intake. He had only worsened the caloric deficit. He was even hungrier than before. The idea of turning back to revisit the food gallery did not thrill him. There ought to have been somewhere else for occasions such as this. And there was. Behold, past the nurse in stockings and an anthropomorphic syringe, was a pub called the Granny Smith's Happy Hour Saloon.

Milton arrived at the door step of the pub and crossed over the threshold. The fog cleared into narcotic injections of fluorescence. Kaleidoscopic lighting effects jolted him with vigor. Musical frequencies rang through the expanse of nocturnal ecstasy. The dance floor motioned with synchronized coordination. Gogo dancer automatons in neon body paint quaked and quivered on elevated catwalks. Cool air seeped into Milton's pores and cleared his sinuses, filling him with mission. He walked up to the bar and took one of the ample seats, resting his arms on the see-thru counter.

A bartender with braided buns around her ears strolled over to him in a hooped mini skirt. She asked him, "What can I do you for?"

"I'll have the cheapest whatever-you-have with a splash of Indoct-"

A petite hand with pink tips covered his own. "He'll have what I'm having," said the woman who had just planted herself beside him. She had on an aqua-colored leotard and pink boots. Her hair was short and volt green, trimmed on the sides, furled at the top. She turned to him and said, free of constraint, "We're together."

"What are you having?" Milton said.

"The Usual," she said.

"Two Usuals coming up," said the bartender and went off to concoct the drinks.

"Who are you?" Milton said.

She leaned in and wrapped her arms around his elbow. "The luckiest lady in the world," she said blissfully. "What about you?"

"I guess you can call me somewhat of a specialist," he said stiffly.

She relaxed her grip and teased, "Give me something to work with."

Milton evaluated the setting of the saloon. His expression fortified. "I hunt aliens for a living."

"You're not the first denizen to tell me that today," she said laconically, "and you won't be the last."

"And here I thought my experiences were unique."

"As unique as every other Joey and Joy Blowhard who comes in through that door, thinking they're a wannabe superhero." A slight smile traced the length of her pink lips. "What makes you stand out from them?"

"Those denizens are zealots."

"And you?" she asked. "You're not emulating it?"

"I never said I'm Trufflehard."

She snuggled up to him once more. "Tell me then, Mr. Trufflehard. Why did you choose such a dangerous profession?"

"When I was young, I wanted to be cool," he said. "But now, to ever suppose that me, this mushroom-headed, little old me is saving the big fat day, seems like..." He trailed off, mulling it over.

"Like it should be a dream come true," she offered.

"Yet it feels..." He reflected with doubt. "... different."

"Immature and jejune," she suggested, "with a touch of vainglory." She gazed deeply into his eyes. "But it's justified. Someone like you needs to be a little like that. Otherwise, the pressure would overcome you."

It already has, he thought to himself. "If someone would've asked me what I wanted to do when I grew up, I would've told them I wanted to be a superhero. Not many denizens get to do what they've always wanted to do."

"Even kids outgrow the chocolate factory," she said. "Especially if they work in one."

"At the time, I felt vindicated for everything. All of my character flaws and past failures. But it was just another romance."

"True," she said. "But not everyone could look into the mirror on their worst hair day and say, 'I'm still saving the goddamned world.'" In a voice that was almost hoping, she asked, "You do, don't you?"

He looked up from the table. "Best believe."

"I don't need to believe," she said, constricting his arms. "I know." Her eyes reflected strobe lights and eternal truth. "That you're not like the other Joes and Joys. That you're a different kind of Blowhard. It doesn't get much cooler than that."

The bartender laid down two drinks. They came in rocks glasses with a stack of sour gummy diamonds impaled by a skewer. The drink luminesced and changed colors as it twirled in her hands. The craft was in the artfully divided segments of the syrupy beverage. The liquids were compartmentalized all on their own like a tri-section petri dish.

"Look at his cheek bones," she said to the bartender. "Doesn't he have gorgeous cheek bones?"

"I get that all the time," Milton said.

The bartender tendered a smile. "Anything else?"

"Keep 'em coming," said the woman on his arm. "Every six minutes."

Milton inserted the skewer inside his mouth, clamped down, pulling loose the candy gems with his teeth, and took them like pills, gulping down the whole cocktail without a break. It was a carbonated tornado of blue raspberry and honeydew and watermelon.

"You're a motherfucker," she said, when he returned the barren glass to the table. "You're everything and all that."

"Come to think of it," he agreed, rating highly of her analysis. "How come nobody else sees that?"

"Maybe you need to dress the part," she said, sizing up his pedestrian apparel. "It's the clothes that make the man."

"You think I'd be any less of myself if I was threadbare?"

"That remains to be seen," she whispered into his ear.

He regarded her intently. "Why don't we take this conversation somewhere more conducive?"

"Take me there!"

"Where to?" he asked her.

"Anywhere," she said. "Just let's get away. I want you to father my daughters. One's eight, the other's four."

"I'll pick up the tab." He got up and groped his pocket. Empty. He felt around himself and felt cold. The kid, he thought.

"Get back here," she murmured sleepily, pulling on his arm, before detecting something amiss. Her instincts were as swift as lightning, glimpsing a subtle trace of inconsistency in his demeanor, a flicker in his hardboiled expression. She narrowed her gaze, turning ten years older. "What?" she asked. "You don't expect me to settle the pecker." An arctic chill swept across her face, putting out the light in her eyes. Her glowing features suddenly appeared windburned.

"I was pillaged," Milton tried to explain. By an eight-year-old. No, seven. That grimy boy. And the mother in the moomoo, she was probably in on it too. His money, his camera, his notes, his entirety was contained in that phone, even my trading card collection and magic eight ball, he thought gloomily. Not to mention sensitive information. He decided they had no interest in any of that, the boy and mother. The phone by itself was worth a pretty pixel. Most likely, it was all they were interested in. Goddamnit still. He would have to access his account immediately and freeze it, before they could override the neurological passcode of the software. But how? he asked himself. I would need a phone to do that.

"It's all under control," he said. "Let me access my account through your phone."

She reciprocated no interest. Her expression indicated so. "Such a shame," she said acridly.

"But I thought you said I was different," he said. "That you wanted me to be a part of your children's life."

"That was a minute ago."

Time flies, he thought.

A group of shoppers passed by, laughing gaily and obliviously among themselves.

Why? he thought. It did not seem so funny to Milton at a time like this, nevermind he could not tell what the joke was. What he could tell was these denizens had no appreciation for the risks he took on a daily basis. They don't care about me, he said to himself. I don't exist to them and never will. What then, are my obligations to defend them?

A marching troop of coneheaded men in speedos and cowboy boots came parading through the promenade. They declared patriotic sounds, bashing and ringing their respective instruments, mostly an electric orchestra of cymbals and triangles, Milton made out. A rumpus of jingles that shrilled his stability, than suffuse him with banded spirit. A united pride that was epitomized by his idol.

Trufflehard had unquestioning patriotism and heroism. The possibility of turning his back on the future of humanity would have never crossed his mind. He was willing to die to save the world. And now Milton was willing to die, too, just not as much in a hurry. There was no gung-ho quest embarked to die for the salvation of others, but more so an estrangement of his survival instinct. After all, if all roads led to death, what was there left to fear?

Milton had often wondered to himself, What would Trufflehard do?

For starters, he would never ask that question. That was a damning realization. Barret Trufflehard always knew what he was supposed to do; it came easy to him, too easy. He was having the time of his life.

There is no thrill for me, Milton thought in contrast. Why couldn't I just let go? Why couldn't I be great? Why couldn't I be larger than life? Like him? Because despite my efforts, I'm not a hero, not technically. Thirteen years ago, I was too stupid to be scared. Now I'm too tired of being stupid. How could I be brave, when I'm fearless of death, of the nothingness?

And yet, I am afraid, even if I'm too tired of being stupid to notice it, that this is all there is, and I'll fade into the night cast by my shadow before I could resolve my own existence.

It was the fear that drove him but could not be rationalized. The phobia was alien to him.

He perceived the thrust of the wind in the atmosphere as he approached dual rows of tall stalks, airheaded and menacing in all varieties of themes and colors. The pneumatic poles twitched erratically and flailed their cylindrical anatomies at him. From its base, a group of teenage girls waddled by. Their necks were strained, their shoulders tensely shrugged from the multiple pastel-shaded bags tightly clenched in each hand, a sense of accomplishment brimming from their faces.

How have we come so far with such a lousy incentive? Milton wondered.

What was Trufflehard's incentive?

What was mine?

It used to be about survival. Fame, even. Glamor. Prestige. Free food. And maybe a home owner, with a wife, three daughters, and an arthropodic fido. Before everything happened.

And now?

He thought hard about it and came up blank. The truth of it was, he had no reasons. At least not anymore, not really. Nor did he depend on the vacuous entitlement of hope. In order for him to continue, he would have to adopt the reasons not his, but what the consumers projected onto him: Their fears, their hopes, their dreams, their demands, their expectations. In exchange for his failures, his faults, his fatigue, his famine, his disappointment. The inevitable transaction, of these cursed shrapnel reflecting and radiating the reaction to every action, of pixilated currency.

What was the point? he asked himself. Why continue under this insidious design, the omnipresence of an unknown threat, monsters lurking beneath the sink, the bed, the floor, behind the shower curtain, the fire hydrant, the closet door, under our supper table, under our noses, under our skin, skulking in the attic, in the basement, in out-of-tune pianos, in jack-in-the-boxes, in our phones, out in the open, out in the media, up in the clouds, up in high places, and in all other forms and devices, un undetectable dark matter that portended to spread to the omega of the universe. Half the population did not believe it. The other half, denied it was them.

I'm not killing jadeites, Milton thought. I'm killing time. My legacy in a nutshell.

He took a deep breath and swore this was his last assignment, and swore this was his last time swearing that this was. Not just because he expected every assignment to be his last, but because he really had no arrangements beyond the assignment that laid ahead. If he got through somehow, he imagined two scenarios: dealing with the economic fallout - the ennui and the onerous realization he was forever indebted to the agency. Or he thought, I'll find a real job, pay off my mortgage, the balance owed, and never look back.

Meanwhile, he predicted Kyra to fill his vacancy with the new and improved recruit, worthy of certification, thereby maintaining her agency. The world would keep turning and churning, and everybody would be better off. That was a possibility. It was also possible, he thought, death would fall upon us. Not only possible, but a certainty. In which case, who would be left to care? Wasn't it true that most everybody would be dead a hundred years from now, thereby forgetting any of this ever happened? A hollow victory in his mind, but not for lack of foresight.

He lifted his head toward the faded sky. It seemed like yesterday that he and Miss Flutterby were holding hands, running for their lives. But it was actually earlier today, he thought. Simultaneously, it felt like it had happened in a wholly different era.

The death and extinction of humanity was not what affected Milton. At the prospect of sexual enslavement, nonexistence would be euthanasia. What perturbed him was dwelling in the finite, the suffering, the torture that came before the inevitable sacrifice for the general population: men like himself, little ones, and ninety-nine-point-nine-nine-nine percent of women, deemed unworthy of birthing a lineage of sexual slaves. What about the zero-point-zero-zero-one who are? he wondered. The select minority would be first to be imprisoned, subjugated as per the Jade Agenda. Cream of the crop, top of the top, dirtbound goddesses, the Flutterbys and the Daras, dare I say even the McVeronica, and the Blacklights. Their DNA would be cloned, no doubt.

His mind returned to the boy and his mother who took him. Where would they fall? he asked himself, before concluding they would fall short of the cutoff. Way short. For sure, they would be eliminated from the inferior genealogy, the infinitesimal of thought he did not indulge, regardless of how well deserved. For what kind of nation would the generations inherit, he wondered, if our worth was measured by the random, anthropomorphic permutations we embodied? Thievery be damned, even marauders deserved to live, not because life was any more quantifiable than death, but because there was always something to live for, even if it was really just the sake of it, the fundamental nature to delay the unknown.

He dragged by Trufflehard, fitted in his heavily padded suit. The model they had selected for the purpose was chiseled and handsome, snapping photos and animated reels, capturing the moment with smiling families. Trufflehard was built like a sculpture, bushy browed and strong jawed, blue eyed with a nook in his chin and diamond studs on his ears, cleancut and provident, charismatic, always knowing what to say, with a fast metabolism and healthy joints, superior in every which way. And Milton extracted from this: I'm nowhere near that damn speckle-free and photogenic. But more significantly, he thought, I would make a destitute role model. And he realized too, I don't have to take credit. For there are those already in place to do that.

I should've known, he thought. And still he could not resist the semblance of disappointment. Even though he had foreseen it, he had expected it to turn out differently.

Meandering through the crowded promenade, he noticed some shoppers had stopped moving. Their throats were stretched out, staring upward. More and more of them were pointing up. Perhaps another promotional showcase, Milton guessed. He lifted his gaze over the undulating skyline of the shopping complex. Between towers of steel rising into the arrangement of clouds that had turned gray, was the train of traffic arrested. Holographic billboards flashed sporadically against a black and white sky. And then, he saw it too. A cloud among clouds, migrating, in contrast of all the other clouds hanging in the background, the orb of vapor shifted directions on a whim, guided by a mind of its own.

Milton broke away from the distraction and started up again, fixed on the path ahead. The archway loomed. He passed through, entering the cafeteria. The tournament was ongoing. The contestants wiggled their bodies, settling the food into their expanding guts, with locust legs and antennae overflowing from their greasy lips. A champion was on the verge of being crowned, but it was nowhere near as loud as it once was. The frenzy had dwindled, as though a mist of sedative had moved in and subdued the masses. The weather around them cast an ashen hue. Milton noticed there were no more explosions; it had been approximately fifteen seconds since he had heard one. The smoke and smell of pyrotechnics lingered. The flashes of light abated. The music waned. The throng of shoppers motioned slowly. They looked bogged down, hushed, with faces fishlike out of water, gasping through the opening and closing of their jaws. The holographic animations had come to a pause. Milton rolled his head back to the eternity and watched the curtain of numerical syntax descend over him.

chapter 21

The chariot of fire that was captivated on Milton Grainjar, ceased the moment her charge of laser struck the anti-gravitational propulsion unit. The critical hit caused a taciturn shockwave to ripple among the crowd. The gathering of stunned onlookers had halted in motion, holding their breath.

Kyra McVeronica watched silently, the cloudy cloak evaporate from the craft. The exposed shell was round and transparent. The craft seesawed pendularly, seeking equilibrium, but it puttered audaciously, and failing to recover altitude, plummeted straight for the promenade. Panicked cries emitted from the crowd of spectators, as they diverged from the oncoming vessel.

Surprisingly, everybody managed to avoid the crash, fleeing from the impact radius. The evasive response however left several casualties trampled by the rampage. Some of them were curled up into a fetal ball, taking cover from the barrage of feet. Others twitched erratically on the floor.

Kyra heard a scream – throaty, high in pitch, with a touch of
monotone. It sounded like Milton Grainjar, possibly. She heard it again,
louder. Could it be? she wondered, spinning around in search of him.
The screams were traced to a woman with a pregnant stomach lying on
her side. One hand protected her stomach and the other reached for the
heavens, shortly before succumbing under the stampede.

Shudders were slamming down on the entrances of the stores. The
shopping complex had issued security lockdown. Alarms were going off.
A riot had commenced between its glass walls. Muffled screams could
be heard trapped from within. Kyra observed shoppers scrambling
cluelessly, collaborating to haul off expensive electronic appliances and
bundles of branded attire with hangers still intact. Collisions,
consequent of balancing stacks of boxes so high they had trouble seeing
where they were going, would cause them to drop everything, breaking
out confusion over ownership. Children joined their parents in the tug-
o-war, holding onto shirt sleeves dearly. Fights were ongoing. Lights
went out. More screams followed.

The pregnant woman was being tended, when Kyra arrived. She
circumvented the scene and approached the grounded craft. Distressed
shoppers lingered at the crash sight, afraid to make any more progress
to its proximity. They stuttered their steps hesitantly around the object
lying at the center of a smoldering crater. The imprint it had left from
impact was approximately twice the size of the craft.

As Kyra got closer, she saw that the entire shell was a geodesic,
spherical window, resembling a drop of water, transparent and made of
something durable. It had not shattered into a million glass pieces,
despite spiraling out of the sky at a harrowing velocity. It was still intact,
with no signs of breakage, not a scratch. A perimeter of jagged corners
perforated its grilled equator. Peering through the glass enclosure, Kyra
gauged the internal compartment was just big enough to fit a full-sized

adult, but no pilot was present. It was remotely operated.

A couple of bystanders joined her in the inspection of the glass cocoon and conferred among themselves, some with their phones out, framing what they saw. Kyra backed away and mounted her trike, as the shell started to blink out.

The search for Milton continued, her engine humming through the promenade. An anxious smattering of shoppers were left over from the evacuation. Tear-struck faces bleated into phones. Fallen shoppers hitched themselves to their feet, injuries permitting. Otherwise, they remained immobilized, floored in a state of shock.

A neck-breaking shriek resounded from afar.

Kyra scanned the distance and rode her trike to the source of the scream. A woman had her mouth open, with both hands wrapped around her cheeks, confronting the fuzzy outline of Milton Grainjar. There he was. Across from her. Bolt upright, briefcase in each hand, visibly shivering.

The high-pitched squeal had attracted gawkers, rushing to see for themselves. "Get away from him," Kyra warned, stepping off her transport. Her order garnered some necks to turn. Some resumed fixated on the public spectacle. Some stepped aside. Anybody apathetic to her trajectory was rendered in the next instant, to the ground, moaning on their knees.

Wading through the crowd, she could see sharply, an indistinct effluvium tracing Milton.

She heard somebody say, "Don't put a spoon in his mouth," as she drew near the frozen figurine hanging in mid-air.

He postured oddly, stuck in stride, briefcases swayed, statuesque, static, yet fossilized by an indefinite state of recoil, as if in the act of being struck by lightning. His head whipped spasmodically to and fro, but his eyes were unmoving, unblinking, staring sightlessly. The briefcases resonated from the violent rattling of his shoulders. The convulsion fluctuated to his lower extremities, which were seemingly locked in motion: his left leg was launching off the floor, and his right leg, bent, jutting forward.

The selfsame voice said, "He's suffering a fit." The man posed as a medical authority. He had glasses with a horizontally-striped polo shirt and khakis. "Probably the shaft of light that provoked synchronous neuronal activity and induced epilepsy."

"There must be something we can do to stop it," said the blonde-haired woman beside him.

"Nothing," said the medic. "Too late now. Let it ride out." He motioned to leave.

"Are you sure he'll be fine?" the woman asked.

"He's not frothing at the mouth. He'll be okay. Seizures are a lot more common than denizens think." The medic left to check on other casualties.

Reviewing the mediocre diagnosis of the spectacle, the small crowd followed suit and scattered away, returning to the frenzied populace.

The remaining members stood at bay, trying to understand the symptoms in an archaic language. Yet Kyra knew the vision before her was not Milton Grainjar, but the volatile vestige of space. He was long gone. This was a visual artifact, residual trails of his memory evident by the processing of the event.

In a blink, the image representing Milton Grainjar was gone.

"Huh," said a scraggy man. He had on a faded black shirt etched with incandescent feline features, and a Rice'n Rise gas station cap draped over his oily hair.

"Where did he go?" the blonde-haired woman asked.

The gas station attendant shrugged. "One second he was here. The next second he was gone."

"Denizens don't just go poof and disappear!" she said, visibly distressed. "There must be a reasonable explanation."

The gas station attendant, swiveled around, appealing to nearby onlookers. "Did anybody see a man toting humongous briefcases?"

"I didn't see nothing," said a man in a light blue button-up with red flannel lining. "If I did, it happened so fast, I was too slow to catch it."

"He must've walked off, when we weren't looking," the attendant said.

"Well, at least he's alright," the lumberjack said.

Another man, wearing a turquoise jacket with dark turqoise elbow patches, chimed in, "Fugginay."

"It looked like he was transfixed by a color wheel," the attendant said.

Someone else was heard grumbling, "I'm too old for this shit."

"My wife and I invested in a shudder last week," the attendant said. "Laser proof. Keeps those pesky jadeites out, the ads say. I would love to offer you all a spot. But you know how it goes. I need to look out for my family."

The lumberjack nodded. "You can't help everyone."

"There's a part of me that hopes fifty years from now, we can look back at this time period and say it was the best time to grow up," the attendant said. "That we were actually a part of something. Something to illicit change. Denizens who didn't just sit back and do nothing. Denizens who fought back."

"Funny you mention it," the lumberjack said. "I was considering that, myself. Maybe we can organize a rally. These are the rare circumstances to get behind each other, bonded by a common cause."

"Ike," the blonde-haired woman called out to the attendant from a few yards out, "are you coming or not? It's getting dangerous. Let's get to the car."

"Yes, dear," the attendant said.

"What say you," the lumberjack said, "you look like good denizens." He looked around.

The man with the elbow patches remained quiet.

The attendant looked at his shoes. "I can't."

"Well why the hell not?" the lumberjack demanded. "Sure you can, guy. Don't say that."

"I'm saying it," the attendant said, dwindling from his previous proclamation, "because there's the other part of me that knows if anything happens to me, it'll crush my family."

"You have integrity, guy," the lumberjack said. "We could've used you."

"Honest-to-God truth, I would've never spouted off like that had I any idea you were scouting for active registration."

"No questions asked," the lumberjack said firmly. "Anyway, it was a spur-of-the-moment, fortuitous development. I have a family to consider as well, I suppose."

The man with the elbow patches spoke up. "What exactly was it that you had in mind?"

"God knows what," the lumberjack said. "God knows."

"Well," the man with the elbow patches said, "it was fun while it lasted."

Kyra got back on her trike and brought out her phone. The neural sensor instantly pulled up Milton's contact and started to dial. It went straight to voicemail. Listlessly, she spoke into the transmitter. "Satellite to Trufflehard. Satellite to Trufflehard. Call me when you wake up."

The blip utility on the holocube indicated Milton's phone was still on the grid. Then why is his phone off? she wondered. Something was awry. She looked for the accompanying cephalic index. There was no detection. For godsakes, she realized with remorse, I've been leaving messages on a displaced phone. The radar indicated the phone was just a few miles away. She decided to pursue the locus and see for herself.

The number of denizens idling the promenade grew sparse, as she cruised on her trike. Most of them had evacuated the premises, racing to the skies to seek refuge. She reached the octagonal intersection of the food gallery. Everywhere, the power was out. The lights that animated the tiles on the surface of the streets, were black and empty.

Kyra saw scrolling colors ahead of her, a holographic sign on tilt. It flashed, perhaps by independent generator, Bi-Monthly Fried Locust Eating Grand Prix. Underneath the disheveled sign, two teens were perched at the center stage, among a drizzle of food particles, discussing the result.

"They were neck and neck, Hiroshi Miyamoto and Toad Fastbender, before they canceled the contest with seconds to go," one of them was saying, shaking her head in disappointment. "Now we'll never know."

Off to the corner, a riffraff of men huddled around a computer linked to various automats. They combined their minds and scratched their heads, endeavoring to manually override the program. "I'm surprised that I'm surprised," one of them was saying. "It happened just like they said it would, with jadeites coming to invade us. They predicted this."

Further on, an elderly woman with frazzled hair, garbed in a dowdy gown and sandals, assorted brown beads draped around her neck, wandered without direction. She called out, "My baby. Has anybody seen my baby?"

Laying on the floor was a copy of the Ekonomicana. Approaching it, she landed the trike to gaze down at the holographic headline: *Jadeite Spaceship Sighted Over Ekonomy Promenade*. She dismounted to one side and picked up the discarded stem from which the issue projected, bringing it closer to her face. She blinked, examining the featured article, trying to make sense out of it.

Xdax deui ufghx eiaquz dd akokl daq eiouegr rieoqoqo aeuirzep cvvzeqx-eoqueui of sdfa. Ojafx dfereck da daiof eyeqea yeajd cmanaoe daw ioeuc poieqaxx...

It registered in her a squall of confusion, and she was seized by a transitory awareness of elements galvanizing within her. She threw the copy down, backing away with suspicion. The quality of writing made her cringe with contempt, and more besides. She returned to her trike and proceeded to accelerate, leafing between the composition of stores cramming her on both sides. Without the invigorating lights to reflect the individual franchises, it felt to her the passage was growing narrower and deeper, slowly being drawn and devoured through the belly of a neverending beast.

Leaning against one of the conduit pipes in a muddled haze, was an Adonis decked out in pearlescent armor. A foam lava gun had fallen to his side. Beside him, somebody stood with her phone out, presumably to consult him for a photo or neural trademark. And beyond, a white-haired man, stumbling and all alone, was heard asking the obligatory question. He mumbled to no one in particular, "Is this how it ends?"

Kyra drove past, wondering that herself. There was a world ending every second, with a new one popping up. We lived in a world of worlds, she thought. This world was just one way of envisioning it. But the world itself would always be there, even if there was no one to witness it.

Where in the world is Trufflehard? she wondered. She was following the coordinates of his phone, but she still could not home in on his neurological ID.

If I was being hard on him, she thought, it was for his best. He came this far, under my guidance and supervision. After all, we didn't invest in him to have him walk out on us.

Operating on that basis, she assured herself he would be back. Even though he requested to discontinue his activities with the Bureaux, she thought, he didn't actually mean it.

Kyra had known him for over a decade, which meant to her, she knew him better than he did. In doing so, she recognized the latest violation of conduct as part of a habitual cycle. It was not the first time he had pulled off something similar, she thought. Dropping off the face of creation, only to resurface with puckered eyes, seeping of cantaloupe punch. God, he had such poor taste in everything.

He just needs more encouragement from me, she told herself. That always brings him back. Even though he almost seemed serious this time. I just have to keep calling. Sooner or later, he'll come around.

What else could he do to support himself, but to support the denizens? she thought. Even if there was, what other employer would tolerate his pathological truancy? Whether he knew it or not, wasn't something he had the miracle of resolving on his own. Maybe later, but not now, she thought, not ever.

Something was unfolding all about her. It was loud and disorderly, but it was an ephemeral outlet. Riots, sirens, and breaking glasses were the sounds and illusions of revolution. The human energy however, was feeble. It could never be sustained. It swayed and puttered from a pleasant disposition. The urge to gravitate toward order was much stronger, even if it meant returning to the way things were.

The same urge was lacking in the jadeite design. The human tendency and desire to seek small comforts, diametrically opposed the Jade Association's limitless, totalitarian ambition. Revolution, true revolution with overnight ramifications, was a fallacy under human direction, but an inevitable verity with the jadeites. For this reason, the campaign to resist the Jade Agenda's influence could suffer no delays for the resolution of a solitary player. The moment their pieces fell into place, the Association would be insurmountable.

Kyra continued the tour of the aftermath, gliding over the inactive, gnomeless surface of vacant tiles, tarnished by foot prints, candy wrappers, bubblegum, and broken condoms.

The spanning shopping complex rumbled with dissent. Somebody had started a fire and triggered the fire sprinklers. Kyra pointed her laser gun at the corner of a faraway gift shop and pushed the trigger. The fire alarm blared through the sputtering shards of glass. Smoke billowed from the entry, and sleepwalking consumers streamed out, wet and coughing.

Kyra tucked the laser gun behind her and pulled back the steering sticks. The trike launched upward and spiraled above the promenade.

She raised the phone and repeated the beacon. "Satellite to Trufflehard. Satellite to Trufflehard." Hang in there, she thought. Wherever you are.

She traced the night air, drifting beneath invisible stars, over the mosaic of a thousand stores recoiling beneath her, like an exterminated spider, festering with spires of black smoke, consumed from the inside out.

Learn more about the author's latest offerings.

ultrakwon.com
twitter @ultrakwon
facebook.com/ultrakwon

Latency Paradox of Barret Trufflehard